MOTOR-PSYCHO
by
Alexandria May Ausman

Book design by Jon M. Ausman
Cover photo by Christian Axel

Library of Congress Control Number: 2022912073

ISBN: 979-8-9862745-2-2 (ebook)
ISBN: 979-8-9862745-5-3 (paperback)

Characters: Book Three

Bob: married to Mary, Psycho's grandmother
Brian Sloan: Julie's father, a trucker
Cindy Sloan: Julie's mother
Crystal: a classmate and friend of Julie
Evans, Mrs.: also known as Porcupine
Ingles, Dr: a hospital physician
Jeff: a local drug dealer, married to Porcupine
Joni: a classmate and friend of Julie
Jordie: a towheaded child, son of Jeff and Porcupine
Julie: a classmate of Psycho, an antagonist
Kevin: son of an emergency room nurse, a schizophrenic
Lauren: daughter of Jeff and Porcupine
Looper: a disembodied voice, usually repeatedly delivering a negative message
Mary: female foster parent and Psycho's grandmother
Porcupine: wife of Jeff
Psycho: a schizophrenic trying to live
Scott, Dr.: psychologist at mental health center
Shirley: an emergency room nurse
Simon Brag: a shard of Psycho
Stephanie: a schoolmate who vacillates
Taggart, Mr.: seller of the Motor-Psycho to Psycho
Tom: member of the Denim Brigade
Vicky: a schoolmate and friend of Julie
Walter: a criminal partner of Jeff and Porcupine

Chapter 34: RADAR LOVE

Good day, Beautiful Family. Are We coming in loud and clear? Should We turn up the volume? Just stand a bit more to the right, hold these tin foil bunny ears for Us, will you? Ah! There, that is perfect, now you are on the right frequency. Look closely at Our homemade X-Rays. Can you see it too? Oh yes, this will be a problem for the mission. Now, no worries, We have a plan to fix this entire mess. All it requires is a bit of mechanical knowledge, Grey's Anatomy, a screwdriver, oh, and lots of towels to clean up the excess fluids. We got this, so you start and We will be there as soon as We sew things up here.

WHY WON'T MY LOVED ONE WITH SCHIZOPHRENIA TAKE OR STAY ON THE MEDICATION?

"55% of Schizophrenics not taking medication did so because they did not believe they were sick: Delusion called-anosognosia. 20% of Schizophrenics not taking medication are suffering paranoid delusions about the medication." -Mental illness Policy Organization.

PROPER WAY TO TALK TO A SCHIZOPHRENIC ABOUT A DELUSION:

"Calmly ask questions about their delusions. Ask them how they arrived at their conclusions, and do not judge or correct them. This will help

guide them to logically re-examine their beliefs and may help them to spot faulty logic. You may gently suggest evidence to the contrary and ask them their opinion. But do not directly tell them they are wrong, or delusional, or tease them about the delusion as it will make them resist working with you. Do not agree with their delusion, or make suggestions: that may add to or even deepen the delusion; (i.e. well, it is possible they are watching you. After all just because you are paranoid does not mean they Are Not After You!)."
-Bright Quest Treatment Center

I was feeling pretty good about having thwarted Julies attempts at making me say I was schizophrenic. I was not sick, and she damned well knew it. I had heard what Vicky said everyone was saying about me. It was very clear that it was the popular consensus that I was indeed Psycho. The more I argued I am not crazy the more they say I am crazy.

Now, my logic was that if you are going to be blamed for something you are innocent of (and no one believes you), then go ahead and do the crime. I knew I was not schizophrenic, not really. However, I could act like I had the disease. Then when Julie makes me say it, I know it is all just an act. After all, Julie had made me say I was liar. Far as I could see it, now I indeed was one. Just like Julie wanted me to be.

As my final class before the end of the school day began, I suddenly had an epiphany. A huge smile spread across my face as I realized I had found my solution at long last.

I will tell Dr. Scott that I was just seeking attention and acting crazy. I will apologize for my bad behavior, take whatever punishment she wants to give me. Then I will have cleared my name. I think to myself barely able to contain my joy at this very simple but effective plan. If I admit that I was faking Schizophrenia she will have to believe me. No one admits when they are lying unless it is truth.

When the bell rang signaling the end of the day, I practically skipped to detention hall. This could really work. Plus, a whole hour more without that ginger haired menace. I was feeling mighty fine. I went into the classroom to sit down but felt a hand grab my shoulder as I entered. It did not shock me. There was no need to turn to see who was there. Only one person could touch me without causing me pain.

My face lit up, "Simon," I yelled out.

I turned to see my beloved friend standing in the doorway putting his fingers to his lips in a gesture of silence. He motioned me to follow him out. There was another fifteen minutes till I would have to be in detention, so I followed him happily. He led me down the hall to the girl's bathroom. I chuckled as I watched the old perv walked right in without even checking to see if it was unoccupied.

Looking down the hall to be sure we were not followed by anyone (especially the evil Julie) I went in after him. He was standing next to the stalls leaning on the back wall rolling a smoke when I came in. I ran right up and hugged him tightly. He was surprised but hugged me back.

"I am so sorry Simon. I will never be mean to you again. I was so wrong. Simon I am in so much trouble," I blurted reluctantly letting him go from the hug.

Simon just looked at me appearing very serious, "Yeah, you will be mean to me again, but I love you anyway. Forget that shit, you have bigger problems indeed."

That scared me. Simon usually did not say things so gravely. "Julie? Her family is taking guardianship and she is hurting me."

Simon interrupted me, "I wasn't talking about Julie. You have a fucking radar tracking device somewhere in your unit. You have to get rid of that or you are stuck with this knuckleheaded bitch for a long time girly." He looks at me hard to see if I am understanding him.

I was indeed. I had remembered Julie told me about the radar. The doctors are tracking me with satellites. I was sure that Dr. Scott would believe me when I tell her I was faking schizophrenia but just in case she did not help me get rid of Julie, I needed a plan B. Plan B would have to be running away with Simon to escape them all. I could not do that if they could track me. Simon was right. I had to find this radar and remove it from the unit of measurement immediately.

I nodded my head yes. He smiled at me as he went back to rolling his cigarette. I smiled feeling some fear at how I was going to figure out where the radar was located. He read my mind.

"The skin will be discolored, or some other sign should be there. Find that and dig it out. Easy as pie. They are not so clever," he said lighting his smoke.

This made sense so I nodded again, "I have missed you, toothless old drunk," I said affectionately.

He smiled wide showing he was indeed without many teeth, "I missed you too, you idiot schizophrenic."

We both laughed at our strange pet names for each other. I would have murdered anyone else for calling me that, but my Simon could have called me anything. He was my only friend and a loyal one at that. He could really do no wrong, even if he was not always right. One would wonder how such an odd ball pair like us had ever teamed up. It was not really important. I had my Simon back. All was finally right with the world. Now, to find the radar, get my name cleared, or run away. The nightmare would finally be over.

Simon suddenly looked at me distressed as he rushed into one of the stalls closing the door behind him. I turned to see Stephanie coming into the bathroom. Shit, this girl never lets up.

"Psycho, who you talking to," Stephanie asks looking about the bathroom seeing only me.

I shrug my shoulders understanding that while I wanted to talk to my friend more, I needed to lead this brain stem away from discovering him in the stall. I briskly left the bathroom knowing she would follow me. Of course, she did.

I went straight to detention hall without answering Stephanie's requests that I slow down and talk with her a minute. I went inside and sat down up front as usual. I internally groaned as Stephanie came in after me and sat in the desk next to mine.

She was panting a bit having tried to run to catch my very fast race to detention, "Psycho, didn't you hear me calling you?"

I shrugged as I reached into my backpack to retrieve my codes. She could sit there if she liked but I was not listening to her drivel. She had joined with the evil bitches in making my life hell. I had nothing to say to her. Plus, that little trick earlier this morning.

She was in on it with Julie trying to make me think I was crazy. Well, fuck her.

She could tell I was in no mood for her bullshit. Stephanie knew me better than anyone other than Simon. I could read her mind. She was trying to decide how to get me to entertain her with conversation. I decided she could forget that. I had 'entertained' her enough. I started working on my codes doing my best to block out her thoughts and voice.

She shifted in her chair and sighed, "Okay, yeah you hate me. You know what? You should hate me. I am a bitch. I was wrong for joining the others picking on you like that. I know you are sick. I have seen how much it hurts you. I know it really doesn't matter, but for what it is worth, I am sorry Psycho. Sorry that you are sick. I am sorry that Julie is mean to you. I am sorry I hurt you with those pills trying to make you better. I am just plain sorry. You don't have to forgive me. I just wanted to tell you."

Her words made me so angry. Despite my agreement with me that we would ignore her I blurted, "You say you are sorry to make yourself feel better, Stephanie. That is not for me. You hurt me, and I am still hurt because of you. You're saying you are sorry but it does not make my hurt go away, it does though for you, doesn't it? Well, go fuck yourself. I am done being hurt by you."

I watched as Stephanie's big blue eyes began to tear up. She knew I was right. I usually could not look into anyone's eyes, but I felt I could live in hers for some reason. My mind rushed back to the day I saw her helpless crying on that bench as Kelly and the thugs tormented her. She was so frail, so small. Stephanie was also so very beautiful. The feeling of her taking my hand before the big fight flooded my chest. The emotion of wanting to protect her crept into my dark consciousness. I recalled her attempt to give me a present, the only one I had ever received for any birthday, and how nasty I behaved. I thought of all the times she did not leave, despite my hitting and cursing her. My resolve to never speak to her again started to pull back, as it always seemed to when it came to Steph.

Something strange was coming over me. I had never felt this way before about anyone, not even Simon. I could not understand why I was even considering talking to Stephanie after all she had done, much less remembering good things about her. The odd sensations were both confusing and well, nice.

"You are in love with this girl stupid," I heard the detention hall attendant say from her seat in the teacher's desk at the front of the classroom.

I looked at the attendant startled, "I am not. Shut up," I yelled out, very embarrassed that this office aide would ever suggest such a silly thing.

Stephanie and the attendant both looked at me as if I had turned into a giant cockroach. My yelling had scared them.

The attendant recovered first, "Quiet over there," she barked at Stephanie and I. No one else was in the room.

Stephanie's eyes were even bigger than usual, "Psycho, you okay? Julie is really getting to you, isn't she? I think she is going to hurt you. You don't deserve that, you are sick. I know you are right about the whole being sorry thing. But I don't know what else I can do to make it right but say it." She started sniffling as she looked at the floor.

I was still upset by the attendant suggesting I was in love with Stephanie. However, Stephanie's obviously honest regret at her treatment of me lately shook off my horror of the foul idea being made public like that.

"Okay, you can start by not doing it anymore. Julie is a bitch. I don't know why she is doing this to me, but you did warn me about her. I will give you that. I did not listen. You were right," I said resolved that if we were to be honest with each other, I had to confess my mistakes as well.

Stephanie looked up smiling through her now erupting tears, "You mean it, Psycho? You forgive me?

I smiled at her childish expression of happiness, "Yeah. I forgive you if you forgive me.""

She bounced in her desk excited with my statement, "I would hug you but I know you don't like to be touched. So, imaginary pinky swear and deal."

"Do you have any idea what the hell happened with Julie and this whole taking over my life business?" I inquired seeing an opportunity to gain some inside information from Stephanie before she had one of her infamous mood swings.

Stephanie stopped smiling and bouncing. A look of anger flashed on her face, "Psycho, you would not take your medications. You got really sick. I was scared you would die or get thrown in jail. You have to take your medications. See...look at you today. You are not mean at all just like I told everyone Plus, you are so funny. What you did at lunch, oh my God. I never laughed so hard. Julie got you because you got so sick and Mary did not want to deal with it anymore. Mary is a horrible person you know. I hate her like you do," she spewed out not even taking a single breath.

I recoiled at several of her statements, "Steph stop it. I do not need medications. I am not sick, damn it. I am faking it. As for Mary, fuck that old bitch. Now, I am asking you specifically if you know why Julie would even wan to take guardianship?" I looked at her to see if she got me this time.

Stephanie almost choked, "Faking? Psycho, okay you know what, never mind. You are still going to take the medication, right? I mean just to keep up the cover and all. Wait why are you faking crazy?" She narrowed her eyes.

I smiled wide, "For attention like you darling."

Stephanie frowned at that, "So, uhmmm, you know, uhmmmm, when people fake they do not do it when they are all alone. They do it when people are around you know. And usually they do not uhmmmm, well do it so....ahhh...well?"

I narrowed my eyes back at her, "What are you getting at Stephanie. I asked you a question. Will you answer or do you not know or what?"

She looked at me hard, "Yes, I do know and you answer me and I will answer you. Why are you saying that you are faking schizophrenia when you obviously are lying to yourself."

Now she was pushing my buttons, but I wanted to know what she knew about Julie so bad I was willing to play this game.

"Fair enough," I said gritting my teeth to bite back the anger at her stupid question. "I wanted someone to care about me. That is why I am faking it. You told me that is why you do crazy stuff. I am not lying. I do not have schizophrenia."

She shook her head now appearing distressed, "Psycho, you know that is not true. I mean I do sometimes do some crazy stuff hoping someone will care. But you are getting hurt a lot with your acting crazy. And it is all the time. I have even caught you when you thought you were alone. It is not getting you the kind of attention that would make anyone fake that. You are sick, not faking. I saw your records. Stop lying to yourself."

My anger was starting to burn inside, "I am not sick. In fact, I know you and the others are trying to make me think that. Like the trick you played this morning. Not funny. I knew you were there, but Julie was hell bent to tell me you were not. She tried to say that I did not talk to you. I know you left early so Julie would look like she was telling the truth. Why would you help her?"

I looked to make sure she heard me this time, "She is holding me prisoner, hitting me and told me she is going to call the law and say I threatened to kill her to get me locked up. She also told me about the radar they put into my unit so that if I run I will be caught. She keeps me from going home to Simon," I was spitting my words I was about to blow.

Stephanie looked away, "Okay, Psycho, you may not believe me, but I was not at Julie's today. I did not talk to you. I was with my Aunt. I can prove it too. If you want me to prove it, I will. If you want to pretend you are not sick, that is okay but don't accuse me of doing that to you. That is not fair. I have tried to help you. What I don't understand, is why is it so bad to just have schizophrenia, take the medication and just be done with it? Why, Psycho? Why not just admit it and move on."

My anger suddenly turned tail and ran from my inner mind like a dog shot with a BB gun. Despair filled the void it left behind as I looked to the floor understanding on some level the truth behind all this. I took a deep breath finally ready to say what I had not even said to myself.

"Stephanie, I do not have a home. I do not have a family. I do not have anyone to care. If I had schizophrenia, I would lose the last thing I have left, hope. There is no cure for it. I would be sick for my whole life and in need of all the things I do not have already. If I had that disease, I would need someone to help me survive. I cannot have schizophrenia do you understand me?" I choked back hard fighting my own tears willing them from popping into my eyes to give away my deepest sorrow.

Stephanie teared up for me, "Oh my God Psycho. I never thought of it that way. I am so sorry," she said as she wiped her eyes "But you are sick. Not wanting to believe does not make it not true. I have seen it. Everyone has seen it. You know it is true. Look at what you just told me. You saw me this morning at Julie's, but I was not there. Psycho, you have to take the medication, you are going to die if this keeps up."

I shook my head no to this lie, "Oh no, you were there. I saw you. I heard you. Julie and you say you were not there. I saw Julie. I heard Julie. Now, how am I supposed to believe that one of you is not there and one is? Do you hear yourself? Who is telling me the truth? Do you see me, Steph? Am I talking to you now? Tell me that I am not! What if I told you I never saw you today? How would you feel when you know you spoke to me." I was livid again having my moods shift more rapidly than even Stephanie's could.

Stephanie's eyes went wide again, "Oh shit. I had never thought of it that way. Is that what it is like for you? Oh my God. So, you see and hear Simon for real? You really saw and heard me this morning? But I was not there. Oh Christ. No wonder you are always hitting everyone. I would die not knowing what is real and what is not." She began to rock back and forth thinking hard on what I had said.

The whole conversation was getting to me. I wanted to end it. Looking at her rocking there in her own understanding of what she and Julie had done to me, I again demanded to know what she knew about the Julie business.

She looked up seeming confused, "Oh, that is easy. She is a spoiled brat Psycho. Julie gets what she wants from her parents who just adore her. She can do no wrong. She has taken a fancy to you. I think she is all turned on by you and stuff. I think she wants to,

14

well you know." Stephanie looked away not wanting to say it.

"Sleep with me," I said for her.

She shook her head yes, "more than that Psycho she wants a girlfriend she like owns. What are you going to do? You are stuck right?"

I kind of knew what she was going to tell me, but it still bothered me to hear it. It amazed me how far Julie was willing to go to get laid. I never understood these delusions, but this was above the cut for weirdness. Even for me. I looked back at Stephanie still feeling both upset and an odd relief we had finally sat down to speak of our shared situations.

"Yeah, for now. But I have a plan. I got this," I assured her.

She tried to talk me into telling her my plan, but I did not trust her yet. I just kept saying I would fix it, and that she should not worry.

"But you are not going to sleep with her right? That is not in the plan, is it," Stephanie pushed appearing curious.

I laughed at that, "Uhm, nope. Not if she called the President himself to report me as a killer."

We both had a good laugh at Julie's misguided amour toward me. I was not interested in Julie like that in the least. Since the onset of my illness, I had not shown interest of any kind in either gender. I had been pretty sure I was not gay per say, but I was becoming aware that Stephanie was making me feel something. What exactly, I was unsure. However, I already knew that males were also of interest.

I had realized I had a crush on Tom way back before the poisoning but had chosen to ignore it. He had not kicked me that night, so long ago when everyone else had. I had always believed the feeling was mutual.

As the hour detention drug on, I watched Stephanie smiling and yapping nonstop as she always does. I was not listening as I thought with surprise of how I had spoken to her of secrets that I would not even tell Dr. Scott. That the attendant may have been right. I wondered if I was indeed in love with Stephanie.

I shook the thought off, chalking it up to the confusion of senses that I seemed to have a lot of as of late. Truth is, Stephanie was definitely straight. If I was indeed becoming interested, like everything else in my life, this would be a dead end. Besides, I had more to worry with then some mixed up teenage crush. I decided to ignore the feelings I had for Stephanie and move on to the tasks at hand.

Julie was waiting at the detention hall door when Stephanie and I came out. She was glaring at me, still likely irritated I had thwarted her little plan to humiliate me at lunch in front of her friends. I smiled at her innocently. This made her angry. I could read her mind. She thought I was an asshole. She believed she would get me yet. That made me chuckle a bit.

Stephanie and Julie looked at me suspiciously when I let out the laugh. "What is so funny, Psycho," Julie said looking at me hard.

I dropped my head looking quickly at the hallway floor. I shrugged stifling the giggling. No need to stir the hornet's nest.

Julie looked at Stephanie, "So, did she behave herself in there? Any crazy shit like, laughing for no reason? What did you two discuss," she turned to me to glare.

Stephanie looked at me and for a second, I felt I could not breath. Would she betray me?

"Nope nothing crazy. I did all the talking. She never says much. She just did homework and stuff. Right Psycho?" I looked up at Stephanie surprised she lied like that (pleasantly so).

Then she winked at me while smiling. To my absolute horror and thrill my heart skipped a beat.

Shit, I am in love with her. Fuck," I though bitterly. "Go figure, you'd be attracted to the crazy ones. you idiot!"

We all three walked to Julie's with Stephanie talking non-stop (as usual). Julie had asked Stephanie to stay over, and I was not happy to hear that. I did not want to be alone with Julie, but now I did not think it wise to be around Stephanie either. I did not need further complications. Stephanie was a distraction from my mission to find and remove the radar. However, as usual there wasn't shit I could do about it.

I tried to stay busy during the walk home listening for the transmissions from 'they' that still had not come. I watched the electrical grid whirling above my head grateful that soon as that radar was gone it would be gone too. I had to spit several times as I kept tasting the dirt from the road we traveled. Lately, I was really having issues with my tasting weird shit like that.

I was also damning myself for telling Stephanie my secrets. She would likely turn on me. Everyone always does. The thought that if I did not have a tongue, I could not do stupid shit like that crossed my shattered mind. This idea got trapped in my unit's cogs and wheels as it looped over and over.

Eventually, it dawned on me that removal of the offending tongue would be necessary. It made perfect sense. If I have no tongue, no way can I accidentally say stupid shit to the wrong people, right? Besides, my tongue would never have done something so dumb. This was apparently not the tongue that came with the basic installation of the unit of measurement. So, removing it was the sensible thing to do. I made a mental note to do this right away.

Once we arrived at Julie's, the other two girls went right to smoking pot and raiding Julie's fridge. I sat down in the overstuffed chair trying to find an excuse to get some privacy to take care of the radar and the foreign tongue.

Julie had been gossiping with Stephanie about the new girl Vicky. She was very obviously doing an inquiry to see if Vicky was evil clique material. Suddenly, she recalled I was sitting there like Norman Bates mother's corpse in that chair.

"That shit you pulled at lunch was not cool," she said blowing out her skunk smoke, "Pull that again and I will beat the hallucinations out of you."

Stephanie looked at me seeming frightened, "Come on Julie, that was funny. Psycho was just having a little fun. Damn cut her some slack."

Julie shot Stephanie an angry look, "Stay out of this. Psycho knows damned well she was fucking me on an agreement." She looked back at me still angry, "My mom will be here tonight. You pull that shit in front of her, I swear I will keep my promise even if you cannot seem to keep yours."

I heard that threat loud and clear. She was going to take another run at trying to humiliate me. I sat there waiting to hear what horror she had planned for this 'mother meeting.' I did not have to wait long.

"My mom and dad are helping your sorry ass out. I expect you to be fucking grateful, you hear me in there you loony bitch?"

She knew I hated it when she called me loony, but I bit back my anger and nodded my head yes.

You will behave. No crazy shit. No talking to people not there. No fucking dancing No calling people Simon!. No yelling for no reason, and no starting shit with me or anyone else," she raised her voice to a yell. It hurt my force shield, making me wince.

She got up in a huff and went into the kitchen leaving Stephanie there staring at me in wonder. Stephanie shrugged looking apologetic. I read her mind. She thought Julie was being too harsh. She wanted me to be careful. She wanted me to run away with her, wait, what? I looked away from her. I decided to stay out of Stephanie's mind. I could not be getting involved with this right now. I had to get that radar and the tongue out.

Julie came back in with a glass of water, baby food and pills, "Take these now. Eat and keep your fucking mouth shut. I am in no mood for your psychotic bullshit."

I looked at the pills trying to decide if I should make a scene and fuck up her plans with mom. My hesitation set her off. Julie put the plate of food and water on the coffee table then reared back and backhanded the fuck out of my face.

Startled I almost fell out of the chair, "Fucking take the medication, Psycho. I am not fucking around here," Julie said shoving the pills at me again while I held on to my now aching jaw.

I took the pills from her and put them in my mouth. She picked up the glass. She shoved the water at me. I drank it finally deciding not to fight about this. I had things to do. A battle would slow it down.

"Oh, no you don't. Open your mouth Psycho. Let me see, you better not cheek those pills idiot." She stood there as I opened my mouth to show her I had swallowed them.

Satisfied, she stood over me smiling with what she thought was victory, "Now that wasn't so hard was it, you fucking cracked moron." That made her laugh, "now eat Psycho."

I looked over at Stephanie to see a look of disgust on her face. She did not like what Julie was doing either but like me, she decided to let the monster have her way for now.

Without any argument I took the plate from the coffee table and ate it fast as possible. I had finally figured out how to get my privacy to finish my mission. As I finished, I excused myself from the two now much more subdued girls. Julie's bullying of me had shut Stephanie's constant prattle up (wow, I didn't even know that was possible).

Neither girl even looked up from the television as I went down the hall to the bathroom. I closed the door and locked it. Now alone I shook off my anger at Julie's latest insults. I immediately opened the medicine cabinet looking for anything sharp. Finding nothing but a small sewing kit for quick repair of missing buttons. I took it as it would be useful to close up the unit once the radar was removed. I looked under the sink and found the tool required. A medium sized slotted screwdriver would have to do. It likely had been forgotten after the repair job was done, but I for one was grateful at someone's disregard for putting things back where they belong.

I removed all my clothing to make it easier for the exam. I sat down on the commode and began to examine the unit for discolorations or signs of prior entry. I checked the legs and feet first, but nothing but the old scars from my home life with mom. Then I moved to the stomach and chest. Nothing but the usual scars. I had a lot of them, but I knew them all very well. In fact, I did my best to forget them as often as possible.

I put my clothing back on. Fear that maybe it was in my back, head or even neck filled me. That would be a trickier surgery. However, to my delight on my left wrist I found the discoloration that indicated there was a radar below. I could even see it glowing blue light just below the surface. I chuckled that I had never noticed it before.

I went to the bathroom sink and put my left arm on the shelf to steady it. Taking the screwdriver, I began to apply pressure to the spot using a sawing motion. Blood welled out of the cut as I broke through. I was almost giddy that in a few moments I would have this thing out of me!

The blood was welling up so fast I was having trouble seeing the target. I opened the medicine cabinet again to find the tweezers. I assumed it would not be very large. The blood made everything so slippery I couldn't get a grip on it no matter how deep I cut.

The whirl of electricity flowed around my head in loud rushing sound. I could see it pulsating blue flashes now. I suddenly realized it was transmitting that I had found it. I dug into the wound with the tweezers trying to grab it before it was too late. I still needed to get that tongue out too. I was running out of time.

"Psycho! Julie, call 911." I heard Stephanie scream. "Stop it, Psychol. Oh God, no. Julie, Psycho has slashed her wrists. There is blood everywhere. Help. Please God, help."

Stephanie had come looking for me. She had called for me, but I had not heard her over the noise around my head. The door was locked but when I did not answer she pushed hard on it. It came open as it was not aligned just right. Someone had installed a crappy door knob, likely using a slotted screwdriver.

That about wraps it up for this chapter. We are having a few issues, but no worries, We still got this in hand. We have the right tools for the job. Do not be too worried about all the confusion. We are sure We can repair the damage done.

CHAPTER 35: CEMETERY CONFESSIONS

There are so many things We would like to say about this but We had better hold our tongue about it. Seems We cannot find Our way through this nightmare of manipulations, hallucinations, and delusions easily. Now with Our Radar gone maybe We will be even more lost then before? It seems sometimes We have to take outrageous risks just to stay one step ahead of the truth. We don't know about all of you, but We are very tired of the constant struggle to discover our true mission. How about We just refuse to move for a moment and catch Our breath? Can you forgive Us just this once if We let you do some of the journey on your own? We knew We could depend on you. Now of course, you all will need to be ready to run at any time. We did not want to mention it but there is a taskmaster driving this insane journey. So, go ahead and start. We are currently 'out to lunch' but will be along very shortly. We are always 'just round the bend."

"To me people out of touch with reality are not nearly as dangerous as those who manipulate it." -unknown

Stephanie grabbed the screwdriver in my hands and wrestled with me for possession of the tool.

I had not removed the radar yet, so I held it tightly, yelling over and over, "Leave me alone. Stop. I have to get this out."

There was so much blood on my hands the screwdriver slips away into Stephanie's less slick hands. I watch in horror as she quickly throws it out the bathroom door. It hits the hallway wall across from the bathroom bounces rolling away far from my reach.

Normally, I would have been pissed and hit her for interrupting this most important surgery. Instead, I realized I had the unit open already. I just needed to use my fingers to rip out the radar. The screwdriver was no longer needed. I had gotten deep enough.

I drop to my knees, holding my left wrist up I use my right and to begin to dig at the gaping wound fast as I can trying to get to that blasted pulsating blue device. Strangely, I notice that my right wrist is also gaping open. Though I find this odd, I ignore it assuming this must have been from a forgotten earlier exploration for the radar. I did tend to forget sometimes.

Stephanie grabs my lower arms. She uses all of her strength to keep my hands apart. screaming, "Stop Psycho. Please stop this."

I was very upset. Stephanie was going to keep me from finishing before the radar could tell of my attempts to remove it. I tried to fight her off but for some very odd reason I was so weak I could barely even yell back. The radar is stealing my energy, I could feel it draining me. I fall backward still on my knees, but the wall blocks me from ending up on my back. Fear fills me as I realize I am doomed. There is no hope left in my shattered mind. It is now clear the doctors know of my attempt to escape, surely the radar has told them. I give up.

Stephanie had used her weight to pin my hands to the wall above my head. I watch the trails of blood roll down my bare lower arms from my wrist. It pools in the cuffs of my rolled-up sleeves. My mind wanders to the imaginary cell that I will soon be throw into now that I have tried to get away. Surely, I would be chained to the floor so that the beasts who live in the criminally insane unit can do horrid things to my unit without resistance. Julie had warned me what would happen if I dared to try and get away. I cannot believe that this will be my fate. I am not crazy but will be locked away with those who are. I find that funny for some reason. A giggling fit erupts that I simply cannot control.

Stephanie was very upset. I could see it in her eyes as the tears fell onto my face. She was standing above me screaming something. I cannot make it out because of all the whispering in my ears. I cannot understand the whispers either. Nothing seems to make sense suddenly. One thing I do notice is how very calm I feel. It is as if time has stood still. I am still giggling as I watch Julie come into the bathroom. She looks angry.

"What the fuck have you done, you fucking loon," she yells at me. This I can understand.

I giggle and say, "Failed." The giggling gets harder as I feel the world begin to spin in the stillness of my inner self.

A woman I have never seen before comes in behind Julie. She is very large with very curly ginger hair sticking up everywhere. She kind of looks like Julie only older, and bigger. I giggle at the Big Julie. Now that is amazing! There are two of these monsters!

The Big Julie pushes Stephanie off me and grabs my arms pulling them close to her face. She is examining my wrists. She yells something to Julie and Stephanie. They leave quickly. She is now looking in my face, opening my eyes wide with her fingers. I shake her off my head. I feel so weak and tired. I just want to go to sleep. She grabs my jaw and shakes me back awake.

"Stay with me, don't go to sleep," she says to me very sternly.

I do not know this woman. She can go fuck herself. I will sleep if I want to sleep. I am tired of everyone telling me what I am to do. No one really cares anyway, so why are they always trying to control me? I close my eyes ignoring her.

The woman shakes me violently, "wake up." I wake again.

I open my eyes to see Julie and Stephanie there wrapping my wrists with white tape. This seems very odd to me, so I try to pull away. The woman grabs my upper arms and holds me still while the girls put the tape on me.

"Now hold down tight till the ambulance gets here girls," I hear her say to Julie and Stephanie.

"Hold what," I wonder as I watch them holding my wrists appearing stressed out.

I am so tired. A hole feels like it has opened within me. I am falling into it, but I am not afraid. I am calm and peaceful as I slowly descend down into the darkness. This not so bad I wonder why I had ever been scared of anything at all. It is the first peace I have ever known. I smile as I close my eyes. No more giggling. No more whispering. No more confusion. No more pain. No more despair. No more chaos. No more fear in a nightmare world. Just quiet, serene floating. I am now merging with the mercy of nothingness. I was just so tired.

I open my eyes. I am in a hospital bed. Dr. Scott is here sitting next to me with her clip board. I am strapped to the bed. I see a bag of blood hanging from a hook. "What the hell," I think.

"Welcome back kiddo," Dr. Scott says with a forced smile that hides concern.

"Where am I? What has happened," I ask, initially very confused.

Dr. Scott sighs, "You tried to kill yourself. I am here to ask you what happened actually."

The look of shock on my face is evident, "I did what?"

Dr. Scott cocks her head. "You did not try to kill yourself?"

I shake my head no, still shocked into silence. "I tried to kill myself? That can't be right. I already did that once. I would never be that stupid twice," I think wildly.

Dr. Scott stands and shines a pen light into my eyes, "Okay, tell me what you remember happened, and we can go from there."

I think on it a moment. It is very fuzzy but finally a memory of the radar. I was unsure if I should tell her but to clear my name of a suicide attempt, I really felt I had no choice.

"Julie told me about the radar you put into me. I was trying to get it out. I know it was wrong, but I did not want that inside of the unit of measurement," I said feeling fear that such a confession would send me straight to the criminally insane hospital.

Dr. Scott's eyes went wide. She sat down appearing stunned, "Julie told you what?"

I read Dr. Scott's mind. She was mad at Julie for telling the secret. She was going to punish her for this. Dr. Scott blames Julie for my damaging the radar in my attempts to get it out. I smile at that. I may get put away but knowing that Julie would get hers made me feel better about my impending destruction.

"Julie told me that you put the radar in my unit of measurement. She said that if I tried to run away you could find me." There now Julie was under the bus.

Dr. Scott looked even more alarmed, "Why would you try to run away in the first place?"

Now that was a harder one to answer without some fear, "Well, she said that I had to tell everyone I was a liar. That I was crazy with schizophrenia (I whispered that). If I did not, then she would tell everyone I tried to kill her. If I tried to run away, then you would track me with the radar." I finished observably shaking in terror.

I knew Dr. Scott would not believe me. I feared the punishment that would come when Julie lies to them and says I did try to murder her. Julie said she would, and I knew she would too.

Dr. Scott let out her breath hard and threw her clip board to the floor with a loud crash. She stood up rubbing her head as she put her hand on her hip. She was obviously agitated. This scared me even more as I began to whimper like a little bitch. Dr. Scott's behavior convinced me that I was going to be tortured horridly for life in some mental hospital hell.

She heard me and looked up surprised as I began to beg, "Please do not send me to the hospital. I am sorry. I swear I did not try to kill Julie. I won't try to get the radar out again. I won't run away. Please. Please," I was yelling hard now in absolute panic.

Dr. Scott began to panic herself appearing to not have expected me to become so upset. She pushed the call button for a nurse as she attempted to calm me down, "Shhhhhh, It is okay, your not getting sent away, calm down. I won't send you away."

It did not work. I knew she was lying to me. I just yelled louder as I tried to get out of my restraints. The nurse came into the room. She had a syringe of medication that she quickly put into my IV lead. The calming effect was immediate. I heard the walls of the room sigh in relief at the end of my terrified cries.

Dr. Scott stood over my bed looking at me with that pity look she sometimes had when talking to me, "Okay, now that's better. Just get some sleep. You need rest. This has been very hard on you, kiddo. I can't even imagine." She brushes some of the wig hair out of my eyes, "No hospital I promise. We will talk before I let you go home though. If you can behave there is no reason to punish you for what Julie did. I will deal with Julie. Now, I will be back in the morning. This will be okay, nod if you understand what I am saying to you."

I did understand her, but I did not believe my ears. Did she just say she believes me? That she is going to get Julie without sending me away? I am sure the medication has caused me to hear what I want to hear. This cannot be real. No one ever believes me.

I give her a weak nod expecting that the next time I open my eyes I will be in chains not just hospital restraints. I watch Dr. Scott leave as the sedative takes me to the land of temporary death of consciousness. I was just so tired these days.

The next time I awake, as promised, Dr. Scott is there. This time I am not restrained. I sit up very confused. "Is she really going to let me go," I think cautiously.

"Morning kiddo. So, feeling rested," she says smiling.

I nod still not trusting this trick.

"Okay let's start with this idea of a radar, shall we?" Dr. Scott settles back in her chair next to my bed and crosses her legs.

I shrug. I am not sure what I am supposed to say to that. She looks hard at me, "Do you really think I put a radar in you to track your movements?"

I nod yes. She looks hard at me, "Think, why would I do that?"

"To keep me from running away," I reply flatly. I am not sure what this game is all about but to keep her placated I would tolerate it.

She takes a breath, "Alright, so I would spend a hundred thousand dollars to keep you from running away? That is what a good radar costs these days you know."

I actually did not know that. "No, you would not. But Julie said you did. I know you don't want me to run away. Maybe you got a discount?"

Dr. Scott chuckled at that, "Okay, so when would I have put in a discounted radar?"

I am really starting to feel pretty stupid after hearing how much radars cost, but I won't trust that this was a lie Julie told me. Not yet anyway, "Uhm, the shock shop?"

She was still smiling at me, "Now the shock treatment would short the radar, wouldn't it?"

Shit, she had me there. I thought on it a bit, "When I was under heavy medication?"

She came back at me quick, "To put in a hundred thousand piece of equipment it would take special surgeons and healing time. Do you remember anything like that? Major surgery?"

I did not of course. I was very angry now. Julie lied to me clearly and there was never a radar in my unit of measurement. Even Simon believed her, damn.

"So, is there a radar inside you," Dr. Scott pressed me.

"But I saw it pulsing," I did see it.

"You saw your heart beat in a vein you were cutting to shreds. I also think maybe you had better consider why you actually did this. Was it really to remove a radar? Think? Or was it because Julie made you admit you have schizophrenia," she said leaning forward looking at me harder.

I shook my head no. "It was to get the radar out. Julie said there was one. I believed her."

Dr. Scott shook her head no. "You know Julie lies. She was going to tell everyone you tried to kill her to get you sent away. If you knew she lies, then why believe her about the radar? You did not remember any radar surgery until this girl says so. Why believe this and not everything she says?"

I look at the floor on that one. She had me there too. Why did I believe her? She is a liar. I shrug feeling that odd sensation of despair coming on again.

Dr. Scott senses I am feeling upset, so she is quiet for a few moments letting me think on these questions. Then in a very soft voice she says, "You tried to remove an imaginary radar from both wrists, but I only heard Julie say there was one radar. Think, why did you cut them both?"

I looked at my wrists. She was right, both are wrapped not just the left one. "Why did I cut them both," I wondered.

Dr. Scott sees me looking at my bandages, "I spoke to Stephanie. She says that Julie was being cruel to you about your illness. That she humiliated you and had others help her make fun of you for it. She also says just before you did this Julie had struck you and treated you like a child in front of her. Is this true?" She is looking to see what I will say.

I nod my head in shame. "I let her do those things so I would not get into trouble anymore. I was not being weak I was just afraid of being locked up again," I admitted.

Dr. Scott sighed shaking her head, "I am sorry I did not listen when you told me Julie was hurting you. Can you forgive me? Can you ever trust me so I can help you?"

I was never going to trust her, but I knew better than to say that, so I nodded and shrugged at that.

This seemed to satisfy her for now. "I have sent Julie to see a counselor along with her parents to learn how to deal with someone properly who has your disease. In the meantime, you have to come to terms with your illness."

I do not answer but look at the floor. I was not sick.

"You tried to kill yourself because Julie forced you to admit you have schizophrenia. She also treated you like a child because you are ill. You believed you were removing a radar to avoid accepting you are sick and, sadly, dependent. Your command hallucination called Simon came and told you to take out the radar, didn't he," Dr. Scott recited softly to me.

I look up startled. "How did she know about Simon telling me to do it?" I think freaked out that she had rudely read my mind.

"Simon is real. He is not a command hallucination. Julie said there was a radar. I saw it," I yell to her now feeling very angry at her suggestions.

She shook her head no. "That is not true, is it? You believed in an imaginary radar to hide your despair. Your disease has split your emotions from your inner thoughts. Those damaged emotions are now a command hallucination you hear outside of your body. You call your emotional self, Simon. Simon told you to kill yourself to escape your pain. This is the reality isn't it." She looked to see if I would accept this explanation.

I was not buying this bullshit. "I do not have schizophrenia. I was faking it the whole time for attention. How do you know there is no Simon? Have you ever bothered to ask to meet him? You want me to believe my emotions are a middle-aged, toothless old drunk? Are you serious?" I start laughing hard at that insane suggestion.

Dr. Scott frowned at my mocking laughter. "Look kiddo, you are not faking anything. You do have schizophrenia. Simon is a command hallucination comprised of your scrambled emotions."

Now I am really laughing at her "Oh, I am too faking. I just wanted attention. I can prove it too. Your stupid medication does not work, does it? Because I do not have the disease! Plus no one in my family has schizophrenia. I checked on it. Mary was lying. My mother was tested. She does not have it. So, I cannot have it either. You have misdiagnosed me, and I want you to fix that right now."

Dr. Scott looked at the floor seeming very sad all the sudden, "Your schizophrenia is very severe because it was caused by lead and arsenic poisoning, not by genetics. You have been told this over and over again. You refuse to listen. You are having trouble accepting that your mother's behavior led to the damaging of your brain. This would be hard for anyone to admit. The one that is supposed to love you not only abuses and tortures you, but then destroys your sanity as well. I cannot imagine how hard this must be. However, you must admit to it in order to start to cope with what can never be fixed. You will be dependent your whole life. Your disease is never going to go away. It may even get worse from time to time or as you get older." She looked up to see what I would say next.

I rolled my eyes. "Again, with this whole poisoning thing. I got better. She missed and I survived. Do we have to go over this every week? I do not have schizophrenia, that is just stupid to even suggest. I just told you I am faking it damn it. Why would I lie about faking it."

Dr. Scott just glares at me mocking her. Despite her harsh look, she very softly says, "You know it is true what I say. Until you face it you will keep having things like this incident happen over and over. You have to deal with this, it is not going to go away no matter how much you want it to."

I keep laughing at her. "You are like a broken record. If you have nothing else to say, then I think we shall just have to agree to disagree. Seriously though, you think the emotions of a sixteen-year-old girl are really a middle aged toothless drunk. That is fucking insane. You need medication, Dr. Scott, not me."

Dr. Scott scowled at this, "You are only making this more difficult for yourself. I am not worried. Your symptoms are acute enough now that you will not be able to deny them much longer. If they continue to deepen, we may even have to consider pulling you out of school. We can look into a long-term placement for the chronically mentally ill as well."

My laughter stopped abruptly as she said that. Suddenly, this was no longer a laughing matter. "Wait! I am taking the pills. Please don't do that." My old buddy fear decided to remind me he was constantly running the show as I felt my bladder may let loose.

Dr. Scott looked at her clip board, "Well if you are willing to take the medication, then we can work on your acceptance later. For now, I am increasing your dose. You need 800 mg a day of the Thorazine. You take that four times a day at 200 and I am adding one more anti-psychotic along with your Benzo and the Pheno."

I sat there not believing my ears again. Is she kidding? If I take all that shit I will be unable to even wipe my own nose. When she finished adding milligrams, I quickly added close to 1800 mg a day of various anti-psychotics, sedatives and anti-convulsant drugs. I wanted to argue further that I was faking but I could tell by her behavior she was not in any mood to hear it. Plus, I did not dare push her on her threat about a long-term placement. I was aware that for now I had no power to stop my doctors from doing whatever they wanted to me. If I gave them too much grief, off to the nuthouse I would go. Still, that was a lot of medication.

Dr. Scott finished her prescription notes, "Okay, you are to be released into Mrs. Sloan's custody. Now I will see you next Tuesday. Next time you are told something about me, do me a favor and call and ask. Also, don't believe the stories of sixteen year old kids either. People will sometimes lie to hurt you thinking you an easy target. We will have to work on techniques to learn how to spot those types of people. Take care of yourself, and take your medication."

I nodded smiling grimly at her. I was already working on a plan to avoid taking all that shit. However, for now I would need to be very careful. This was a near miss to another inpatient treatment. I was not in the mood for another stint staring at the wall in a straight-jacket or riding the lightening. For now, I was fucked (sorry, but that is only word to describe it).

Cindy Sloan was there to check me out of the hospital that morning. Julie was at school. Cindy was an LPN who often was not at home as she attended her dying mother's bedside. She was likely a good person at heart if you had a legitimate physical ailment. However, when it came to my alleged disease, she had no tolerance. Cindy believed with all her heart that mental illness could be controlled by the sufferer. She also believed if you can't see it then it is not really there. She had taken me in because she had a good heart and wanted to help me stop acting like an idiot. I know all this because after she checked me out of the hospital, she told me on the way back to the Sloan's house.

I was trapped in her old tan Plymouth forced to listen to a lecture about how "I had better straighten up and fly right." I was informed I just needed a little 'tough love' and 'discipline.' Well, fuck me who knew? lol Turns out I was not sick at all. I just needed to be spanked regularly, and treated with indifference. I also obviously had been far to spoiled. But no worries, Cindy assured me those days were over now. I was going to learn gratitude by keeping house, taking care of Julie (who was a saint I just discovered), and doing yard work. If necessary, she "would not spare the rod no matter how old I was."

You see Cindy set me right. Idle hands are the devil's playground. Hands that clip hedges and do slave labor "have no time to cut open wrists with screwdrivers." Wow, I sure was happy to know I did not really have schizophrenia. I was just a "spoiled rotten brat who had been treated with too much affection." Sorry beauties, I have to just sit here a minute and laugh a bit. It is funny because this is all true.

I for one was so very grateful to Cindy. Had she not come along when she did, who knows what may have happened? Likely, terrible shit like me taking my medication, adjusting to my nightmarish life, or even worse excelling at school! Now, we cannot have that bullshit now can we?

Instead, I began my fall to a deeper level of hell than ever previously found since the onset of the monster schizophrenia. Julie and her family would prove to me that there are worse things than admitting to a crippling mental illness. I was about to receive painful lessons in the true meaning of loss of identity and personal freedom. I would wish hundreds of times that Dr. Scott had put me into that long term treatment center before the next year had finished out. It certainly could not have been anymore soul crushing, or life devastating.

See beauties told you We would catch up eventually. Sorry about that, but sometimes even We are cut...errr...worn to the bone. Now, We are about to start a new section of this long journey towards the Goth Queen. Is everyone ready to put on their 'holy shit' running shoes and head for the finish line? Oh damn, We just remembered, that line up ahead is Our breaking point not the end of the race. No worries, We will get there someday...promise.

CHAPTER 36: THE LUCID ZOMBIE

Well hello Beautiful Family! Aren't you all a sight for sore eyes! Well, here we are again on the journey to what seems like nowhere. Awe, don't you worry your pretty little heads over this latest failure. I promise you we still have plenty of those to keep us in stitches for several years to come. In the meantime, let's all prepare for the heat of summer and all the surprises it has in store for us. Don't you just adore a warm summer season? No school, long crazy, I mean lazy days, and of course plenty of time to hang out with your fiends...Ooops I mean friends. Ah yes, those were the finest of times. Young, strong, a whole life ahead of you, oh and crushing psychosis, what could ever go wrong. Ready to find out? Well, then for just this once do what the voices say and follow me through the looking glass. Now, watch your step, that first one is a doozy. Just remember to stop, drop and roll if you slip. I would catch you, but I have to go and put out something that has gotten out of control. So, be careful and hopefully I will see you again.

"Many people with schizophrenia are withdrawn and don't make friends easily. ... Some people with schizophrenia may also have movement disorders, like muscle twitches, repetitive motions, dance-like tics, or general clumsiness."
- Living with Schizophrenia article

"The only thing worse than not knowing where she belonged...was knowing where she didn't."
-Tessa Shaffer

My sophomore year had been a total nightmare. Actually, there is not a word strong enough in the English language to truly describe the atrocities that I had endured. From extreme abuse, a poisoning, life altering suicide attempts, pneumonia, numerous hospitalizations, Mary, then the queen mother of fuck jobs, the onset of the horrid schizophrenia. Only the Gods know how I had managed to survive to the end of that school year. These many difficulties had caused so many days of missed school I had failed the courses soundly.

So, as Cindy drove me to her home to embark upon my latest of misadventures, she informed me that Dr. Scott had excused me from the final three weeks of school before summer break. No reason to bother, I could never catch up now. I would have to repeat the 10th grade beginning in the fall. Cindy went on to tell me that Dr. Scott believed that lowering the level of stress in my environment would help the high doses of anti-psychotics get my symptoms under control.

I merely listened to her drone on about what a problem I was to everyone, as I watched the world go by through my window. It is not that I did not care about the bombs she was dropping on my already overburdened shoulders, it was just that the medications had already begun to put me into a mental straight jacket. Try as I might, I could not muster up enough inner strength to even respond to her most cruel accusations, derogatory statements, and generalized negativity regarding my continued existence in her house.

I had not asked her to take me in, now had I? I did not ask Dr. Scott to take me out of school, or to put me on tons of medications that required constant monitoring. I had not asked anyone to do a thing in regards to my personal anguish. I did not have schizophrenia, but everyone appeared hell bent to believe I did. Everyone also seemed to be sure they knew better than I did how it should be handled.

Cindy and Julie would have to go to counseling for the entire summer twice a month over my little "radar" incident. Cindy was super pissed at me about that. She said many nasty things about my character because I "was a shit stirrer to bring Julie into my drama." Cindy told me that she and Julie were to attend a day class on how to handle a schizophrenic person. Interesting, I was not sent to any fucking classes to learn about it. Now, that would be silly though, now wouldn't it? After all, since I was supposed to be a psychotic. I could not really ever understand anything anymore, right?

Well, I admit that really pissed me off. I wanted to know why everyone kept trying to say I had this disease. I was not sure what symptoms I was 'faking' that had caused them such a conclusion. I did not even know what the fuck schizophrenia was. Oh sure, I had a complete list of myths, bias, and stereotyping like everyone else about crazy people. However, what was it exactly that I was doing that made everyone so damned sure I was sick with it was beyond me.

As I sat there, I decided soon as I could, I had to find a way to look up the disease, its symptoms, and the testing used to prove it. It would likely be the fall school year before I could get to it, but regardless I would find out. I quietly cursed myself for not destroying those records Mary had thrown at me, and for not following up on the lies contained within. Had I done that, perhaps I would have tried to fake a less horrible disease, or at least not have accidentally faked this one.

We pulled into the Sloan's garage, and I got out of the car waiting to see if Cindy was going to start the 'tough love' shit or wait and ambush me later.

She got out frowned at me standing there. "Get in the house and clean the kitchen. After that, you have medication to take. I am going to relax and watch some TV do not let me hear a word out of you. Julie will be home in a few hours. You will leave her alone too. I think you have done enough damage already. In fact, I don't want to hear or see you at all as long as I am in the house. There is plenty of housework so keep your ass busy and out of my way." She walked into the house leaving me there thinking on what she said.

"Okay, so I can do that. No speaking and avoid everyone in this house. It will be my pleasure you stupid bitch." I smiled as I thought this. "I will be going home soon. This has to be the way to win back my clean records. If I do not speak ever again, no one can call me crazy anymore."

I do not know why I had not thought of this before. Just stop talking to the delusions. So simple, so easy. Now this has to work and Dr. Scott will see I was faking it the whole time. I so wished I could talk with Simon about it. For now, I would have to trust he would agree with me.

As I entered the house, giving Cindy enough time to settle, I received my transmission from 'they.' I had begun to worry but to both my horror and joy I was informed that Green was the color of disgust and Yellow of death. Nodding my head, I went inside to do my chores sure that this mess could still be all cleaned up.

Julie came in just as I took the pills Cindy had left out for me on the dinning room table. I would have to work a way out of having to take this unnecessary shit, but for now I was determined to comply. I was simply tired of fighting everyone all the time. If I did not fight maybe I would stop getting hit all the fucking time, or even get to go home without having to connive so much. Either way, I did not want to push my luck for now. I needed time to rest and regroup.

Julie looked at me with her eyes focusing on the bandages on my wrists. Cindy was on the couch asleep in front of the TV snoring loudly. Julie put her things down and walked over watching me take the pills. I did not make eye contact. I rarely did anyway but today I made damned sure not to even by accident.

"You are so fucking stupid Psycho," she sighed. "Do you have any idea how bad you fucked up?"

I nodded yes, because I was very aware, trust me. She sat down at the table as I stood there looking at the floor trying to decide if I should run, stay there, die, or what?

"Mom is pretty pissed at you. If I were you, I would stay out of her sight." She looked to see if I heard her. I nodded again.

She just sat there waiting, I think, for me to speak. Julie could wait till hell froze over, wasn't happening. I turned and went back into the kitchen to find a broom. While I stood there, I had decided in order to avoid Julie I was willing to sweep floors, scrub toilets, wash windows and rip open my wrists with a screwdriver...wait, what?

I found the broom rather quickly then went right to it. Julie had followed me watching. She leaned on the counters finally she could take the silence no longer, "why did you tell Dr. Scott I told you that there was a radar inside of you? That is fucking crazy, Psycho. I never said anything like that."

I kept sweeping refusing to answer her. However, my thoughts were swirling with panic, "Wait. Why is she lying again. She did say that. I heard her. Simon did too. She is still fucking with my mind. Damn her. It was suddenly very hot in the room. I felt sweat begin to roll down my face. What was her game? She won! Why is she still screwing with me.

"Psycho, I know you are listening. You need to be honest with Dr. Scott and tell her I never said that. You hear things all the time. You were just hallucinating that shit. Now I am in trouble because you are a fucking schizo. Why are they even taking your word over mine? You are nuts," she was red faced trying to bully me into saying I would tell Dr. Scott I had lied about the radar.

She did say there was a radar though...right? No way she was going to convince me she did not, I think to myself, "I have too much proof! Wait! why am I even justifying this? Simon heard her; I certainly did not fucking just make it up. I am not schizophrenic. She is angry that she is having to pay for her lie." I move my sweeping to the dining room.

I suddenly hear a woman voice whisper in my ear, "You are insane. It is possible Julie did not say that. You believed in a hundred-thousand-dollar radar. Maybe you were hallucinating like she said you were. You are schizophrenic and you know it too."

I was so startled by the voice I dropped the boom and almost ran into the wall behind me trying to get away from no one. There was no woman there. I was horrified to realize I just heard a voice without an owner, or did I? Julie saw my "startle" and came in with her hands on her hips smiling at me grimly.

"Hearing things are you there, Psycho? What did you hear this time? That aliens are landing tomorrow night next door? Maybe you should go run and tattle to Dr. Scott that I am from Mars? Or whatever the voices are telling you about me. I know you are hearing them. You talk to them constantly." She started laughing at that, "You are a God damned train wreck."

I picked up the broom and begin to sweep the floor hard. I was fighting back the urge to yell back at her that I am not Psycho, that I do not hear voices, and that she did say that radar was in my unit of measurement.

"She is trying to confuse us," I think to myself. "Ignore her. She is playing tricks on you. Throwing her voice and everything Why is she so mean."

Julie walked over and stood in front of my broom's path, "You can ignore me if you like. Sooner or later, I will get you back for this. You hear me, Psycho, I will make you pay big time for fucking with me. You tell Dr. Scott you lied about my saying you had a radar in you, or I suggest you watch your back, you crazy bitch." She then turned and went to her room closing the door behind her.

I stopped sweeping to lean into the wall a second. I was just so tired of all this. I had not done a thing to Julie; she had come for me. She was not having to leave her home, work like a house slave, or take horrible medication. All she had to do was take a class and do some counseling (which the way I saw it, I felt sorry for the counselor).

My mind was struggling with both the terror of the possibility that she might be telling the truth, and with the smothering effects of the medication that was quickly taking hold. It seemed that my perceptions of reality were being questioned so often by so many people that now I was beginning to question them myself. This was causing me to become confused. Their attempts to make me believe I was crazy were starting to work.

As I used the wall to hold up my suddenly very heavy body, I wondered, "could I actually be schizophrenic? Maybe, I am not faking? How can that be?"

I feel the world tilt as I look down at the bandages on my wrists. For the first time since the poisoning, pure lucidity returned. With it I also had a sudden insight into the reality that had been so elusive over the many months. I thought I may faint as the whirling cogs in my mind suddenly froze up with a most horrid revelation.

I felt as if someone had struck me in the back of a head with a baseball bat as I think, "Oh my God. What am I going to do? This cannot be happening. I am schizophrenic. I have been hallucinating. I did believe in an imaginary radar. I am fucking insane."

I felt an explosion happening within my chest as my heart began to ache with these horrible realizations. I had to get out. I dropped the broom again and quietly left the house running fast as I could for the cemetery across the street. Once inside the only type of real estate I had ever known as home I fell to the ground on my knees. I felt I may die right there, I wished I would die right there. I looked up into the sky obscured slightly by tree branches. I could hear the birds telling each other of my presence. No sounds but that of the woods and the earth. It was the right place for my reckoning.

Sorrow was overtaking my inner self as the tears broke loose from their cage behind my eyes. I wailed loud and long reaching for that God that never cared much for me, "Nooooooo, please, nooooooo. Take it back, please, please, please. I will do anything. Please take it back. I am so sorry."

Tears streamed down my face as I begged God to take away my madness. I promised any and everything I could think of and made up things when I could think of nothing else, to offer. My bargaining did not yield results. I did not see an angel sent to heal my brain that had been raped and shattered by a mother that never loved me. No redemption was granted no matter how much I plead for mercy.

Eventually, the intense sorrow turned to anger as I then stood up raising my fists to the very same Deity that I had just hoped would cure me. I cursed this God, saying the foulest things I could think of, and again made a few up when I ran out of the usual. I then cursed humankind, the world, the trees, the cemetery, and most of all myself. I yelled and railed, kicking the headstones, the trees while hitting myself in the head for being "defective." I growled like an animal and shouted unintelligibly until I finally was spent of all my energy.

I fell to the ground pulled up my knees and like I had seen Stephanie do so many times, I cried into my lap rocking back and forth. Nothing worked. I was still schizophrenic. I was never going to get well. My mother had successfully murdered me. I had suddenly realized I had been correct all along since my riding the lightening. I am a walking type of death. I truly am undead. Unable to live, but still had a heartbeat. A body with only enough mind to know it had no mind and no hope of a real life. I was lost forever and could never again find myself.

Cindy and Julie had not come looking for me, so I did not go back to the house. I spent the entire night rapidly shifting from grief to anger and then after sleeping a bit I would start all over again. To this day, few nights have been more horrific. Acceptance of one's fate is a bitch no matter what the devastation is. Finally understanding you have a crippling, progressive, mental illness is likely not much different than coming to grips with learning you have a terminal illness. I really believed all was lost. For the first time in my life, I did not try to develop a plan, nor did I try to solve for X. No, this time, I gave up. There was no longer any hope in my heart.

The sun rose the next day, as it always does, but in my mind, it was forever night. I did not appreciate the woodland residents calling out good morning as I had always done. I felt empty and hopeless. I left the cemetery not much different than the zombie I tended to resemble with my outlandish dressing style. Nothing seemed to matter anymore as I entered the house to find the Ginger twins glaring at me from their breakfast at the kitchen table.

"Where you been, Psycho," Julie said growling angrily.

I pointed to the door shrugging. I then went to the bathroom to clean up. I did not say a word. Julie could chase me down and beat the stuffing out of me if she wanted. I no longer cared. Maybe I would get lucky, and she would kill me. However, I seriously doubted it. I was never lucky.

The next three weeks I continued to take the medication as prescribed. I never said a word no matter how much Julie threatened me. Every day, I did the chores around the house, without complaint or fighting. Cindy had taken a three-week respite from her mother's bedside to make sure Julie was able to finish the school year without "this Psycho" upsetting the household further. She and Julie would often just sit around smoking pot together and watching TV.

They really were a lot alike in many ways. Big, mean, and arrogant. When I heard them talking, they were always trying to one up each other with tales of 'how awesome' they were as people go. I was often left wondering how anyone would come up with such a conclusion when they obviously had no awards, celebrity, or proof otherwise. No, these two believed they were hot shit just because they were breathing. It truly was amazing.

Julie's dad Brian came in one every other weekend, but I avoided the man altogether. I did not trust men (well, not women either come to think of it). I had not had good experiences with them and this one was a big guy. He frightened me. I would catch him often just staring coldly at me whenever I accidentally came across his path. I would quickly exit keeping my eyes down caste. I wanted nothing to do with that noise for sure. I had enough trouble of my own without inquiring into his.

Every night I would go to the cemetery after Cindy and Julie went to bed. I spent the entire three weeks going through bouts of begging for mercy from God, to kicking the shit out of myself. I slept the rest of the time on the benches or wherever I would just finally wear out after having thrown a fit regarding my illness. I was feeling more and more washed out. There was no hope of any life in me anymore as the medication locked down my mind and put out my fire within. I no longer heard voices from nowhere, or transmissions from 'they.' I could no longer read minds or see the delusional world tapestry. In fact, I could not see anything at all but grey bleakness of a world of nothingness.

By the end of the third week, I decided I was turning into stone. A living statue devoid of emotions, reason, and thought. Sometimes, I would just sit and stare at the wall for hours at a time, thinking and feeling nothing. I was not even depressed about it. I did not have enough life force left inside my stone flesh to even want to kill myself. Apathy had replaced my anxiety with a whole new type of hell. If this was the life schizophrenia offered, well then, they may as well put me in a cell and lose the key.

I was supposed to see Dr. Scott every Tuesday, but that did not happen. She had been called off to a family emergency, so I was given a bit of a reprieve from her stupid attempts to make me believe there could be any kind of hope for a future. I already knew my life was over before it had even begun. I did not even have the motivation to care that much. It was, however, too bad that she was not there to see the "real me" she had always wanted to know.

Dr. Scott had decided not to hospitalize me. She instead managed to put me in a padded cell inside my own head. Dr. Scott was sure the medication would somehow glean out some extraordinary person from under the piles of psychotic symptoms. Well, she was wrong. If you took the psycho away, nothing at all was at the center, just a compliant meat puppet.

Of course, that was what they wanted. The comfortable peace of their not having to deal with my lashing out from my nightmare is all they cared about. If they did not care that my lashing out was caused by pain, they certainly did not care that my not lashing out was caused by worse. It was never about me. After all, with no cure, they could offer me only heavy sedation. Sedation did not end my horror, only theirs at having to deal with it. This was something I finally understood. They were not trying to help me. They were trying to help themselves.

I finally realized that I was not even as important as a beloved pet. I had heard more than once a family struggle with the decision to put down their dog or cat so that it did not "suffer" in pain, as that would be cruel. I was suffering in unbelievable pain but instead of putting me down, they sedated me so I would not scream or try to escape my agony anymore. It seemed to me not only was a schizophrenic not even really human, but it was also not even high enough in humans collective consciousnesses to be given the love and concern granted a dog or cat.

The three weeks finally ended, and Cindy went back to caring for her mother. She was satisfied I was "on a leash" and felt fairly confident Julie could now manage the Psycho alone. I would have been afraid knowing that Cindy was leaving me to Julie's care, but truth is I no longer cared. Nothing Julie could do to me was worse than what the disease and its useless medication already had.

Cindy barely pulled out of the driveway before Stephanie, Joni, Vicky, and Crystal showed up driven by Vicky in her shit box Buick Skylark. The girls came through the door like gang busters. The house that had been sullen and silent for the last three weeks was suddenly filled with laughter and loud talk. I was in the kitchen sweeping as usual as I heard the ruckus in the next room. I did not bother to go look, join them, or even care. Not my problem. I hated those girls and they hated me. I kept on my tasks ignoring them as I saw Julie head for the living room to join the evil clique for this "end of school" girls sleepover party. Besides, I was not invited.

The girls were talking loudly of boys at school that were 'hot' and of gossip of all kinds. I tried to block them out, but it was impossible. They got even louder as I heard Julie start passing a joint. I knew the girls were smoking from that horrible smell of skunk, plus all the coughing. I just shook my head and started cleaning the counters for the thousandth time. I did not want to try to make a run for the back of the house or outside till I was sure they had all calmed a bit. I was in no mood for teasing. The medication had given me the curse of lucidity.

Lucidity was a curse for me because it did not come with an end to the stigma. It did not matter that I was not Psycho for the moment, they would treat me like her. As Psycho I could at least fight back. As this meat puppet I was helpless against them. So, I was stuck for the time being.

Julie pretty much had ignored me the past three weeks after her initial threats, but I did fear today she may get back around to feeling it her right to make me her bitch. I held my breath hoping she would continue to forget I even existed. Instead, it was Stephanie who remembered me. To my horror I heard her ask Julie about me.

"Oh, that dumbass is in the kitchen scrubbing some imaginary dirt off the walls, I think. Who cares," Julie said to Stephanie after a coughing fit.

I heard Stephanie get off the couch. Her footsteps were coming my way. I looked around trying to think of something to do so I would not have to interact, but there was nothing.

"Oh my God, Psycho," Stephanie said happily, "You look great. I have missed you. How are you feeling?"

I shrugged and looked at the floor. I had promised not to speak. This promise had held well, no way I was going to break it now. Not even for Stephanie. Now that the medication was working, I no longer believed I was in love with Stephanie. That had been a confusion of some sort caused by my illness I had finally realized. There never had been any desire to date her, or anyone else for that matter sadly. No interest in sexual/dating/love relationships was just another nasty part of my curse, I had recently discovered. Wishing for such interest in anyone, even if it was Stephanie, had been a delusion sadly.

As she stood there looking at me bright eyed and happy, I realized I did indeed love Stephanie. But I was not "in love" with her. There is a difference. I cared about her and wanted the best for her like one would want for a sister or best friend. I was grateful I could at least feel that kind of love even if it was not the passion that makes life worth fighting for.

This kind of love is important, but it was for the other person's benefit and not for the pleasure of oneself. It certainly was not the lust that makes one's heart sing and soul soar. No thanks to my disease I was forever banned from such inner joys. The secret of schizophrenia is the inner self is damaged beyond repair. I could no longer have such emotions because I no longer had a true sense of self.

Stephanie had kept saying we were friends. I loved her because I believed she loved me. She was not the best person in the world. Stephanie messed up sometimes. So do we all. Despite it all, I also believed she had cared when no one else had. She did the best she could given her limited age, lack of knowledge, and own problems. That was my definition of love.

Apparently, even psychotic, I had understood that to some degree, even if I had gotten it a bit mixed up. I was glad to see her, to my surprise. However, I did not want to talk to her. I had hurt this girl far worse than she ever had hurt me, even when she was misguided in her efforts to "help" me. I could never hope to pursue any kind of friendship or relationship of any kind as this thing I was. Without a true sense of self, I was sure to harm anyone who got too close. I would suspect them of wrongdoing, hit them, or just fear them.

Stephanie meant too much to me to do that to her. I had done enough already. I wanted nothing more than hang out with her and do all the things she had once wanted to do with me. I now understood why anyone would do such things, but now even with that understanding, I did not have the ability to enjoy any of it. I had lost that when I got sick. Now seeing her reminded me of what had truly been lost the day my mind shattered. I simply could not bear it.

"Hey, Psycho, come into the living room and hang out with us. I want to tell you all the stuff that has happen since you had that accident. Hey, are you like okay now? Julie says you are taking the medication like they told you to do." Her eyes go to my mostly healed wrists.

I did not respond. She eyed me appearing upset. Julie walked in just as Stephanie's began to ask another question. She turned and looked at Julie, "Hey what is with Psycho? She is just standing there calm and stuff. Is she on those downer pills or something?"

Julie snorted at that, "She is on enough sedatives to knock down a fucking elephant my mom told me. I like her better like this. No talking to people not there. No crazy shit. Nothing. She doesn't do shit anymore, but clean and keep that trap shut. Hey, maybe you should take some of her pill Steph." Julie began laughing at that idea.

Stephanie ignored the insult, "Well I don't like it. I mean she needed to get some stuff to calm down some of that crazy stuff, but this is too much," she finished pointing at my still form.

Julie glared at me, "Shut up Steph. I planned on cutting off that heavy dosage they are giving her soon as Mom got off my ass. Psycho is not any fun like this. She just sweeps and stares. Give it a couple of days, then we will have some fun."

My stomach lurched a bit. "What the fuck is she talking about? Seriously, Julie is not going to make me take the medication? Now that would be too much to hope for. This must be a cruel joke of hers. What did she mean have some fun," I thought it but if I did not say anything?

"Psycho, go out to your cemetery. You are a wet blanket like this. No one wants you around anyway. Go ahead, beat it. Come back in the morning and make my breakfast," Julie barked at me.

I just nodded. I did not have to be told twice. I hauled ass out the door never looking back. For once I was grateful to Julie. It was maybe the only time I had seen her be merciful.

I am sure the girls all had a good time that night gossiping and smoking their pot. I spent it staring into the sky wondering what would become of me. Now that I understood the extent of the damage, I could not imagine that there was any chance at any life of value. I could not even hang out with girls my own age and do regular teenage things. Even on the highest doses of medication I was still choosing seclusion in a cemetery to social interaction. What could I possibly do now but look with dismay at an empty future with years of isolation trapped with my own negative thoughts and memories of a life ended far too soon? I wished I had successfully removed that damned radar and bled to death, or even been a better suicide diver.

The thoughts of suicide were so heavy that I decided maybe I should think of something else. It occurred to me that I should try harder to make friends. Surely, if I faked a life, I could at least lie to myself that I had one? Maybe create a delusion that could work in my favor for a change. I did want to die, of that there was no doubt. However, there was still a part of me that could not let my mother be the winner. I needed to find a way to beat this thing she had done to me. Sleep overtook me that night as I tried to figure out how I could function in a world where I just did not belong anymore.

I awoke to find Stephanie standing over me smiling. "You are so pretty when you are sleeping," she said giggling.

I was a bit startled rising fast enough to cause Steph to back up in a bit of fear. That made me feel bad. I had hit her so many times. She had reason to fear me. I looked down in shame at that, finally deciding to break my silence to make sure she understood how sorry I truly was,

"Steph, I am not going to hit you. You just scared me is all. I know we already apologized a few weeks back, but seriously I am sorry I hit you all those times. You didn't deserve it. I am sick. You were right, but I would not listen."

Stephanie gasped while staring at me in disbelief, "You are admitting you have schizophrenia?"

I nodded looking down at the ground. My heart was still aching every time I even thought of this horror. Stephanie had earned the right to see that true pain. She had tried to help me, even shared her own mental health issues, and I had been an ass in return. So, I owed her this.

"Oh, Psycho, I am so sorry. I know how you feel, well I mean I don't, but I know what it feels like to have something so bad happen you just think your life is over," she sniffled appearing as if she may cry. I could see her empathy was real.

"I don't know what I am going to do Steph. I don't even know if I can live like this. What should I do? I am so lost." I covered my face as I began to cry quietly.

Stephanie was startled by my tears, "You can cry. Well, I would cry too, Psycho, I would." She came forward and tried to put her arms around me.

The shock was horrid, I recoiled and yelled out instinctively, "don't touch me."

Stephanie jumped back scared to death, "Please don't hit me Psycho. I was just trying to hug you not hurt you. Why won't you let me hug you," she was screaming at me.

This made me really begin to go into a crying jag, "Steph, your touch hurts me. Everyone's touch hurst me. Everything inside my head is all mixed up. I have brain damage. God damned me."

This confession surprised Stephanie, or maybe it was my utter break down as I fell apart before her in total despair. Whatever the reason, she sat down quietly at a short distance, speaking very gently with her own tears on her face, "I am beginning to understand. You are all alone, and no one can make you feel better. You can't even have a hug when you cry, so you don't cry."

I am in hell as I hear her say those words. She had just done what I had only three weeks earlier, she had found insight to the true horror of this illness. The schizophrenic is trapped in a world with things attacking them that no one can see. No one can save us from the things inside our heads, and no one can comfort with something as simple as a hug.

I do not know how long it took for me to get a grip on myself, but eventually I did. Stephanie waited for me patiently weeping on her own over the things that could not be fixed.

Finally, when I had settled down, she spoke, "You should go back to your cemetery, Psycho. Julie is not good for you. The medication has made you sick in a different way, a worse way, I think. If you go home, you can be with Simon again, and I will come see you."

I did want to go home. I looked at her as I recovered from my pity party, "Julie will come after me. I have no money. How will I survive? If I don't take the pills, I will get crazy again. How Steph, just how?"

She smiled, "Psycho, you are still crazy, just a different and sad kind. Even mean, I like you better without the pills. I will help you with money. I know people who will give you work this summer for more. Julie is a bitch. Her family just wants the check. If you stay out of trouble she won't even bother. You are no longer something she wants. That's the only good thing about the medication, it made you a bore." Now she laughs.

I laugh too. She was right. I was not acting a fool anymore. Julie loved drama. One thing about the medicated me I could say was there was nothing interesting about a silent, sulking teenager.

Then a thought came to me that stopped my laughter, "But Dr. Scott? How about the probation officer I have to see next week?"

"I got you there too. I have a driver's license now. I can use my aunt's old Volkswagen whenever I want long as I put gas in it. I am babysitting but I can work out driving you to those appointments if you can pay me back gas money when you get work." She was smiling, proud she had all the answers to my situation.

I thought on her idea, finally deciding this could actually work. Maybe I just needed it to work. Whatever the reason I decided I was going home. I had also decided to quit the medication. I was ready to quit not because I did not think I had schizophrenia, but because the medication made my quality of life so bad, I would rather be dead, or psychotic.

Julie and the other girls were still asleep. Stephanie had risen early. She helped me slip quietly through the house and gather my property. I thought briefly of asking her if she knew where my missing records were, but I decided that it no longer mattered. I was sick. Having those records did not change that fact.

She and I took off for my cemetery home before any of the evil bitches stirred. As we walked together, it felt good to be out in the world again. I even had a friend at my side. She of course talked non-stop the whole way but this time I actually enjoyed listening to her. We arrived at the metal gate in record time having moved quickly before Julie could discover we were gone. As I touched the metal a feeling of relief poured over me like a warm shower. I closed my eyes enjoying the rare positive sensation. Stephanie was still talking but that did not matter, all was right with my world, for at least this moment.

Once inside we discovered the place needed a woman's touch. It had quickly overgrown, and my supplies had been scattered by animals all over the place. Not that there was much there to begin with.

Stephanie helped me all day as we cleaned up my home. She did not complain a bit but never stopped talking for even a second. Sometimes, I would chuckle at it wondering just how anyone could come up with so many words but actually say almost nothing. I did love Stephanie before that day but now I also respected her. She did not have to help me. She did not have to try to understand. She also did not have to care, but she did all of that and more.

On this day, she proved it. To this day it still makes me smile bitterly the memory of those days with Stephanie. I would soon realize how much this small bit of kindness truly spoke of my absolute inner desperation and loneliness. I had waited my whole life for someone to give two shits. Simon came and did that, but Stephanie did even more. She actually sacrificed her place in Julie's world, to hang out with a Psycho.

We both knew Julie would retaliate, but Stephanie told me I was worth it. Now that was something I had never heard before. I was worth something to someone. I wished that my mind would crack again right then and there so those words could loop like words used to. It was the finest day of my young life. And to know it was only because I had a friend, and a cemetery shithouse says a lot about my life up to this point doesn't it. My bar for happiness was a bit low to say the least.

When the sun set my friend Steph had to go home to take care of dinner for her aunt. For once I was sad to see her go. I spent the first night back home smiling and listening to my precious mad box reflecting on the possibilities of a job, a car, maybe someday a family. I knew I was lying to myself. I was used to lying to myself. I am a schizophrenic, hell, we are fucking experts at it. However, it did not hurt anyone for me to wish I could live in their world, be well, and have all the things others take for granted. For this moment I had some reality, but a little unreality was always there just under the surface, thanks to my illness.

I fell asleep with a big smile thinking of what kind of house I would like to live in one day when I saved enough money from my imaginary job. Why shouldn't I have that? After all I had made a friend, I maybe could find a life despite it all.

Stephanie returned the next day and the next to hang out with me as we worked on restoring the cemetery to its former glory. By day three, it was beautiful as it likely had ever been. The outhouse was back in order all was as it had been. Steph and I even had time to dance to music enjoying just being two stupid kids hanging out dreaming of the wonders that awaited us in our futures. It really seemed like just admitting I was sick to her had done the trick. I was feeling better every day. Each morning I awoke to less zombie feeling as my thoughts became clearer.

Of course, I had not taken my medications in three days. By day four I started to feel very odd. Though I was expecting Stephanie, I felt like someone was already there with me. As I walked around my boneyard, I swore I saw something run behind a tree.

I was startled to pure panic. Something was sneaking around watching me. Stephanie showed up shortly after to find me agitated looking behind every tree in the cemetery for the 'thing.' This seemed to upset her a bit.

"Psycho, I think maybe it is time to try to get some of those medications back from Julie. I think you are getting sick again." She looked concerned.

I shook my head no, "No, Stephanie, believe me there is something here, I saw it."

She would not be swayed, "There is nothing here. You can't go forever without medication, you know that."

We began to argue about my mental health which pissed me off to the core. I really liked Stephanie but her questioning my sanity was not okay. Eventually, I felt that she was trying to get inside my head as she kept staring at me hard. This feeling kept growing with each accusation she made about my past fiascoes.

Finally, as she continued to argue with me, I was sure that Stephanie had only pretended to be my friend but really was there to get me in trouble with the Sloan's.

"Okay, I see it now. You are working with Julie. I am such a fucking fool. You are a backstabbing bitch. Get out Stephanie and tell Julie she can kiss my ass. You are just like her a fucking liar," I yelled at Stephanie.

She stopped arguing as tears welled up in her eyes. "Okay Psycho, I will leave. I see you are already sick again. It is my fault. I should have brought the medications in case. I will fix this. Don't do anything stupid till I get back."

"Are you fucking deaf or stupid? I said fuck off, "I screamed, now finding myself pacing back and forth with extreme anxiety filling me. All this drama was making me feel very nervous for some reason.

Stephanie took off running never looking back as I started to talk to myself about 'Judas's everywhere.' I did not bother to even go to the gate to make sure she had gone.

As I paced back and forth, I suddenly noticed a transmission coming in as the trees began to glow and pulsate with the many wavelengths lighting up from 'they.' I heard that Green was still a problem as well as Yellow. I nodded that I understood.

My head was aching in the center as my pacing increased in speed. I could hear the earth sigh a breath of relief that my powers were returning. They were indeed and rapidly too.

By noon, I could see the tapestry of the delusional like a spider's web spreading out covering the real world just below it. I could once again hear the whispers of the dead residents as they discussed my most recent difficulties like I was today's headline news. Their gossiping about me made me very angry.

I started to hurl insults back at them and tell them all to "shut the hell up."

I began to feel the need to sway my head, push out my arms over and over as if I were on a cross, and stomp overcome me. My anxiety within became terror that was replacing my blood supply with a circuitry of errors. All my senses became acute to the point of pain, then by dark they blew. I fell to the ground trying to hold my head together as the static and cicada bugs called my name. The pain was excruciating as I felt my brains leaking from my ears. When the static was done with me, I stood up, Psycho once more.

Thank Goth that we all survived that nasty fall. Guess we just found out that there are things worse in the grey than ever could be found in the dark. Make sure to return for the continuation of this part of the story in the next chapter as things are about to get hot!

CHAPTER 37: LIAR! LIAR! YOUR HOUSE IS ON FIRE!

Well, so we had a meltdown, no surprise there. These things are just bound to happen when you are behind the looking glass. You see reality is always based up the shared perceptions of everyone around you, usually. The trouble here in this delusional world is the perceptions of others who say they understand reality, are likely also out to get Us. We all learned that though the radar transmissions didn't we, or did we? Join 'Us' as we once again are left scratching ou4 head watching the world go up in smoke. We ask ourselves; did We just lose it all, or did we never have it to begin with? Now, you all start while We make sure to place the lightening rod just right. The shocking ending of this chapter will be worth all the pain you have all endured to get here. I see a storm coming, can you hear the thunder? Great! See you below!

"Believing something existed and then finding out it didn't was like reaching the top of the stairs and thinking there was one more step."
— Francesca Zappia

That night that Psycho returned, I did not sleep. Instead, I danced to the sounds of the night and my mad box. Inside my head millions of thoughts, sensations, ideas, and memories swirled like an F-5 tornado. Nothing was coming through correctly any longer as I could smell what I saw, heard what I thought, taste what I felt, and feel what I imagined. My nightmare was back in full force and this time I had no intention of waking up. I had been awake to find I still did not function correctly. At least in this world I had some power. In the real world I was a zombie enslaved to the monster Julie. In the delusional world, I could rule.

When the sun rose again, I had expected to see Stephanie return with Julie and an army in tow to drag me back to the zombie world of heavy medication and cruel degradation. I was quite nervous about it, but no one had come even as the sun began to climb into the sky.

Around late morning my best friend Simon finally showed up. He told me he had been waiting at the schoolhouse for me, but I never returned. I laughed at his stupidity.

"You know damned well you can read my mind. Why did you never come to visit the cemetery across from Julie's," I demanded to know.

He apologized, "I could not find your mind. It was blocked." Simon looked confused by that.

I looked at the ground ashamed of having yelled at him, "Ah yes, Simon. It was the medication. It was like cotton on my powers. I could not send you any messages."

He looked surprised, "Why were you taking the medications? You are not sick."

I shook my head no, "Simon, I am sick. I have that disease schizophrenia. You have told me several times. You were right. I figured that out. None of this delusional world is real I am told. I am crazy, there is no doubt."

I was most unhappy to admit that to my friend, but it was a truth I had to face.

I hoped he would not leave. Maybe he would not want to hang out with an insane person. My heart seemed to stop as I awaited his answer with trepidation. Instead, he began to laugh at my statement.

"You are not a fucking schizophrenic. I was only saying it to piss you off. You are not crazy. You are confused. I am here to fix that. You do not need medication; you need to stop believing liars. You have special powers, and they are jealous of it." He started rolling a smoke while glaring at me to see if I understood.

Well, he had a point. I can read minds, see the tapestry, hear the dead, and get transmissions from 'they.' I had even more power than that, but these were the big ones. His answer made perfect sense. The medications made me feel bad because they were blocking my circuits. I did not have the disease, I was 'enlightened.'

I was so glad not to be schizophrenic I could barely contain my relief as I hugged Simon tightly telling him 'I had missed him a lot.' His explanations always made my confusion clear right up. Now that I had him back, along with my powers, I was sure all would be well. Let Stephanie and her wolves come calling. We would be ready for them.

The only real problem I could see with my plan to stay home with Simon was the need for food and other supplies. Mary was no longer in the picture, so no way I could blackmail her into helping out to protect her precious reputation anymore. Besides, apparently everyone thought me insane. My antics and living conditions would no longer be judged as Mary's fault most likely. No, these simple towns folks would likely chalk it up to 'what crazy people do.'

By mid-day I was wishing I had not been so harsh with Stephanie. She may have been a backstabbing liar, but I really needed the job, money and help she had promised in order to survive on my own. I was beginning to think I may need to apologize to her, to see if there was any hope left of a compromise. This became a possible scenario in my shattered mind. However, by late afternoon there was still no Stephanie.

Simon had noticed my anxious pacing as I continued to watch the gate for her return. He had kept my mind busy all day telling me of the old days" "when he worked as a brakeman for the railroads. I found it all very interesting but in truth I was missing my friend Stephanie. She was my age, my gender, and well my generation too. Simon was great, but Simon was not what I really needed to learn to navigate in this delusional world. He was an awesome distraction from boredom. He simply could not compete with the excitement of what I desired more than anything. I wanted a life and I wanted to be friends with the delusions. This was my world, his was real. I did not belong in the real world. I was not satisfied living through the memories of a life already spent.

"She is getting Julie to come fuck you over. Stephanie is not your friend," Simon said looking hard at me.

I nodded my head yes. I know Simon is right. She was betraying me as I stood there. I could tell, but still I wanted to have a friend more like me so bad. Simon read my mind.

"You are not like them. You never will be like them. When you accept that and stop wishing for things you can never have you will start feeling better." He put his hand on my shoulder. You can't even touch them. They are not real. You have to stop putting yourself through this."

I wanted to argue with him, but I did not. He was right. I could not even touch one of them. All they ever did was hurt me, so I would hurt them back. The ability to reach out to the delusions was crippled by our vast distance from each other. I was not like them in anyway other than appearance. I did not even think like they did. Most of all they did not even like me.

One does not see dogs hanging out with wolves, but both are canines. I am like that to humans, I look similar, but I am not their species. Though this is painfully clear to me, it did not stop my desire to run with their packs anyway. Dogs who try to run with wolf packs get killed and eaten. This was just natural law. I am not above the laws of nature any more than the delusions are.

"If she does bring Julie, what are we going to do," I asked Simon still nervously watching the gate. I already knew Julie was coming, I could feel it. It was another of my new powers, sensing trouble hours in advance.

Simon shrugged, "Fight."

I looked at Simon when he said that. I had grown tired of fighting all the time. Julie was at least three times bigger than me. Even with Simon's help I doubted I could beat her easily. I looked at my healing wrists and all the scars visible from previous attacks, abuse, and accidents. I did not want to fight with Julie again. A small moan escaped my throat before I could stop it. That made Simon glare at me.

"You had better get over that shit quick. You were born to struggle. It is your lot in life. If you don't like it, well too bad for you. Be a little bitch if you like, but I will be here waiting for you when you grow a pair and stand your fucking ground." Simon had read my mind. He stormed off back to the outhouse.

In the distance I could hear a car coming. What was left of my pathetic gut began to roll into a tight ball. A chill in the breeze entered my unit of measurement through my neck and reached down my spine. I knew that sound. It was Vicky's shit box Buick. Julie had arrived.

I saw the car pulling into the short driveway in front of the gate. It was the Buick as I had feared. For a moment I was frozen to the spot in terror, but finally my feet tore themselves free of the earth as I ran to the outhouse after Simon. Surely, he would help. However, I looked in and he was not there. He had left me to deal with this alone.

"Simon, you coward," I yelled out knowing full well he could not have gotten far. He could hear me.

I turned to see the horrid sight of the evil clique in their full glory walking together through my boneyard. Vicky and Joni were on the left with Julie in the middle and Crystal to the right. The only member not there was Stephanie. All of them were wearing cruel smiles on their faces. They had me cornered and they knew it. I was afraid I could not beat Julie alone. I knew I could not beat all four. No wonder Simon had skipped town.

"Well, well, look what we have here. A Psycho and her Simon," laughed Julie as all the girls started to chuckle, "Why did you run away? You know I could have called your probation officer on you Psycho."

I was not really listening to Julie. I was aware it would only be a string of insults and threats anyway. No, I was desperately looking for an escape route. There had to be a way out of this that did not involve more stitches.

"Hey, hey, you in there. Did you hear me? I could have turned you in," Julie repeated.

I saw an opening through Crystal. She was the smallest plus I could tell she was afraid. In all of the fights I had with these idiots I had never really seen Crystal get in too deep. She was a full on toadie, but not willing to get her hands dirty. I decided to make a mad dash through her if Julie and the demons got any closer.

"But you didn't, did you? Why don't you go fuck yourself Julie? I seriously wish you would go die...I mean...No, I do mean that go die please," I said smiling now that I thought I could indeed escape this probable beating.

This caused Joni to drop her jaw dramatically and cover her mouth as if surprised I ever dared to say such things, "Jesus, Julie you going to take that from this idiot? Look I have shit to do. Can we just move this along, beat her ass and get back to the house," said Joni?

I readied myself for my attempt to flee. My shifting of position caused a generalized nervousness among the pack members.

I could feel the mood had changed suddenly from cockiness to fear, "That is interesting," I think to myself, "they are afraid of me?"

"Shut up Joni! Let me handle this," Julie yelled at the now less sure of herself Joni.

Julie lowered her voice tone to soft and gentle, "Okay now, Psycho think about this. You need your medications. You cannot sleep in a filthy outhouse. Come back with me and we can just forget about this. Mom and Dad don't know. You will not get punished for it. Promise." She looked at the ground not making eye contact.

Her strange demeanor pissed me off. Had it been anyone else I may have fallen for it, but this hateful bitch was trying to talk to me the way Dr. Scott does. A sudden burn began inside my chest. I recalled that Julie had gone to a class to learn how to deal with "crazy people."

"She is treating you like a schizophrenic,' I heard one of the dead souls of the cemetery whisper in my ear, "She is trying to trick you, beware."

I nodded my head to acknowledge I understood this was correct information.

Julie looked up at me suddenly, "What was that? What did you hear, Psycho? Did Simon say something to you? Tell Simon I said you need to go home with me right now."

She started to focus her eyes as if looking behind me. I did not look behind me, this was a trick to distract me. I could feel it. I also did not like this game.

"Who is that standing behind you, Psycho? Is that Simon," Julie said as Vicky snickered unable to keep a straight face. Julie was mocking me and my friend.

"Ha, ha, Julie. Forget it. Not going to work. I am never going back. Where is that Judas, Stephanie? She too scared to face me," I challenged Julie back, keeping my eyes on her.

This statement made all the girls look at each other surprised. Even Julie appeared startled by my question.

"What? Are you serious? Psycho why would Stephanie be here," Julie inquired as she narrowed her eyes.

"Oh, I get it. You can tell Stephanie it is not going to work. I know she came and told you I came home. For your information it was her fucking idea, so she is not your friend either. Stephanie is all about

Stephanie," I said spitting the words out as if they tasted bad.

Julie's eyes widened. Joni gasped. Vicky covered her face with her hand. Crystal looked as if she was about to cry and pee her pants. Their behaviors were starting to get on my nerves. They were such psychotics. I had given up a bit ago trying to understand them.

"Your running away was Stephanie's idea," Julie could not hide her shock at this revelation.

I nodded laughing hard, "Yeah, I bet she did not tell you that when she came to rat me out to you yesterday, did she. Well, surprise."

Julie ran her hand through her ginger hair appearing distressed, "No, she did not. You are right there."

She turned and looked at a very surprised looking Joni. Joni made that circle motion around the forehead indicating crazy" that I hate so much. Vicky was staring at me like I had grown whiskers and wings. Crystal was now defiantly scared. Her eyes were as big as the moon.

Julie turned back to me, "Psycho were you taking your medication the whole time before you left the house to come here? All of it like you were supposed to," she stood there seeming to be sincerely asking and not being sarcastic.

I was still laughing but that question really made me laugh, "Uhm, yeah. You made me, remember. Who is the Psycho here Julie?"

Julie was not happy to hear my response, "That can't be true Psycho. You must have been cheeking it or something. You missed a dose or threw some of it up," she was now talking more to herself than to me, I could tell as she was looking lost in thought.

"What is your damage, Julie. I took the damned medication. I did not cheek it or miss a dose, so what? Now, I will ask you nicely, leave or else you are not going to like what I am willing to do to make you leave." I stood my ground taking on an aggressive stance ready to go through with my threat.

Julie looked at me bitterly, "Okay, Psycho, we talked about this. Stephanie and her aunt moved away over two weeks ago. Remember, her aunt got that good job out in Oklahoma City?"

My laughter stopped. Now this was low even for Julie. I looked at her as anger filled me to my core, "Bullshit, Julie. Stephanie and I came here just a few days ago. Look around. She helped me fix the place up. She helped me sneak off that morning and has been here every day since. You are not going to try to make me think I am crazy anymore. I will not let you."

"Psycho, she moved away. I can prove it. Come with us and we will take you to her house. It is empty.

She even came by and said goodbye to you the day they left. How can you not remember?" Julie was staring at me hard now.

I began to feel terror replace my anger, "This is not true. Julie is lying to you like she always does. Remember the radar? This is a trick to get you into their car without a fight," I think trying to reassure myself as my shattered mind started to whirl. It always does that when I am "unsure" of information provided to it.

"Fuck you, Julie. It will not work. You are not going to lie to me ever again. I am not a fool. Stephanie did help me run away, and she did tell you on me. She did not move to Oklahoma. Now leave me alone." I doubled up my fists ready to fight.

No more plan to run. I have had it with this whole trying to make me look insane shit. It was time to make her pay for being so cruel. I had not done a damned thing to her and yet, time after time she had interfered with my life. Julie stood there still appearing to be in disbelief.

"Psycho, I am not lying. Stephanie moved away, you idiot. You know she did. Your just as fucking loony on the medication as you are off it. Fuck me," Julie yelled as she and the girls all started to laugh, well except Crystal. She was still visibly frightened.

Their laughter was the last straw. I ran at Julie full boar fists flying knocking her to the ground. Dust flew into the air as we rolled struggling to gain the advantage of the top side. The other girls just watched yelling chants of "Julie beat her ass" and "Knock some sense in that nut."

Initially, it was not looking good for me at all. Julie was so much bigger. As we struggled, she got several good slaps, punches, and kicks into my unit of measurement. However, my desperation was high, so I took her blows, able to ignore the damage and pain.

Finally, I got her under me. I grabbed her ginger hair with my left as I began to plow into her face with my right. I spared no strength making every blow count as her blood began to gush up like Texas oil from a drilled well. Julie was grunting and moaning as I hit her wildly. I was now relentlessly letting lose all my pent-up anger at this toxic girl. I was even believing I may win this battle.

However, I had forgotten about Joni and Vicky. They saw Julie losing her bid to subdue me and stepped in to assist the now flailing ginger haired monster. Joni jumped on my back as Vicky grabbed my right arm. I could not hold both of them off, so all three of us went to the ground off of Julie into a pile.

I tried to get free of them. Joni, who was as big as Julie, was still on my back. She wrapped her arm around my neck. She started to apply pressure cutting off my air supply from "panting with effort" to "couldn't breathe for shit" level. Vicky held my arms to the ground keeping me from grabbing Joni to break her grip. I could feel my energy leaving me as each breath yielded less and less precious oxygen to aid my unit in its struggles. Within a few more minutes I could not even keep my eyelids open as I felt the darkness coming for me. There was no doubt I was about to faint from this 'choke hold.'

I vaguely heard, "Okay enough, she is done, I think. Get off her Joni, Christ. You'll kill the idiot. Get off," from a voice that sounded a lot like Julie's.

Just as it was about to be 'lights out' I suddenly could breathe again. I rolled over onto my back sucking in the precious air like a thirsty camel drinks water after a hundred-mile hike through a desert. I was still very weak but slowly coming back from the brink of unconsciousness.

A shadow suddenly covered my view as I looked up to see a very battered and bloody Julie standing over my unit of measurement. My situation was not lost to me despite my most recent near pass out. I rolled fast to my hands and knees taking off to a full-on sprint like a professional track runner. I nearly tripped right away to a face plant in my last-ditch effort to escape. I have no idea where I got the wind in me to even get up much less run like a jackrabbit straight for the gate.

"Grab her, damn it," I heard Julie yell.

I almost turned around but thought better of it as my knees wobbled under me still weak from lack of oxygen supply. I was not fast enough. Joni easily caught up to me before I reached the gate grabbing me from behind and throwing me back to the ground. I tried to get up again, but she kicked me in the stomach ending my bid for freedom. I was down this time, no chance of getting back up. Joni stood over me as I writhed in agony from her blow.

"Shit, you are too much fun, you are a crazy bitch," Joni said as she grabbed my jacket by the back and hauled me to my feet. "Got her, Julie," she called out, chuckling under her breath.

She held my jacket so tight I could not even struggle out of it to try for another run as she pushed me along in front of her, back toward the awaiting Julie. Vicky and Crystal were looking in their purses for something to help Julie clean up her face of all the blood. I smiled at Julie as Joni, and I approached. It was funny to see her bleeding like a stuck pig.

Julie looked at me angrily, "Something funny, Psycho?" She reached out and slapped the holy crap out of me.

My face snapped at the force, but I quickly looked back at her and smiled again, "You know, red is your color darling," I began to laugh.

This infuriated Julie. She slapped me hard several more times calling me every term for "psycho" she could recall. I was actually surprised how many there are.

Joni, Vicky, and Crystal got a good chuckle at Julie's angry slap fest while she demonstrated her expert grip on English idioms and slang terms. I am glad someone was having a good time. It was bad enough to have my face smacked to the point of thinking maybe she had broken my jaw, but worse still I realized I was going to be hauled back.

I found the whole thing oddly humorous. My laughter kept getting worse with every connection of her hand to my cheek bones. I was pretty sure I finally qualified as being 'flak happy.' Yeppers, I had left the building no doubt. My insane laughter started to scare Julie so finally she relented.

"What is so fucking funny, Psycho," WHAT IS SO FUCKING FUNNY PSYCHO!" Julie shrieked in my now very numb face.

I could hardly answer, I was laughing so hard, "I don't know, Julie. Guess you just slapped me silly."

Julie just shook her head at me appearing not to appreciate my sense of humor (some people are so damned serious you know). She told Vicky to go to the Buick and grab the rope they had brought. It turned out they had come prepared for a fight. Julie was ready to haul me back to her home even if she had to tie me up and drag me the whole way. Well, she was going to have to tie me up because I was not going to go voluntarily.

Vicky came back with the rope. Joni held me as she and Crystal tied my hands behind my back then wrapped the remaining rope around my waist tying it off so that I was without the use of my arms. Julie watched me watching her. I continued to laugh as they did their best to secure me so I could not hit any of them anymore.

"You know this is kidnapping, Julie," I said chuckling as they finished their shitty tie job.

Julie rolled her eyes at that, "You are our ward, idiot. You can't kidnap what belongs to you, stupid. Besides, look at my face Psycho. That is assault and battery."

I really started laughing hard again, "No, Julie that is art. Let me go or I will do enough art to start a museum if you catch my drift."

Julie ignored me as she and the girls pushed me along with them to the outhouse. Julie's face, and mine, were a mess. She told the others she needed a break before they headed to the house. They drug me to the back of the outhouse. They pushed me down on my tied hands to the privy bench as they gathered blocking my path to the door with their bodies. The outhouse was very small, and five teenagers were quite a squeeze job. I barely had enough room to keep any of them from touching me much less get enough room to run again.

Julie had finally found a handkerchief to quell her bleeding nose, lips, and cut forehead. I sat there giggling admiring my work. At least she would have a scar I thought to myself. She pulled a joint from her purse as the girls all started to get high.

Now I was the one rolling my eyes. These gals seemed to be using a lot of pot. I did not understand it. However, I was not stupid as Julie thought me. I quieted myself hoping they would get so high I could overpower them and attempt to get away once more.

My hopes increased as I watched Vicky roll another one before they even finished the first. I thought of Simon and wondered if he would come back and help me out just this once. He was always calling me a pussy, but I could not recall him ever fighting at my side. I snorted at those thoughts as I swore, I heard the sound of God in the distance. He was laughing at my latest humiliation.

I strained my ears to see if I am imagining it, but I was not. God laughed again, closer this time. I saw the outhouse shake briefly with his powerful chuckle. This time, I noticed the girls heard him, too. Crystal pushed her way out the outhouse door. She returned as the next burst of Gods laughter rocked the ground.

"Damn, Julie, it is a big storm. It is almost on us," she said appearing a bit anxious about it.

I saw the cracks of the outhouse light up with the flash of Gods sword as he came to enjoy this show. Soon the skies would open, releasing the tears of God on the ground that was already dry from the heated breath of early summer.

I used to hate it when God came to laugh at my nightmare, but today I was actually glad to see the fellow. His need to rub it in guaranteed Julie and the evil pack would not be able to haul me back to her house for a bit longer. Any time I could buy to formulate a plan of escape was appreciated. Even if it meant I had to be the butt of a cosmic joke.

The first tears fell with a pounding on the old roof of that shit house. The girls were very high, so it seemed to make them frightened or marveling (I was not sure) at the noise. I had sat through so many of these God shit fits I just sat there glaring at Julie.

She finally noticed me willing all my hate into her with my eyes, "What the fuck you staring at you tipped bitch? When I get you home, soon as mom goes back to grannies on Monday, I am finally going to beat the crazy out of you."

I started laughing at that, "I am not crazy, Julie. I am enlightened. I am never going back with you. Do you hear me? I will use my powers to burn your house down if you try."

I do not know what made me say that it just sort of popped out. Still, I laughed hard at the thought of it.

Vicky gasped, "Julie, she just threatened to burn down your house Shit! . What if she does? She is fucking bat shit crazy. She may do it." She was visibly shaken as was Crystal.

Julie's turn to laugh now, "No, Psycho is full of shit. Arson would get a fucking fruit loop put into prison. She is bluffing."

She looks at me hard, "Powers? What fucking powers. You schzio motherfucker." She took another drag of her joint on that comment.

Joni then pipped in her two cents as she did not like to be left out, "Well you had better give her higher doses of medication, Julie. Crazy bitch thinks Stephanie is still around. I think that shit isn't working or something."

Julie looked at Joni suddenly, "Oh, you are right. I had forgotten. Come on everyone, we are leaving, now."

The girls all looked at each other. They began to complain that it was storming but Julie would not listen. I was grabbed by my upper arms and drug out into the storm by Vicky and Joni. Everyone began to run to the Buick. I tried to struggle free, but the bitches held tight. I was shoved into the back of the car between Crystal and Joni as Julie took shot gun and Vicky drove. She backed up rapidly into the now increasing storm. God's sword struck hard and lit up the darkened landscape as I watched my gate disappear into the distance as we drove away. I felt my heart let loose its own tears as I began to lose hope that I would ever get to go home again.

Before we headed back to Julie's house, Vicky made a single stop. She pulled into the driveway of Stephanie's house. Julie turned in her seat to look at me.

"Look Psycho. Do you see that? Stephanie moved. She left weeks ago you crazy bitch. Look." She was pointing wildly to the house.

It was indeed abandoned of all signs of occupancy with a For Sale sign out in the front yard. However, this did not prove a thing far as I was concerned. Stephanie may have moved yesterday.

I smiled at Julie, "She moved because she knew I was going to kill her for betraying me. She was afraid of me like you had better be. You had better watch your back, Julie. I will not stop till I make you pay," laughter erupted from me like lava.

I could feel the storm raging within my soul as deeply as it raged outside the car. This seemed to unnerve Crystal, "Please Julie I want to go home. Can we just leave?"

Julie nodded. Strangely she did not respond to my statement. I decided to read her mind.

She was frightened like Crystal. She had not considered I may retaliate. She is also upset she thinks the medication did not work. Julie thinks I am just crazy enough to maybe carry out my threat. I stop reading her mind with great satisfaction.

"Please Julie, I want to go home," I parroted Crystal even using her voice tone. "Please Julie, I want to go home," I continued to laugh wildly.

I could feel every nerve in the car come undone. I was scaring them. Good, I was wild with my need to be free of my restraints and back home with Simon.

As Vicky backed out of Stephanie's driveway, she looked back at me briefly then to Julie, "Hey, just send Psycho back, huh? I don't like this shit. This is not funny anymore. I think maybe she is not kidding here," her fear was like honey to me, sweet and thick.

Julie looked at Vicky angry, "Stay out of this." She then turned back to me, "Psycho, cut the bullshit. You are scaring everyone. You are going home. To my home, where you live now," she was screeching now.

I stopped laughing and looked at her with an evil smile, "You have taken away my home. So, I will take away yours. Watch your back Julie," I started laughing again.

Julie turned back around as Crystal moved closer to her door. Joni just glared at me as we rushed onward towards Julie's.

I saw the red before the others did, then the yellow, as it lit up the stormy night. Black columns rising into the sky like fingers from the hands of God. I smiled. I already knew. I could smell it a mile away. God had come to strike me down with his sword, but he chose the wrong home. He thought I lived with Julie. He missed again. Julie on the other hand did not get missed. In her haste to own me, she forgot I have a curse. She now owned that too, and tonight it came for payment.

Every girl in the car screamed as we pulled into the cemetery driveway across the road from Julie's house. Every girl but me. I laughed harder than ever with the reflection of Julie's house engulfed in flames in my eyes. Julie jumped from the car wailing as she watched everything she owned going up to the heavens in God's black fingers. The other girls bailed from the car all running to restrain her from running into her now lost home.

The fire department was there in the driveway trying to put out the inferno, but it was too late. Every part of that house was engulfed by the southern element. I smiled with intense joy at the beautiful sight of that house of horror melting away into charred tinder of used up energy.

I watched as a neighbor approached the inconsolable Julie to tell her that lightening from the storm had struck the house. The remodeled home did not bother with the old-fashioned lightening rod. Without a conduit to remove the sword of God's power safely into the earth, the electricity had blown every circuit in the house. Within moments of the hit, the entire house had simultaneously burst into flames. The neighbor had reported both Julie and me as likely dead in that house fire to the fire department. After all, we were supposed to be there at home. The fire was so sudden no one inside could have escaped it.

The neighbor was "so happy" to see we had been somewhere else. What a miracle she said. She was hugging and thanking God for Julie having been spared. I chuckled at that. Where were my hugs?

Julie finally came back to the car and sat down in the front seat. She appeared confused, "What are we going to do. All I have is the clothes on my back. Where will we live now?"

I laughed hard at that, "Where are you going to live, Julie. I am going home like I told you I was going to do. I warned you if you fucked with me, I would use my powers!"

Julie jumped from the car and reaching into the back seat she dragged me out. She was kicking and yelling like a crazy woman as I did my best to duck my head from the blows. Vicky and Joni saw Julie's fit. They quickly pulled her off me.

Joni glared at me as she held Julie back, "I think you had better leave. You are not welcome here. Don't you ever come back, Psycho."

I smiled at those gorgeous words, "Untie me and I am gone."

Crystal was told by Joni to untie me. She did not argue. Within a few moments I was free to go. I tipped my imaginary hat at them as I smiled, quickly walking away, never looking back. I was going home finally. Julie no longer had a home to hold me hostage in. I was free.

I was just about out of earshot when I heard Julie scream after me, "fucking witch. How did you do it, Psycho. How did you burn down my house? You are a fucking witch."

That was one of the finest nights of my life. However, it was only a mild detour on my highway to hell. Julie still had plenty of pain in store for me but for this night I entered my cemetery gate to the sounds of the weakening storm in the distance. I saw Simon rolling a smoke by the outhouse smiling wide. I knew he had talked to God. Simon may not have fought those girls in hand-to-hand combat, but he had pulled favor with the deities so that we could stay together. He was my best friend, even if he was a toothless old drunk.

You know beauties, it just doesn't pay to get some people all hot and bothered, does it? Well, our dear Julie and friends just learned what it means when they say 'it is by the grace of God go I' now didn't they? No one really knows when their own fortunes may change. Sometimes, the shoes one has used to kick another with are now on the feet of those that have kicked. You thought Karma was the hippy chick your brother used to date. Nope, beauties she is really a bitch. We do admire her work. Too bad about Stephanie though. Guess sometimes we can want something so bad we will do just about anything to get it. Even 'make it real' when it is not. One of the only good things about schizophrenia is that you can always 'make' friends whenever you need them. Just to know, did you already figure out Stephanie was never there as our best friend? That we were hallucinating her?

CHAPTER 38: SURVIVAL OF THE SICKEST

We are back, in a new and improved condition. New and improved in that We now realize the extent of Our amazing powers. Riding the lightening may have had its advantages. So, now what? It would appear We have everything We wanted. No more Stephanie, no more Julie, no more school (for now), what could go wrong? Oh, wait...We forgot the unit needs to eat. Our dear Simon is not very helpful in acquiring supplies, now, is he? Whatever shall We do now? Isn't that always the problem behind the shattered looking glass? Nothing is ever balanced, is it? Well, let's all put our shards of Our mind together and see if maybe We can solve this latest quandary before Our time runs out. Get ready to drop all the shatter pieces out on the ground. We have to fit them together perfectly to make the winning pattern. Oh, and ignore that picture on the puzzle box. We are going to make Our own up as we go along. If the corners do not fit, just force them. So, you all start, and I will go and find a hammer to help you pound together this perplexing mess. We want to make sure it adheres to what We really want.

"You don't ask people with knives in their stomachs what would make them happy; happiness is no longer the point. It's all about survival; it's all about whether you pull the knife out and bleed to death or keep it in..."
— Nick Hornby

I told my dear Simon of how I had walked slowly through the darkness toward my cemetery home savoring the brilliant smells of Julie's burning dreams. I knew deep down I should have felt some pity for her since she had just lost her entire life of worldly goods. However, I searched inside myself and came up empty.

It was God's choice, not mine. I really believed Julie had stuck her nose into a war between myself and this deity. I did not bring her in. She had pushed her way in. Now she was collateral damage. I really did believe God hated me. While I never quite understood what I had done to earn his wrath, I no longer questioned it. Did it really matter? I thought not. In the end, all that mattered is she and Cindy would have to rebuild. For the moment the last thing on their minds was me or the difficulties I appeared to bring all who are dumb enough to get involved with my pathetic life.

Simon and I finally had the life we thought we needed to be happy. We did savor the moment. The first few days were indeed awesome. I danced with him, we told stories, and enjoyed each other's uninterrupted company. Summer was on full blast with hot southern days and warm muggy nights. It seemed that for once I had won a bit of peace. Each sunrise brought with it a smile on my face. I had actually forgotten I even could with the long year and all its many nightmares. However, I found I could indeed still smile. I started to believe in a future again despite all that I had seen, endured, and knew. Funny how no matter how much badness is heaped upon one's head, a few fantastic days could renew so much hope for what one thought was lost forever.

As usual, I was not really living in reality. The reality was that there was no longer a source for supplies. I had no money, no job and no one was helping me out with it either. By the fourth day I began to become dizzy with hunger. Water was easy, I got that from the hose from the school in one of my old water jugs. Food, now that was an entirely different matter. The reality that I was hiding from was that I would starve to death very shortly if I did not find a way to get food. Not to mention, while bathing had never been my strong point, not bathing in the muggy summer heat, add in my need to overdress, and numerous vicious bug bites, I had also developed a skin infection. Things were starting to go downhill in my peaceful delusion rapidly.

I looked over the pus- and blood-filled lesion on my shoulder washing it down with water from my jug, "Simon, it looks worse. It is spreading too. It is all over my back and chest. I think I may be getting sick. What should I do?"

He looked at it closely, "Damn, that does look bad. Maybe you need antibiotics, but I am not a doctor you know."

I just glared at him, "How useless can you possibly be? Can't you go and find us some food and supplies? You know I am stuck. Julie and her family have all the money that the state sends to care for me, and do you see them here? I need help Simon." I grimaced as the lesion burns and tingles to the water running over it.

He just frowned at me, "You could go to the lake to bath you skanky schizo. As for supplies do I look like a grocery store? What the hell am I supposed to do about this?"

I growled at him while covering back up my wounds. He was great to talk to for fun, but when it came to the important stuff, he was often lacking in good advice. I needed to figure out something, but without a car I knew my chances at finding work were slim to none.

On day five, I realized I would have to find food wherever I could. Even if I had to steal it. I was weakening fast. Despite Simon's complaints I took off walking for town early that morning. I did not know where to even begin, but surely in a rural community I could find something growing in a garden, or maybe a pie in a window cooling off like I had seen on a TV show once when I was little. One thing was for damned sure, if I did not find something fast, I would be as dead as my roomies.

I had of course fixed myself in my finest so that any town people I may accidentally encountered would not freak out. My idea of finest was my best make-up job with my long black duster, and black clothing with my trusty black wool derby hat. I looked like a demon corpse, showing my most extreme lack of insight into what other's find socially acceptable in one's appearance.

This was quickly demonstrated as I walked past a home with a small group of teen aged boys playing a game of basketball in their yard. As I walked by, all activity stopped as the young fellows stared jaws gaping open in what appeared to be terror. I just smiled and tipped my hat. They screamed and ran into the house abandoning the basketball behind them. Their screams startled me, so I took off in a run till the house was out of sight. I certainly had not expected that response.

This town was tiny, so my run almost put me right out of the town limits in only a few moments. This nowheresville was completely rural, a schoolhouse and a post office were all it had to even demonstrate it was indeed a community. To my horror, I realized I would have to travel much further to find anything to eat, or even civilization of any kind. The town homes did not even have gardens with anything ready to pick. I found the main road as it was the only paved one around. I headed east as I began to walk toward the next town. The single road sign promised the town was seven miles ahead.

I hoped it at least had a store. I was not a shoplifter or thief of any sort, but desperate times called for desperate measures. There was no doubt in my mind the first store or gas station I could find, I would get those supplies anyway I had to get them. Even if it meant being dishonest. In my mind I was already condemned anyway. So, may as well go for broke. I could not possibly get any deeper in hell anyway, right?

Even in morning hours the black pavement of the road, summer sun and my heavy clothing made the walk miserable. Sweat began to pour from my pores making me feel I would surely pass out. On occasion a car or truck would pass by and often they would swerve though I was alongside the road not in it. I could see the drivers staring at me with looks of shock. This was strange to me, but then again, these small towns people were strange. I would just shrug it off, ignoring it. I kept walking until finally I saw what I had hoped to find.

The next town had a population of 500 souls. It also had (I could see it even from a distance) a small rural gas station and to my joy a small country cafe. My heartbeat faster as I realized I may yet still survive this loss of support after all. Now all I had to do was figure out how to get what I needed so badly without getting caught.

First, I walked to the gas station. I could see inside it had only oil, filters, engine belts, and car stuff, no food or other supplies. I was looking in the window when a silver haired toothless man in overalls came out looking me up and down as if I had landed the mother ship at the full-service pump.

"What in the Sam Hill are you supposed to be? Girly, you lost? It t'ain't Halloween for a couple months ya'll should know," he drawled out, appearing irritated.

I just smiled at him and walked away. I was not stupid. He would call Dennis and Boyd if I stuck around. Just as I turned to head for the café, I heard a woman speaking. She was not talking to me but to this man.

"Carl, that must be that nutcase from down round Rover we keep hearing about. I heard she looked like a clown from Halloween from our oldest boy Jesse. Best watch out and keep her away from here. She is trouble," she said in a loud whisper.

I turned around to see a very heavyset woman with salt/pepper hair pulled back severely in a bun. She was wearing a washed-out blue dress with the rolled down knee stockings and slippers. I chuckled as she was looking me up and down with awe and fear in her eyes.

"Halloween clown? Nutcase? Really? Have you seen your own reflection lately, ma'am?" I then tipped my hat as she gasped and grabbed her chest as if it was offensive that I had politely called her out.

"You'all best git on outta here girly! We don't want yourn types round us decent folk," Carl said making a 'shooing' motion with his withered arthritic arm at me.

I just chuckled tipped my hat and smiling wished them much luck and happiness in their future business endeavors by saying, "You all have a nice day, you hick motherfuckers."

Carl and his woman shouted they would call the cops as I turned and rapidly departed. Some folks just don't appreciate good manners.

My hopes actually were starting to sink fast. Now all I had left to investigate was the very packed country cafe called "Wanda's" across the road from this shitty little gas station. I crossed the street and train tracks, but I already had realized I could not shop lift a meal. I suppose I could order one and run but apparently based upon my short conversation with Carl, I was already well known in this town too. Someone would call the cops and then I would be in for trouble. My summer of freedom would become a summer of Thorazine shuffling to the sounds of the ECT machines if that happened.

I stopped in the outer part of the parking lot and counted over twenty-five cars and trucks there. This was a happening place. Seemed like all the towns people must be inside. This made me decide against going in. I had already noticed my appearance was not setting well with the natives. It seemed best to give this idea up and either find the next town or go home and die.

As I stood there trying to decide which to do, I noticed around the back a large green dumpster.

My spirits raised a bit. Perhaps, like most people, this rural bunch were wasteful. I decided to try to sneak into that dumpster and see if I could find anything I could eat. All I had to do was not get caught doing it.

Luckily, no one had exited the establishment, so no one had seen me approach. I moved quickly running behind the building hoping that no one was out back having a smoke break. To my joy no one was. I stood there lurking around the back corner of that small cinder block building watching the customers come and go for about half an hour. None of them appeared to look my direction. Most were in a hurry to just leave or go inside when they arrived. I was very hungry, but caution overrode my need to eat. It appeared that most of them would come in and stay about thirty minutes then leave. So, with much anxiety I finally made an attempt to see if I could find something of worth in that garbage can.

I walked to the front of the dumpster watching all around for any prying eyes. Believing no one was looking I opened the dumpster lid and found I had hit pay dirt. This place was wasteful indeed. Several bags of half rotten potatoes, crushed up oatmeal containers still half filled (with oatmeal and meal bugs), and half eaten pancakes were right at the top. I was thrilled!

I grabbed the bags of potatoes, bagged up the oatmeal while I snarfed down the tossed pancakes. I was not someone who put much stock in good hygiene, and my extreme hunger made me less than interested in hygiene of food either. One thing was for sure, even if half rotten with bugs, this food was not tainted with LSD or poison. It was just dirty. Dirty did not bother me.

Having gathered enough for a few days and deciding I could not carry more, I dropped the lid and hightailed it for home. The trip was long but the payoff awesome. I almost felt like dancing all the way despite the heat as I believed I had solved my problem. I would not starve at least. School would return in six weeks then, if need be, I could find a way to get lunch closer to home. I never eat much anyway, so it all seemed like it could work out.

Of course, the dumpster at Wanda's would not solve my need for other supplies like batteries, matches, and antiseptics. Now that I had found the value in dumpster diving, I decided to start to check the trash cans in town for other things I could use. The oatmeal and potatoes would require cooking and I was out of a way to light a fire, so first on the agenda was a lighter. I did laugh pretty hard as I walked the miles back to my cemetery as I thought of

Stephanie's curse that I spend my life living out of trash cans. Looks like she was right.

The memory rattled my mind to the question to why she had not come to visit and help me out like she had promised. I decided once I had stored my items, I would go see her and ask her myself. She had told Julie where I was, but I had forgiven her now that Julie's house was gone. I was not one to carry grudges. Besides, I could really use a job, and Stephanie had promised to help me find one. Not to mention, I need a ride to see Dr. Scott and the probation officer. I was not sure what they would do to me if I missed those appointments, but I was not wanting to find out.

I got home just after noon to a very thrilled Simon. He saw my haul of half rotten food and smiled proudly at me,

"That's my girl! You have enough here for days. I hope you can get more when this runs out."

I smiled at him, "Yeah, I found a source for the food problem. But I still need a job and a ride, Simon. I am going to see Stephanie see if we can't work something out."

Simon grabbed my arm as I started to store my cash of food stuffs in the outhouse box, "Hey, not smart! Stephanie is bad news. You go over there and there will be trouble! You had better come up with another plan, leave Stephanie alone."

I shrugged off his grip, "She is our only hope Simon, you idiot. Not like Julie or Cindy are going to get us to our appointments. What the fuck am I supposed to do? Walk thirty fucking miles?"

Simon looked at me hard, "Yeah you had better get used to walking thirty fucking miles. Stephanie is a dead issue; do you understand that? Or are you really that stupid? She did not help us. You just thought she did. Really Stephanie was out for Stephanie, can't you stop your fantasy bullshit?"

That pissed me off, so I pushed him, "Shut up Simon. Stephanie is my friend. You are just a jealous drunk."

Simon pushed me back. I fell on my ass dropping the potato bags on the outhouse dirt floor. "You are worse than a jealous drunk. Do you know what you are? You are a skanky, dumpster diving, schizophrenic. That is right, you are psycho." He made the circle motion around his temple indicating crazy.

"Fuck you, Simon. Get out, get out," I yelled from my sitting position. I could not stand it when someone called me that and he knew it Simon had crossed the line.

Fuck you, Psycho," Simon said back at me laughing.

Suddenly, the entire cemetery started to laugh with Simon. Horror gripped me as the residents began to mock me from every corner of the bone yard.

Whispers filled my ears like buzzing bees. The fifty or so residents were all saying ugly things about me, and everyone was laughing about it too. Worst of all they were repeating these things in a loop over and over, and all at one time. The whispers were deafening.

"Psycho, die, Psycho," a man called out while laughing deeply.

"Hold still, this will hurt you more than it hurts me, whore," a woman roared out chuckling.

"Schizophrenic! Go and hunt for radars. Do the voices tell you how stupid you are," another woman chortled?

She is crazy because her mother didn't love her. Hahaha. Who could? Look at her," called out yet another disembodied voice of the long-forgotten dead.

I grabbed my ears with both hands trying to drown out the insults, the laughter, the mocking voices of those who would judge me for my short comings, "Please, please, shut up."

I felt as if my head was splitting down the middle. My brain was trying to liquefy. This feeling was now well known to me. I was melting down. I had to get out of there to make this stop. I stood up knocking

Simon down as I ran to the gate still holding my ears groaning in intense pain from the noise of their criticisms.

I was blind with rage, pain, and terror, as I crashed through the gate not ever taking my hands from my ears. I felt blood start to pour down my chin from my nose as I had busted it opening the gate with my body slam rather than my hands. This did not stop me from continuing my blind run straight to Stephanie's house. I had to talk to someone, anyone. I needed to get some help somehow before I did something stupid. That was very clear despite my very apparent confusion. Stephanie, I just knew would help me. She was not always on my side, but at that moment I would not have even refused the Devil's aid.

The sounds of the cemetery dead still rang in my ears as I saw Stephanie's house in the distance. Relief poured through me. I finally removed my hands from my ears and did my best to wipe the blood from my nose and mouth. I did not want her to see me acting Psycho." She did not care much for some of my behaviors and today I needed her to listen and help me.

I ran right up her porch and began to knock on the door hard. I was grateful to see the chairs she and I had sat on replaced there. The night Julie had tried to convince me she had moved Stephanie had taken them inside apparently. Now, in the daylight I could see that this house was full of furniture and no for sale sign. I had known it all along, Julie was playing a cruel joke telling me Stephanie had moved away.

I waited as I heard Stephanie's footsteps come to the door. I smiled big and tried to look "normal" as possible. In truth, I was so upset, I was ready to yell and bash my head into the light pole in front of her house.

The door opened and a short woman of around fifty answered. She had mousy brown hair and big glasses. She was wearing an apron and I could smell she had just left her kitchen as the scent of a cooking ham wafted off her person. I was as surprised as she was as we both stood there staring in disbelief at each other.

"Is Stephanie here." I finally stammered, still trying to figure out who this lady was.

She just stood there shaking her head no. This lady was looking me up and down, ready to run, like I was some demonic Jehovah's Witness.

"Do you know when she will be back." I asked still thinking this lady would give me some information I could use.

The lady finally came to her senses and in a rough, low voice said, "There is no Stephanie here, weirdo. If you mean the girl who used to live here, she has been gone for weeks. Get off my porch and slink back to whatever hellish hole you crawled out of." She then slammed the door in my face.

The bang of the door sent me to a cower as if I had just been hit. The stun of hearing Stephanie was not only gone but gone for weeks made my shattered brain whirl like a car high centered in a mud hole.

"You are a liar," I screamed at the shut door as I saw the woman peering at me from her window shades.

I sensed she was going to call the cops, so I did not wait around for her to argue my challenge. I hauled my ass out of there like the four horsemen were on my tail. I headed for the school grounds.

Once there, I went to the picnic table I had not so long ago had all the trouble with. I sat down spent, confused, and terrified. Stephanie had moved away just as Julie had told me. That meant that she could not have helped me run away that night, and she never came and hung out with me. More than that, she had never promised to help me out.

I could not wrap my broken mind around this horror. The idea that I had been tricked by my own mind was beyond what I could accept. Everyone around me was a liar, and now I realized the biggest liar of them all is me.

As I sat there, I thought of all the things I had believed to be true. I thought of the horror of no longer being sure of what truth really is. I wondered how I would ever be able to know what was real and what was not real. It was beyond terror to realize that if Julie says something it may be a lie, it may be the truth. That my Simon could be real or could he be a trick of my mind. It was then I also decided I myself may not be real. I could be anywhere, and this was all just the dream of an abused child wishing to be free of torture. Perhaps, I was the delusion of a lunatic locked within a padded cell in a straightjacket wishing she were free.

These thoughts sent me into overdrive with a total melt down of all my senses. I paced, yelled, kicked, rocked, and laughed uncontrollably until dark all alone in that school yard.

Simon had been right after all, going to see Stephanie had brought me nothing but trouble. By dark, I was spent. I sat on the picnic table rocking and mumbling until finally sleep overcame me. I knew I could not go home that night and deal with the possibility of more derogatory voices of the dead. So, as I drifted off, I gave into the fact that I was indeed insane, and no longer could I trust my own mind to be honest with me.

The rising sun found me still laying on the picnic table unable to find the will to get up and face the nightmare my life had become. No matter how bright the sunlight, I was trapped in a dark world of suspicion, fear, and confusion. I laid there for some time thinking on what to do now. Death was definitely an option. I doubted I could continue now that I knew the truth of my inability to tell the truth to myself.

However, I could see my mother standing before me laughing. She had done this to me, and she loved that I would die as she had always wanted me too. I watched as Mary join her. They stood there, hand-in-hand, jeering me to do what they wanted me to do, "kill yourself." I could even hear the two of them chanting "go die bitch" in my ears.

I felt my old friend, anger, rising in my belly warming me even more than the strengthening summer day. It burned away all my apathy with a new dose of willpower. I would not give these two demons what they wanted. I found the strength to get off that table and fight on despite my most recent discovery. Somehow, I would find a way to discover if what I believed/see/hear was truth or lie. How to do this was only in the details.

So, hungry again, I started my twelve-mile walk (twelve from the school, seven from town) to the next town for breakfast. As I endured the jeers of passing motorists and the unforgiving southern sun, I worked on a plan to keep my reality in line with. well reality. I decided that Simon was of no use. He was now suspected to be a trick of my mind for the first time ever (which scared the shit out of me). I would require someone I could verify as real to help guide me through this very confusing world of the delusional.

Slowly, I was beginning to realize I had been correct about this world being delusion to some extent. I just had it backward. I was the delusional not the damned world.

I had just discovered there really are two worlds, the delusional one that I lived in, and the real one that belonged to everyone else. It seemed that once I had known the real world myself, but then something went wrong, and I no longer remembered. I had somehow gotten lost.

My mind again painfully danced with the idea that I may indeed be schizophrenic. Simon had said this was not truth, but I was not stupid. Thinking that someone who had moved away was the friend you had always wanted is, well, nuts. I could not ignore that no matter how much I wanted to believe I was not crazy.

I was so deep in thoughts like this that when I arrived at Wanda's I almost got spotted by a customer leaving. I saw him before he saw me, and I hid quickly behind another car. He left as I went to the dumpster hoping to be as lucky as the day before.

I opened the lid to find today I would have to do some digging as all that was topside were items such as bacon, ham, and pork chops. I could not eat any of them with my stomach so as I frantically dug deeper, I almost fell into the thing.

I finally found some pancakes half-way down that were covered in coffee grounds. I decided beggars could not be choosers, so I grabbed them and did my best to shake them off. I stood there eating my foul meal leaning on the dumpster as I noticed something very odd.

A small towheaded boy who could not be more than four years old had come out of Wanda's unaccompanied by an adult. He was looking at me and smiling while babbling like small children do. I smiled back with concern.

"Where is your momma little one," I called out to him.

He just put his hands to his eyes and smiled with a big spittle bubbling as he gurgled in child speak. Then without another word he took off running for the road. I looked around and saw no sign of a mother, father, hell anyone This kid was headed straight for a road where people hit dogs, deer, and anything not fast enough to escape their racing egos of being kings of the world. Terror hit me as I began to realize he would surely be run over!

Without thinking I took off after him. He looked back and saw my frightened person running after him, so he laughed thinking it a game and picked up his pace. I yelled for him to stop as I pushed myself with all I had to catch up (kids are fast little devils)! I managed to catch up to the baby just as he hit the shoulder of the road. I grabbed him by his shoulders as he squealed like a stuck pig. I pulled him to me cradling him as if he were my own precious child.

The shock was beyond painful, but my heart almost stopped as a huge truck sped past us without slowing down. The wind from the speeding vehicle blew dust in our faces as I spun rapidly to run this child back to Wanda's. Had I been a bit slower, not seen him, not decided to chase, that child would be no more.

My knees were weak as if filled with water at the thought of this beautiful child laying smashed on the road, as the baby in my arms laughed and grabbed my wig playfully tugging it bubbling and gurgling. He did not even know his life had almost been over.

Slowly, it dawned on me he surely had the worst mother on earth to not notice this happy little fellow was missing. Had he been mine, he would never be out of my sight as a treasure beyond value. This made me angry as I thought of how little people care about others, even their own.

My skin was sending signals of pins and needles everywhere that our bodies connected but I did not care. I marveled at his big blue eyes, his tiny fingers, and chubby rosy cheeks. He laughed as he saw me admiring him as I walked him back slowly. The sound was like pretty wind chimes blowing in a gentle breeze. I could have looked at him forever. My eyes filled with rain as I saw how pure and perfect, he was, even with his syrup sticky face.

"A child is the world when it was pure," I heard a woman's voice say behind me. I turned but I already knew no one was there. I finally understood, I do hear voices of people who are not really there.

The child and I arrived back in the parking lot. I knew I would have to go inside and find his mother. I stood there outside that door trying to decide if I had the strength to face the hate, I would surely find from everyone there.

Luckily, I did not have to go inside. All of a sudden, a small black-haired woman with big green eyes came flying out of the door with a fear in her face that could only indicate this was his mother who finally figured out he had escaped her.

Behind her a very tall skinny man with a mustache and goatee. He was holding a girl child with golden hair that was almost the spitting image of the child I held myself. She was older by a year or so, but also very young. These two were a handsome couple with two beautiful babies indeed.

"Oh my God, Jordie," the woman said as she scooped the child from my arms.

I looked at the ground. I figured she would call the cops seeing me holding her kid like some monster that had crawled out from under his bed.

The woman was tearing up appearing very upset. "Oh my God. Thank you so much. I thought, I thought, oh my God, Jordie," she held the child tight as tears ran down her face.

The man was looking at me bemused. A small cat like smile on his face. He did not appear as upset as the woman, "Porcupine you have to watch him closer. I told you Jordie is a pistol. What if he had gotten into the road!"

The woman he called Porcupine cuddled Jordie, "Shut up, Jeff. I know, God help me, I know."

I decided that maybe it was time for me to haul ass myself. So, I turned to leave as Porcupine said to my back as I started walking away, "Hey, I seriously thank you for saving Jordie. I am so sorry if he caused you any trouble. He has ADHD and is always sneaking off. We thought he was in the bathroom, but he snuck out somehow and got past us."

I just nodded and stretched out one arm in a wave to signal I heard her loud and clear. I did not look back as I headed for the road to home.

Jordie was an accident, and it was truly a pleasure to hold that child, but it was time for me to get back to my own hell. These two could call the cops if they wanted to but the cops would have to come looking for me. I was out of there.

All the way back to my cemetery I thought about Jordie and how much I would like to have a child someday. I knew that was not going to happen. After all I could not even take care of myself, much less a kid. However, holding that child was the first time in a long time I had felt truly satisfied and well love.

I decided I would speak with Simon about my chances at being a mother someday, even if I could not tell real from fiction. Maybe he could offer some advice. I had already forgiven him for being nasty to me. After all, he had been right about Stephanie. I just had refused to hear what he was trying to tell me.

I arrived at my gate but heard a sound that I had not heard around there in some time, a car was coming. Unsure of what to do I went past my gate and kept walking so that whoever was coming would not see me go inside. The car pulled up slowly behind me, then pulled up next to me and stopped. I was scared to death. It was not a cop car, not Mary, not Vicky nor Julie nor even Cindy. I had never seen this small black Chevy. The driver looked at me smiling a small cat like smile. I recognized him; it was Jeff from Wanda's.

He got out of the car as Porcupine the dark-haired woman exited on the passenger's side. Both were smiling at me. I was about to have a heart attack. To be honest I thought they had come to retaliate thinking I had tried to hurt Jordie.

I put up my hands in a display of surrender, "I am sorry ma'am and sir I swear I only ran after Jordie to save him from being squished in the road. I did not mean him any harm. I was bringing him back to you, honest"

Jeff looked at Porcupine and they both laughed. This made me sure I was toast. My pleas were of no use.

Jeff looked at me as I tried to decide which way to try to run, "Hey, I am Jeff, and this is Porcupine. You are Psycho, I presume? Sorry, but you left so fast Porcupine and I had to ask around to find out who you are. You are well known around these parts," he chuckled at that. "We wanted to thank you for saving our boy. What you did for us can never be repaid."

Jeff held out his hand for me to shake. Completely stunned I took it blindly ignoring the shock but grimacing a bit at the pain of it. I was just so relieved they were not there to beat my ass I seriously would have let him hug me if that would have made him happy.

"Uhm, no problem. He is a very adorable kid. I am glad he is safe," I stammered as I looked at the ground keeping eye contact away from Jeff and Porcupine.

"Really, we thank you. Where are you headed? The least we can do is give you a ride home," Porcupine said sweetly.

I shrugged at that, "Oh no, that is okay. I am okay with walking. Thank you though. I hope you two have a great day." I kept my head down. They were making me very nervous.

Jeff and Porcupine just stood there in an uncomfortable silence. I could sense they were looking at each other trying to decide what to say. I was going to read their minds, but Jeff spoke up before I could.

"So, uhm, Psycho. We are looking for a babysitter. Are you working anywhere? The pay is good, but the kids are hyper, so you know the job is sort of tough." He chuckled at that.

I could not believe my ears. Now, I had just realized only a few hours before that I would make shit up to suit my own desires. I needed work really bad, so this weird offer in the middle of the road was, well, looking a bit unrealistic. I shook my head believing I had discovered one of my delusions. I was trying to play a trick on myself. No way this was real.

I looked up at Jeff flatly, "Okay, very funny. You know damned well I need a job. I know damned well this is bullshit. You are not real so please go away now and leave me alone. I will not be tricked again. Fuck this."

Jeff and Porcupine looked at each other appearing confused by my irritation with them, "Seriously, are you interested in the job," Porcupine said a bit less sure sounding than Jeff had been.

I laughed at that, "You expect me to believe that you asked around Wanda's and found out I am called Psycho? Right. If that were true you would have heard the other rumors like how I got that nickname. No fucking way you are chasing me down and offering a job babysitting those two beautiful babies to a fucking schizophrenic! What rumor did you hear exactly that made you sure I was the right psychotic for that job? The one where I kill cops or the one where I bash lockers in with my head? Humm?" I stopped laughing and glared hard at them both, "Now leave me the fuck alone. You are not real."

I turned around and went through my cemetery gate, slamming it shut behind me. Jeff and Porcupine were left standing there in the road appearing stunned by my berating them for such an obvious attempt by my mind to play a trick on me. I no longer worried if they knew I was living there, after all they were delusions like Stephanie had been.

As I walked to my outhouse I chuckled bitterly while talking to myself, "You are going to have to do better than that Psycho if you think you can fool me twice!"

I went into my outhouse to settle in as I heard the sound of a child's laughter. Startled I ran out to see Jordie and his sister chasing each other around the residents. I also watched as Porcupine and Jeff walked holding hands and smiling toward me.

"What the fuck is this," I yelled at them, "get out, all of you.

They did not stop smiling nor did they leave. I watched helplessly as they continued toward me as if this was a family get together. I suddenly realized I was seriously sick and really in need of medication. Fear gripped me as I understood that my delusions could be powerful indeed.

They finally arrived within talking distance and as they looked around still smiling Porcupine spoke first, "Look, yeah you got us. We did ask around. Yes, we heard...well things about you that...well were crazy. But we actually need someone like you. You are someone who is not going to call the cops, talk shit, or well interfere with business."

I narrowed my eyes, "What is this nonsense? If you are going to have a fucking delusion, Psycho, at least have one that can talk fucking sense," I said to myself out loud as if these two were not standing right there.

Porcupine and Jeff looked at each other with concern. Jeff then asked, "So, it is true? You are schizophrenic? Not that it is an issue, just wondering?"

I laughed out loud at that, "Great. Now I am asking myself to say it, really," I kicked the ground still laughing, "Okay, yeah, I am fucking schizophrenic. Are you happy now?

"Yep, crazy as fuck," I yell loudly with my arm outstretched in a "bring it on" pose so that these delusions would see I meant business.

They both started laughing as I continued to yell, talking to myself while pacing and saying I was, "psycho, nuts, crazy, gone to lunch, bats in my belfry" and everything in between.

"You are fucking hilarious," Jeff said appearing to enjoy my self-depreciating talk. "Look, clearly you are on a bad trip. We don't care. We are used to people tripping out. Porcupine and I are the biggest dealers in this town. People come for miles to buy our pot and its great pot. So, yeah, we don't care if you are crazy. Porcupine just needs help keeping up with our little devils while we do business. She would always be around, so it is not like we are leaving you for a fucking day trip to the spa or anything."

"Wait...what?" I was stunned into silence at this revelation.

Porcupine who was still laughing as well said, "Yeah, I need help keeping them from escaping the house is all. We need someone who will keep their trap shut, not steal our shit, and to be honest you are one scary looking bitch. We think it will help to keep customers in line having you around. Your reputation alone would keep some from acting like assholes. The pay is good, so you interested or what? Do you live here," she finished looking at my outhouse suddenly appearing concerned?

I blinked my eyes, the two were still there. I rubbed them, yep, they were still there, "So this is real? You are real? You are hiring me to scare people?"

They busted up laughing again, both nodding their heads. Now this I could believe. Being hired to upset people was surely the only thing I would be good at. Somehow, I had managed to find a bit of luck. I had never been a lucky one but this day my ship had finally come in.

"So, you interested or what? And shit do you live here? Damn that is wickedly fucked up. Look take the job. You need it no doubt," said Jeff.

I nodded my head, "Yeah, I will take the job, but I don't have a car. I also have to tell you I am on probation for assault and court ordered to psychiatric treatment. I may be in the criminal unit soon since I cannot get to my appointments on time. So, I will take it, but I may not be able to keep it." I had to be honest. Especially since they had those two cute kids.

I was sure that information was going to be a deal breaker for this job offer.

Porcupine looked at Jeff then at me, "No problem, sweetie. One of us can get you to your appointments if you can tell us in advance by a day or two. We work from home. So, someone is always there to look after things. Can you start tomorrow? I will pick you up around noon. The job is from noon to midnight by the way if you can do those hours."

I again had to shake my head not believing my luck. I nodded my head and smiled big at them. They smiled back and gave me a thumbs up in approval. They decided to hang out with me for a bit as they discussed the details of my first job.

I was basically a door guardian. I am to keep the little ones inside, and was to show myself to clients and well, behave as if unstable (I had that down, so piece of cake). Jeff told me he and Porcupine only sold pot, LSD tabs, peyote or shrums. Jeff did not deal in heavier drugs due the age of his children. He told me that he had seen too many coke and heroin dealers get shot by clients and by bigger dealers, so he kept it small. However, his business in this small town was booming as there was nothing in this town to do but, "fight, fuck, or smoke the dope."

I really did not care much for drugs or drug dealers, but a job is a job. The fact that they dealt with illegal substances allowed a schizophrenic a chance to earn a living.

After all both drug dealers and schizophrenics were part of the underworld no one in the real world want to see, admit to, or do anything about. It made perfect sense that this dark union was offered, at least it did to me at the time.

As Jeff and Porcupine finally left, the thought that I would likely always be trapped in a dangerous world of the illegal, hidden, and taboo thanks to my illness, was not lost on me. I shook my head both elated to have finally found a solution to a big problem and sadden that it was one that came with more stigma and evil connotations.

As I fell asleep with that most foul thought on my mind I did have to laugh, at least it was more prestigious than dumpster diving.

Yet another strange turn in this shattered looking glass trip. So, goes to show you if you dig deep, you may just find the good stuff hidden below the surface. Are you ready to see what we will find once we have all the tools required to do some serious mining? Awesome! Join Us soon, as this shaft is bound to collapse.

CHAPTER 39: SPLIT SHIFT

Good day, Beautiful Family. Here we are yet again spinning in circles. It would seem that We are unable to drive in a direct line but continue to take left turns whenever We thought we had finally taken a right one. It is the confusion of the road dust in our eyes that keep Us from following the straight and narrow path in life. However, that is simply the way of things for those of Us trapped behind the shattered looking glass. Up is down, down is backward, and tomorrow never comes. Are you sure you want to keep trying to find your way back with Us? It is now getting rather monotonous as you realize you really are on the road to nowhere. The scenery changes, but the trees are plastic and the people mannequins. Oh my, did you actually believe any of this was meaningful? Goth no! This is what We do to pass the time till Our next long rest in a white one-armed jacket. Here in Our world the bad guy is the good guy, and you are the villain even when you have done nothing wrong at all. So, ready to pay for crimes you were the victim of rather than the perpetrator? Wait...what's that? Not fair, you say? Ah, well this may be true, but what do We actually know about truth? In the end, truth is determined by those who have the power of persuasion, and We are just not that good at that. Tell you what, this one time We will hold them off by distracting them while you try to escape. Run fast, and We shall be along as soon as We can. Often, we get lost and forget which is the right road to take. We will see you below as soon as we can figure out which direction is correct.

LOSS OF INNER SENSE OF SELF OF THE SCHIZOPHRENIC:

"A sense of self is defined as one's perception of oneself. Each person's sense of self is directly related to how they feel about themselves, their levels of self-esteem, and confidence or lack thereof. Numerous researchers have pointed out over the last decades that there is a loss of the sense of the inner self in schizophrenia. A person affected by *schizophrenia* feels *lost*, as if his "*self* no longer belong[s]" to him/her. ... Patients fail to recognize that their actions, thoughts, or *feelings* are initiated from within the *self*, leading to delusions of passivity and being controlled by an outside force or even another person. Some schizophrenics develop delusions that their inner self is a separate person altogether. The reasons for this are still largely not understood but research appears to indicate some likely hood of damage or poorly connected pathways in the frontal lobes as one of the factors involved..."
-Schizophrenia Bulletin-2011

I dedicate this chapter to Simon who will always be my very best friend. I would like to take a moment to thank him for helping out with this part of our story and granting his permission to tell it.

I awoke the next morning to the sounds of the birds calling out good day to each other, and the stinking smell of Simon's home rolled smoke. As I open my eyes, he flashed a smile at me. He likely was ready to apologize for our latest squabble. I smiled back at him. I was ready to forgive him. Simon is my best friend, we fight sure, but in the end, he has always been there for me. I can forgive him almost anything.

"Where you been Simon? What time is it?" I stretched while wiping the sleep from my eyes.

He smiled bigger, realizing I was no longer angry, "It's early. I went to town to walk it off a bit. Look let's not fight about something as stupid as that girl Stephanie."

I looked at my friend as he cast his gaze to the ground appearing sincere. No, you are right. I should have listened to you. I went to see her, and it caused trouble like you said it would."

He looked up concerned. "What do you mean," he tried to read my mind, but I felt him there. I blocked him from it.

"I do not want to fight about this, Simon, but I think we both know what happened when I tried to see Stephanie. Stephanie was never here. She never helped me. I imagined her. Now, I have to be afraid. I have to be afraid that you maybe are imagined too. No one else can see you. No one else believes you are

137

real. I think I am really a schizophrenic like everyone says I am. I think you already know that I insane but keep lying to protect me from that truth." I look at the ground taking a deep breath as I ask the questions I have been dreading since realizing the friendly Stephanie had been a delusion.

"Simon, are you only inside my head? Who are you really? Am I telling myself another lie? Am I lying to myself believing you are real," I struggled to get the words out? I could not even look at him as I confessed my biggest fear.

I heard Simon take a deep breath and hold it. I was already very sorry to have brought it up. To question the only friend, I ever believed I had, well it was horrifying to say the least. If he were imaginary would that end my being able to enjoy his company? I already had lost everything else in the world, I could not tolerate the idea I could lose him too. Those awful thoughts were all I could think in a loop. I wanted to retract the questions, but it was too late. I had asked and now the fearful answers were coming. Now, all I could do is wait to see if I had just destroyed the only good thing left in my shitty world.

Time came to a standstill. Everything inside that cemetery seemed to be watching us. Silence covered the world like a blanket on a cold night. Simon just stood there smoking and staring into the quiet distance as the terror began to build within me.

Finally, he finished his smoke and crushing it on the ground looked at me hard.

With a mournful sigh he begins, "Sometimes, it is better to just believe, isn't it? Has the truth ever done anything but hurt you? So, before you decide if I am real or not real, or who I am really, ask yourself, who has always been there for you? Is it those people outside our world? No. It was me, your Simon."

I shudder as I realize there is something horrible, I have missed here, I wanted to run away but I could not move a single muscle as my chest began to ache. I moan under my breath. I had already heard enough and really did not want to hear the rest of this truth. but still I could not will myself to run.

Simon looks at me hard as suddenly tears of hidden emotion roll down his sunburned cheeks in a waterfall of pain, "I will tell you the truth, the one you have hidden all this time because it is one you have realized by asking this in the first place. Get ready, this is going to hurt. Now focus your mind best as you can and see with your heart not your eyes."

I concentrate as he told me to do (thought I did not want to anymore) as I looked deep into his flooding eyes. A sudden feeling of deep despair washes over me. We can read each other's minds. I heard the answers to my questions without him uttering a single word. Those answers were now threatening to shatter my already very disabled mind. Now, it was up to me to decide if I would turn my back on it or accept the facts. I could not unlearn the truth and could no longer ignore our shared reality.

Simon stood there waiting in hellish torment that I could actually feel in my inner stillness. I suddenly understood he was right. I had always known the truth of who Simon really is. It was there all along and I had blissfully ignored it but that moment, I knew the full extent of the tragedy of his existence. As I looked at my Simon with my heart for the first time ever, I saw the true him. He was no longer the drunk, toothless, middle-aged brakeman. He began to morph into something beyond beautiful. So, beautiful I had to shield my eyes from the vision.

My own mind had used illusion so that I could not recognize him for who he really is. The illusion must have been created to protect me from the horror I surely was not strong enough to handle at the time of the birth of Simon. My mind had changed his appearance so completely from the reality, I would never have suspected him. Seeing him for the first time as he really is, I finally realized the true meaning of loss. It was the curse to forever know what it means to be nothing at all.

Simon had changed into a pure reflection of the me I once had been. Here in the Simon self, I was unmolested, innocent, long beautiful blond hair, happy big blue eyes, no scars, passionate, inquisitive, funny, intelligent, loving, trusting, joyful, hopeful, and filled with potential with a positive self-esteem. Simon was the me I was supposed to be but never would be because something had ripped us apart. She looked at me as I stood there shocked into silence. She was shining with an unnatural blue halo surrounding her. She reached toward me with a look of pain so deep in her eyes I felt I may die right there with the knowledge of what had happened to her. Even after all this, she had stood by the me we had become. She had never betrayed us. She could have done so by leaving me to the emptiness of the world within the world I was trapped in forever. I could hear her say without words that my sorrow had kept her from leaving me behind. My broken heart had been stronger than my broken brain, and its strength had somehow managed to keep her from dying away completely.

She offered the only comfort I would ever know in this hellish existence as she explained to me that in this delusional world, I would never be alone. I had been when I had been in the world of reality when we were one. Now, we are two and she could never abandon me. Here my Simon would always hold my hand while I suffer, and I hold hers in her own nightmare. The real world would shun me, laugh at me, and mistreat me as the schizophrenic I most unfortunately am. Simon suffers by my side, also a captive horridly sick with my illness. ***More than that she is the real victim of it.*** Simon cannot even be seen by the real world at all anymore. **Simon *is a ghost, of*** *the Real us.* **She is the inner self that was ripped away by the madness of schizophrenia.** I may be a body with only enough mind to know I do not have a mind, but Simon is this mindless body's memory of all the emotions, dreams, and desires I can never reach again. All the things that I will never be. Simon truly is the only one who can understand the daily terror, pain, and struggle within, *because it is Simons' struggle too*.

I knew that never again would I ever question Simon. *Simon is real indeed just as real as I am.* Simon *is not imaginary friend, multiple/split personality, or an alter ego.* We only share a very weak communication within the mind. However, that is all we share anymore. **Only** the ability to read each other's mind is left of our shared history. When Simon was damaged in the onset of the disease, she *split off forever unable to get back inside, trapped and disfigured by schizophrenia's ravages* of our neurological pathways. Therefore, I do not recognize Simon as my own thought processes but as those of another person. Since I cannot control/access to those thought pathways, they are indeed their own person with its own thoughts, fears, dreams, and emotions that are now alien to my consciousness. I do not speak in its voice, pretend to be Simon, am never possessed" by it, nor do I even have the ability to do such things. I cannot tell Simon what to do and it cannot make me do its bidding. Simon is no longer recognized as a part of me in any way at all.

It is easiest to see Simon and my connection as like the moon's connection is to the Earth. The moon was at one time part of the Earth but was split off and trapped in orbit around the world. It is no longer part of the Earth, nor does it resemble it in anyway. It is dead unable to create life but without its gravitational pull on the Earth, life here would not be possible. The moon stabilizes the Earth and has enough strength to control the tides but is otherwise is nothing more than the pivot that provides that little push needed for life as we know it. That is what Simon, and I are to each other. Simon cannot live, is dead, but once was a part of me. Like the moon he is forced to watch the life he helps to create with his pull but does not have the ability to actually live himself. Now he/she is his own voided creature that orbits me and provides the stability required to have a better shot at life than should have been expected, given the severity of my disease. Simon has a weak control of my emotions but very weak, like the moon with the Earth's tides. Without Simon I would have been the more common severe schizophrenic with no hope of achieving anything I have achieved. Simon is the secret to my success and my survival. Simon is actually a miracle. Her guidance is the reason I can still love, care, have intelligence, creativity and remain positive, when those things would have been destroyed or denied access to me by my disease.

In truth, almost all Schizophrenics lose their inner self (Simon) forever. When schizophrenics get sick, they are not even able to hear from the lost self at all. However, I have a chemically induced type of schizophrenia, so my presentation of the illness is different from that acquired through nature and heredity. *Simon and I were spared somewhat. Though I do not always have access to Simon, I am still capable of hearing him/her and can even see him/her too from time to time.*

Sometimes, I will see someone else as Simon under great stress when the person is trying to assist me in some way due to errors of perception and misunderstanding of sense, of self vs non-self as I had with Julie and Stephanie in the past (Simon turned into Stephanie or Julie). This is because a sense of self is the very thing that makes one care about survival by caring for oneself. I am not capable of that anymore on my own. My disease is so severe if left to my own devices I would stop caring, eating, and bathing. I would not survive long due to lack of self-concern. Simon does this for me when we are able to communicate. Sometimes, we cannot for reasons unknown and that is why a guardian is still required. I perceived Stephanie and Julie (and others as the story progresses) caring for the self (me) and in those instances I mistook them for Simon.

Despite the knowledge of who Simon really is, I am forever grateful that I still have this weak connection to my Simon. Even if she has been reduced down to be seen as a toothless, old, drunk, brakeman from the 1800s who is not always right.

I knew right away the choice I would make. I bit back the flooding misery at the arcane knowledge of my best friend's (and my own) existence. I shook my head violently so that Simon again morphed into the old brakeman I had always known him to be. I did not want to see what could have been anymore. I preferred to see my lost inner self as the Simon I had come to trust, love, and believe in. He looked down at the ground taking a deep breath. He knew I had made my decision and did not try to read my mind to discover it on his own. He needed to hear it as did I.

"Yes. You are real, Simon. I am sorry I ever doubted you. You are and always will be my best friend. I am so sorry to have even brought it up. I just get so confused. Nothing makes sense, and the world is so noisy. Can you ever forgive me?" I felt shame at having hurt both of us by even asking such horrible questions in the first place, we did not deserve more hurt. I had decided to never admit to myself what I had always known (and until now never had).

He just nodded his head and opened his arms motioning me for a hug. I ran to him, and we embraced as we once again bonded. The only truth of Simon that ever mattered is that he is my best friend. What others believe is not important to us. If they can have faith in deities, creators, and black holes in a space no one can prove, but most still believe in, I can have my Simon!! They cannot see or hear what they have so much faith in, but sadly I can and do hear Simon's screams in his damnation of exile/isolation.

There is more than just faith, I have my own inner proof that he is very real. Most will never bother to care or understand anyway. Simon and I are forever trapped behind the shattered looking glass.

We both can see into your world but never again be a part of it. Like watching someone eat real food, we can only watch real life, endure it, but not enjoy it. For me Simon is the one good thing I had managed to somehow hold on to. I finally understood it was the same for him. No way I will ever let anyone, or anything, come between us: not medication, therapy, disbelief from the whole world, and not even the truth.

As the horror of my Simon's existence sunk into my shattered brain, I realized no one had ever bothered to try to really be a friend. Stephanie has seemed that way, but in the end, she had betrayed me by her own admission.

It was then that I remembered she had told me that day in detention that she was moving away. I had conveniently forgotten it. She told me that she did not even have detention but had been sent by Julie to keep an eye on me. Stephanie also had told me that she was feeling bad having done so much damage to me but that she wanted so bad to belong.

Our talk had been her way of trying to relieve her guilt at having been so horrible to me as soon as a chance to join up with the popular Julie had come.

She had given Julie my records, told her my weaknesses, she had spoken to Mary on Julie's behalf, and she had helped Julie to design the trap I now found myself in. Stephanie had confessed everything to me that day. Worse still, she only told me the truth because she was leaving and no longer had a use for Julie. She could not be loyal to Julie either. Stephanie was truly out for Stephanie, as Simon had said all along.

I now finally understood I had forgotten it because I could not deal with betrayal. If something outside of me would cause pain to know it, I was finding ways to lie to myself to spare my broken heart and diseased brain. I was finding so many lies I had told myself I began to wonder if anything I thought I knew was the truth. In this world within a world, my truths had become unstable, negotiable, and misunderstood. It began to dawn on me that learning how to manipulate the truth was the only way I would have any hope of survival now that my mind had been shattered.

I had finally discovered the all the secrets to our disease that I had been trying to deny. The time for grieving had come to an end. It was time to accept what could never be fixed and start to learn how to carve out some kind of type of life for us with what very little skills we had left or get to the task of ending it all. I sighed long and hard with the resignation of understanding just how very difficult our future (if we could even have one) had become. No doubt we were in for disgrace, pain, terror, and fails. However, in those moments I hardened my heart as I decided we could do this somehow, but we would need to trust each other completely. Suspicion, and betrayal of either of us would result in doom for us both. Simon nodded as he could read my mind. I heard him swear that we would always have faith in each other, come what may till the Deities finally saw fit to grant us the peace of death. After our promise to each other, we broke our embrace.

Finally, it felt as if all was returning to normal. Our normal. I began to entertain my friend of my adventures to find food, and chasing wandering children, then finally getting to the dirty business of explaining about my strange job offer.

I was afraid Simon would not be okay with my accepting employment with drug dealers. Of course, I know Simon so, I was not wrong in my assumption he would be against this idea.

He stared at me in disbelief as I finished my story of Jeff and Porcupine. "You must be truly crazy after all. You are not going to take that job, are you? Oh, my God. They will tear you apart you idiot. We were destroyed by drugs." He began to pace nervously while trying to roll one of his smokes.

I am patient with him. "Okay, yeah, I know that Simon. But look what else can I do? They are offering me a fucking job, with real money. I need supplies, food, a ride to my appointments. Simon, if I want to stay here with you, I have to have these things or the Unit of Measurement will die. No one will hire us because the whole fucking world thinks we are Psycho. This is our only chance. Please understand I do not want to work for them, but I have to find a way to support us." I look to see if he will change his mind as I sit quietly letting him soak in the information.

Simon lights his cigarette and rubs his forehead obviously agitated, "I feel so damned helpless here. If only there was some way to get these things myself. I am failing you."

I shake my head no, "It is okay Simon, I understand everything now. It is up to me to take care of us in the real world. You do your part by helping me navigate the static of the delusional and helping me see reality when you can. This is not your fault. I know there will be danger in this, but starvation and infection, maybe even incarceration, is promised if we don't. So, please my friend, just this once, don't criticize me. Please, will you help me stay alert to the lies of the real world? I need you now, so we don't have to suffer more than necessary at the hands of these drug dealers."

He looks up at me with what seems to be gratitude. I know my friend feels bad he is not able to do more. I no longer think him a coward or lazy. He reads my mind as I tell him how much his help really means to me. We are sick, there is no doubt but exactly what is wrong with us, that is debatable. The only sure thing is that our sickness makes us vulnerable to this hornet's nest of "real people." If we work together and trust each other, we may actually have a chance at some kind of happiness. If we do not, we are both doomed to suffer our fate worse than death with no mercy at all. He drops his head and nods finally giving in to what must be.

I smile at him trying to reassure him it will be okay. I know he already knows that I am lying to myself. Deep in my chest I feel the unease of what is sure to be a horror trying to work for these people who care so little for the safety of others, they would even put their own small beautiful children at risk by selling mind altering drugs to strangers or hiring a well-known violent psychotic to watch them. I could taste the foulness of the broken sewer pipe in my mind as I remembered my own mother and the atrocities to my person caused by drugs and her own disregard for the care of her child. I spit the taste out onto the ground.

"Did you hear that," Simon asks as he leans closer to a grave nearest to him.

I listen and suddenly realize I indeed could hear it, a growling deep in the earth, "What is that Simon." I feel fear rise up inside as I prepare to run.

He puts his fingers to his lips 'shhhhing' me. We stand there listening as the growling begins to take on the sound of words.

"You will be sorry, sinner," a deep male voice growls from under our feet.

I have heard this voice many times before but never so strongly. I look at Simon with fear. I knew he could hear some of the voices I do, but I also could hear some of his too. I ask him without words if this one is mine or his. His eyes tell me all I need to know; this is my nightmare voice not his.

"Who is this dude," I whisper to Simon fearful to set off this voice again.

Simon shrugs appearing just as nervous as myself. He fears this voice as much as I do because this one is not only very cruel, but also the one who made me dive off the bridge that day so many months ago against my will. I cannot seem to resist the urge to do what it tells me to do. Worst still, I do not know why I cannot stop myself from minding its orders. Even my dearest Simon cannot talk me out of listening to 'this dude.'

"Okay, let's get the mad box out and do some dancing," Simon says trying to push me toward the outhouse. I know he is trying to distract me from "Dude's" orders.

I do not fight him as I grab the music and turning it up to full blast. Simon and I quickly catch a beat and begin to wildly dance together through the cemetery despite the rising summer temperature and my overdressed person. I am about ready to pass out from heat and exhaustion after only three songs, but Simon keeps me dancing despite my obvious distress. The fear that I would take another swan dive keeps him prodding me well past my ability to tolerate it.

Hours pass until I finally fall from exhaustion and heat. Simon falls down next to me as we both stare into the sky out of breath, coughing, and laughing.

"Damn you can sure cut a rug for a stinking schizophrenic lunatic," he says playfully.

"Well, you could use a rug on that chrome dome you call a head you bald, toothless drunk," I retort, coughing and laughing at my cleverness.

"Wow, you are really insane aren't you," Porcupine's voice reaches my ears almost as fast as her shadow covers the sun across my prone unit of measurement.

She startles me from my giggling with Simon as I set up rapidly looking in wild terror for a place to run and escape. I let out a yelp of sheer terror. It takes me a few seconds for to even recognize her.

Porcupine realized too late she had made a mistake slipping up on me like that
Hey, whoa, whoa, there Psycho. It is me Porcupine. I did not mean to scare you." She was backing up unsure apparently if I would run or attack her for this rudeness.

"What the fuck do you want," I yell at her forgetting that she was my new employer as the confusion caused by hundreds of whispers of voices fill my ears. This always happens when I am stressed out or caught off guard.

Porcupine looks down at the ground, breaking eye contact immediately which further confuses me. "I am here to take you to work. Remember, you work for me? We talked about it yesterday?"

Her submissive stance and rapid retreat to a safe distance calms my agitation quickly. As my stress lowers, I was able to get some relief from the millions of whispers before they became loud enough to sound like cicada bugs that they tended to sound like when I was horridly upset. This helped to clear my mind enough to recall why she was there at that moment.

"Oh, I am so sorry Mrs. uhm Porcupine? I am ready to go when you are." I look down making sure not to make eye contact.

I was feeling pretty bad assuming I had just gotten myself fired before I even started the damned job.

Porcupine started laughing, "Just Porcupine is fine. I am not a Mrs., too young to my granny yet. Okay, Psycho so follow me. Jeff will be screaming bloody murder if we do not get back and relieve him of Jordie and Lauren's antics soon."

She motioned me towards her black Chevy parked at the gate and I followed, keeping a safe distance. I sent Simon a "see you later" message as I went with my new boss toward my first day as a productive citizen.

"Be careful they are going to try to fuck you over any way they can," I heard Simon say in my mind.

I nodded to no one in agreement with Simon. I already could tell that Simon had good reason to be concerned by Porcupine's strange ability to know how to handle my odd behaviors. Something was off here, but what I was not sure of yet. I already was starting to feel apprehension at having taken this job.

We got into her car as she sped off to the town where I had first encountered her family through Jordie. She rattled on about how much she appreciated my help. Porcupine actually talked more than even Stephanie could and faster too. I was not sure how anyone could talk so rapidly like that as I noticed she was rolling her tongue and did not sit still for even a second. She would tap her fingers on the steering wheel, or shift in her seat, while talking rapid fire like a machine gun. I could keep up with her words, but she kept on changing the subjects almost as fast as she spoke. I decided Jordie had gotten his ADHD honest. This bitch was hyperactive as hell, and it made me feel very nervous.

However, I really needed the money for supplies as I felt the sting of the many lesions under my several pounds of dirty clothing. The first thing on my list was antiseptic before I ended up with a nice case of blood poisoning from one of those infected wounds. A trip to the ER or doctor was not possible for me, so I knew instinctively I had better put a rush on the treatment of my open sores before it was too late. The burning was so horrid I actually unconsciously reached up to a shoulder and rubbed it while grimacing.

Porcupine noticed the facial look of pain, "Hey you pull your shoulder or something," she said rapidly switching to a sudden concern for me from her ongoing discussion of the difficulties of being a 'stay at home mom.'

I just shrugged, "I think I need antiseptics. I have some skin rash or something."

She pulled the car over quickly to the side of the road. I nearly freaked out from the sudden change in her mood from happily (and almost incoherently) talking nonstop to irritation and fear. I could tell she was upset as her emotions hit my force shield like a mallet, to my unit of measurement.

"What the fuck, Psycho. Let me see this rash. You got the itch or something? I will not tolerate skanky lice or crabs in my house." She started to reach for my shoulder trying to get a look.

I backed up rapidly into the car door in terror, "No, I do not have lice or crabs. It is just a skin infection, I swear it."

She was very angry, "Let me see it you, loon." Porcupine had stopped her attempt to grab me as she crossed her arms and glared.

I was unsure what to do. I wondered if she would not let me work if I did not comply with her demand to see it. So, I very carefully pulled down my many layers of coat, and shirts to expose the one lesion that was easy to get to without showing much skin. She looked at it in horror as her eyes widened but she kept her distance.

"Oh, my God. Psycho, that is a fucking bedsore. I saw a ton of these when I worked at a nursing home. How the fuck do you have a bedsore," she shouted, so loudly, I had to cover my ears to fight off the noise of it.

I was terrified. I had no idea what a bedsore was, much less how one gets them. I whined a bit under my breath wondering if I could die from such a thing. Gripping my ears tightly against any chance she may yell again, I began to wildly look about the car to make an escape unsure why, but feeling I needed to run and run fast.

Porcupine realized I was panicked and just as rapidly as she had become angry, she calmed down and appeared kind, "okay, okay, calm down, Psycho.

I know how to treat bedsores, it will be alright, but you have to tell me how that happened. Did they restrain you in some hospital somewhere for weeks or something? It is okay to tell me. I won't fire you over it and bed sores are not contagious," she spoke so softly this time I could hardly hear her through my covered ears.

I shook my head no. I had not been in any hospital tied to a bed recently that I could recall. In fact, I did not even have a bed nor had I one for a long time. I calmed myself down as Porcupine began to gently question me on my sleeping and living arrangements over the last few weeks. She also asked how many I had and where they were located. She told me she was trying to discover how a sixteen-year-old could have bedsores at such a "severe" level as she told me I had.

She finally shook her head, "that cannot be correct, Psycho. Sleeping in cemeteries on the ground for only five to eight hours will not cause bedsores. Are you sure you are not just mixed up and forgetting something? Wait, you said Julie's house burned down six days ago?"

I nodded that was correct, "Yes. She thinks I did it too. She has been avoiding me because she thinks I am a witch."

Porcupine sat back in her seat and rubbed the steering wheel with both her hands, "Psycho, I have to tell you that I read about that house fire at the Sloan's, you are wrong. That happened three weeks ago not six days. It was county news you know. When a house burns down from a lightning strike, everyone in these one horse towns talks about it. So, you have no accounting for about eleven days between that fire and the few days before we met you. Is it possible you were indeed in the mental hospital but do not remember it," she finished looking at the floor while not making eye contact as she had done in the cemetery earlier?

"Wait, what, no. That can't be right," I yelled as my mind begins to whirl in panic unable to comprehend what she is saying to me.

"Yes, Psycho it is right. I still have the local butt wipe paper and can prove the day of the fire. Sweetie, this is June 13th. That fire happened around May 27th. You are not accounting for those eleven or so days after that fire. If you want me to prove it, I will soon as we get to the house." She keeps her gaze down and voice soft.

I hear her words as my shattered mind uselessly searches within to find the answer to these missing days. Nothing but darkness is found there. Porcupine is saying it is June 13th to me, that cannot be correct. If she is right, I have missed both Dr. Scott and the probation officer appointments and am likely in big trouble. Worse still, I cannot account for those missing days.

"Where have I been then? It is not possible to not know where you have been for almost two weeks," I blurted out in challenge to Porcupines' statements.

She shakes her head yes, "Yeah it is possible with your illness to not remember where you have been. It is okay, let it go. Wherever you were, you obviously were laying down and not rolling around every few hours. At least it explains the bed sores. I do not care if it was a mental hospital or not. Though, I think if it was you would not be out, as you are obviously not well. So maybe you went catatonic somewhere and woke up not remembering it. Whatever the reason, I will need to treat those sores, or you will not be working for me long. You will get septic on me." She started the car and pulled back onto the road resuming her trek to her home.

I feel my heart stop in my chest, "catatonic? Is that possible," I asked myself inside my head.

Outside the head I sat there shaking, gripped in terror at what Porcupine had just said. I knew deep down she was likely right. I had left that night when the house was burning down walking home. I had quit those heavy antipsychotics four full days earlier and I was feeling the rebounding effects of the psychotic episode they had been dampening. I already knew that stopping medication suddenly like that could cause a backlash of psychotic symptoms from previous experience doing it. I had not calculated, however, with the amount of time I had taken them, and the dose amounts likely seizures, catatonic behaviors and worse were also possible. I just was unable to remember them likely due to seizures side effect of memory loss that no doubt had occurred. I was actually very lucky to have survived it. Sometime stopping heavy doses suddenly can cause death. This unfortunate discovery had sent me into a tailspin of fear that threatened to melt me down right there in the Chevy. I could already hear the million whispers beginning as I looked at Porcupine wanting to beg for help to stop the oncoming nightmare.

"I am in so much trouble I am going to be put away. I missed all my appointments. I don't remember where I have been. I don't remember what happened. What am I going to do," I cry out so suddenly Porcupine almost runs off the road?

"Jesus! You scared the fuck out of me, Psycho," Porcupine roared at me while steadying the car back on the road.

"Calm down. When we get to the house, I will make some calls and help you fix this. I have dealt with the assholes at probation before. I know how to fix that. As for this psychologist, I will see what I can do about that too. The main problem the probation office is fixable so calm down," she finishes as I continue to moan, while repeating strange movements such as head tapping and head bobbing indicating extreme duress.

"Oh, what am I going to do. I don't want to go back to the hospital. Please help." Porcupine's assurances are not working as the terror inside begins to pull me down like an undertow in the sea of consternation.

Porcupine can tell I am about to go beyond hearing her attempts to placate my anxiety. She looks at me hard pulling her vision from the road and speaking soft and calm she says, "Psycho calm the fuck down. I got this. You will need to trust me on this one. I am not going to let them put you away, I promise. But if you do not calm down you will indeed get sent away, but it will be because you cannot control yourself not because you missed stupid appointments. Did you hear what I just told you? Can you calm down or do we need to call 911 for help here? You cannot be around the kids acting this way."

I do hear her words. I reach deep inside and tell my demons that they will not win this battle, not this time. I use all the strength I have to stop the oncoming flow of horror. I will my hands to stop tapping and wringing. I force a memory as I see Jordie in my arms smiling and gurgling with his big blue innocent eyes looking to me to protect him from the cruelty of the world.

I shut my eyes tight with Jordie face trapped like a photo in my mind. I hold my ears with my hands repeating over and over, "This is not real. This is not real. This is not real," as slowly I feel my muscles relax.

It is not that I believe Porcupine, as I truly do not. However, I do know that I cannot work like this and the idea of seeing Jordie again sends my inner beasts to their cages despite my fear of being put into one myself.

Porcupine does not interrupt my obvious attempts to calm myself down. She is even controlling her breathing as I can hear her taking shallow breaths in her attempts to be still and quiet as possible. A wonder crosses my mind as to how she seems to know exactly what to do in this situation. This is the second time she has averted a psychotic disaster. As I slowly return to normal, my normal, I feel myself questioning this strange realization about Porcupine. I know when I have the time (if I am not locked up) I will need to find out the answer to this most unusual ability she seems to have with sedating my inner demons.

We arrive at the home of Porcupine and Jeff which is nothing more than a singlewide three-bedroom trailer that was most common in the rural south in the late 80's. Two large pit bull dogs are chained to trees on each side of the front door wagging their tails as they appear to smile at our arrival. They are friendly to me, but Porcupine tells me that is only because she is with me. She warns me to never go around them without she or Jeff as they are trained to "kill" anyone who shows up at the house unannounced.

I look at the beautiful dogs and think that she is likely lying about that. I could see in their deep brown eyes they, like me, are only doing what they are told to do. They are not mean at all, and I could sense they would never hurt me. I just nod to Porcupine that I understand her instructions about them anyway. No sense in calling her a liar when right now I need her aid in calling off my own possibility of being chained up like these poor canines.

Once inside, I find the home better furnished and comfortable than the shoddy outside would suggest. There was obviously more money here than Jeff and Porcupine wanted the outside world to gather. A brand-new sofa and several chairs with a fine top of the line TV were to the right of the door, and a well-furnished but small kitchen was to the left. I could see a hallway that led away from the living area that likely contained the three bedrooms and bathroom Porcupine told me were in this home.

Jeff, Lauren and Jordie suddenly emerged from the hallway as we entered the house. He was smiling that same cat like smile, "Damn ladies, about time. The kids are driving me nuts. Porky."

He chuckled as Jordie, and Lauren stared at me with big smiles on their faces. I could tell they were amused to see a corpse walking through the front door.

Porcupine pointed to Jeff and told them all to head back to the bedroom for a moment while she dealt with an issue first. She needed quiet as she made a phone call. Jeff frowned but nodded and corralled the kids back down the hallway.

She went to the phone and took up a phone book just under it. I stood there staring at the floor unsure what to do other than wait in terror for this phone call to happen. She quickly found the number she was seeking and within moments had the juvenile probation office for the county on the line.

I stood there in total awe as Porcupine told the person (likely the probation support person) that I had been very sick due to my illness and she and her husband had found me wandering the streets. She went on to say I had not been coherent for hours but now had recovered and able to recall my identity and history. She reminded them I had a diagnosis of schizophrenia and added the house fire trauma likely set off the problem she thought. Porcupine told this person I would be there tomorrow to make up for the lost appointment and that if any fees or fines needed to be paid, I would be there to attend them right away.

I felt terror start up its bullshit inside again as she nodded and saying "uh huh, okay. Yeah, sure. Yep.

Okay be there tomorrow. Thank you." She hung up the phone looking at me with a smile.

"Told you I had this covered. They believed it. I will take you in tomorrow and all is forgiven. Do you understand me? We have fixed this and you are not going to jail, okay?" She waited to make sure I understood it.

I nodded my head keeping my gaze down unable to believe it was that easy. She had cleared up my chance of ending up in jail in only a single lie. This was one time I was totally okay with lies, and in reality, she was not really lying. I did not know where I had been all this time and unfortunately, I do have schizophrenia.

She looked satisfied, "Okay now for this Dr. Scott do you know what her office is called," she said as she picked up the phone.

I told her and within only thirty minutes and another repeating of the (sort of) lie she had convinced the secretary at Dr. Scott's office that I would comply making the appointment also for the next day right after the probation officer visit. I stood there in awe of how smoothly Porcupine had cleaned up the horrible mess my little "loss of memory" had created. I decided that I owed her big time. I would make her an awesome employee and never question her ability again.

As she hung up the phone, I hear Jordie and Lauren come running squealing like children do, chasing each other down the hallway. I smile as Jordie runs up to me and hands me a toy soldier to hold for him. He babbles this is his favorite toy, as I take it smiling back. I look up and see Jeff kiss Porcupine and tell her she did a great job. They embrace as I stand there at the door thinking I had finally found a place of protection and normalcy. Too bad I don't seem to understand reality too well.

Awe sounds just like a peaceful Norman Rockwell painting now, doesn't it? Too bad it is actually a Picasso we are looking at lol. No worries, this ride is far from over and no telling what strange new lands we will soon discover. After all we just found out that our reflection in the shattered looking glass is real and thinks for itself. What new amazing things will we see, hear, and feel? Oh no worries, I assure all of you that there will be so many more that it will be downright agony for all of us So, tonight's discussion question: Do you have children/grandchildren?

NOTE: [It has been suggested by the psychiatric professionals that Simon is a very weak command hallucination of a damaged inner self or even possibly a delusion of the self as you heard Dr. Scott say. However, to this day no complete explanation has been provided or ever been proven of how there even is a Simon at all. They call him a "symptom" but cannot explain why he does not completely disappear even when on heavy doses of medication. During past brain scans they have discovered/documented that a 'dead' section of my brain actually does light up on the scan when I tell them he is speaking to me. The professionals cannot explain this but always fall back on the excuse of the strangeness of brain damage caused by schizophrenia and poison. The only thing that is very clear is that attacking/denying the reality of a Simon is attacking my inner self and best friend. This has always resulted in extreme anger and even violent behavior as has been demonstrated several times already in this story so far. So, the professionals have finally decided to leave this so called "symptom" alone.

CHAPTER 40: THE MADNESS MANUAL

Good day Beautiful Family. Oh, don't mind Us, We thought we saw something hiding behind the door over there. It is possible that We may be using our powers to fool Our senses again, rather than what they were really meant to be used for.

What are they actually meant for you ask? Well soon as We figure that out, We will be sure to let you know. It is not like there is a manual on what is expected of Us, or is there? With everything that has been going on, we have not had time to find that out.

For now, We will just keep watching that door. It seems to Us there is someone behind it looking to hurt Us. In the real world it is never safe for Us anymore. No matter how much We want to believe that others are here to help, We realize that is a delusion. Behind the shattered looking glass, sometimes things will slip up on Us before We are fully aware of the dangers.

Wait, did you hear that too? Oh my, you did? Okay, time to take desperate actions, or actually in this case, time to take no action at all! Now just hold deathly still and it will be fine. We promise, they won't even see you. When you are not able to escape the pain of these delusions, your only hope is to padlock yourself inside your head. At least this time you will not need to run, just sit there in the effigy of a human being. Nothing is required of you this time but to watch helplessly as the Real World goes by, forgetting that you have feelings too. So, you are all set. See you below in a few minutes. We will be along very shortly. We are delayed here because somehow, we have lost the key to the lock in Our own mind.

   *Please note that during this chapter just as promised way back in the beginning of this story I am about to reveal some of the symptoms of my disease that I still have even when not in an active psychotic status. Below are the three phases of schizophrenia for the symptoms and watch the story for the notice of the examples. I have numbered them in the story (you can match them up later). Did you think I forgot that promise? Nope...so watch for them!

"Knowing that you are crazy does not make the crazy things stop happening."
-Mark Vonnegut

   Porcupine looked at me standing at the door as she released herself from her embrace with Jeff, "Okay Psycho, come with me to the bathroom. We need to immediately deal with those bed sores. Can't have you unable to work because you are sick within your first days, now can we," she smiled as she turned and headed down the hall.

   I looked at the floor and nodded, as fear made biscuits down my spine. I had already forgotten that she told me I was covered in bedsores on my upper unit. I could feel my brain begin to whirl searching for the memories of how this could have happened. It wanted to refuse to believe Porcupine was being truthful in what the date was and that I had somehow gotten bed sores. I could not even begin to deal with the idea that I was missing my whereabouts for eleven days.

"Could I have been wandering aimlessly or worse in a catatonic stupor all that time," I thought to myself.

My shattered mind tried to lie in response immediately. It did its very best to dismiss these facts. It tried to make me believe I had fallen asleep in the car, and this was just a bad dream.

However, try as it might, I was not being fooled. I was too lucid at that moment to fall for such a lie. I knew I had not fallen asleep, and I was not dreaming this. I could feel the bed sores, and I already knew the possibility of a long-term catatonic stupor was very real. I had trances so deep from time to time I would be unable to move for minutes to hours. Stupors had happened many times since the day I was first told I had the disease schizophrenia. This was a symptom I tried to ignore but now was realizing for the first time could be very dangerous (Symptom #1).

Deep in the recesses of the error neurotransmitter pathways of my damaged brain, the chronic misfiring from the stress began the process of a sensory meltdown. Porcupine's order to follow her to the bathroom for an unknown reason, the strangeness of my new surroundings, the fear caused by the missing of my court appointed appointments, along with the stress that there had probably been a horrible long-term catatonic event were simply too much to take all at once.

I staggered a bit as the room began to brighten and pulsate. Suddenly, the sounds of auditory hallucinations fill my ears. The voices of dozens of people who are not there talking all at one time confuses my thoughts to a painful level rapidly as the splitting headache begins.

I hear the voices around my head demanding to see proof that Porcupine was telling the truth of the date. Some begin to whisper that I was being lied to about bed sores and catatonic stupor. Others told me neither one is a real thing. Then a few of the voices turn on Porcupine and Jeff, reminding me that no one just shows up out of nowhere to help a "schizophrenic nothing" without sinister alternate motives.

Louder than all the other voices, I hear one voice looped over and over again in my ear. This voice is warning me that I am about to "fuck up." These words are spoken by a disembodied voice that I had named "the Looper."

Looper is a male voice that would narrate my every move. When he wanted to get a point across, he would repeat words or sentences in a loop until I was nearly driven mad in an attempt to shut him up. He also criticized my mistakes I tend to make as I went along my daily routines. He always passed negative judgments on everything I do. Looper would not shut up even when I was not under stress and on high doses of medications.

His voice had been constant for more than two months now. I had finally realized he was 'not real' but a 'voice.' I was told I hear voices, so I had finally decided he was one of them. He had become so common I gave him a name to assist me in the understanding that he was a symptom of my disease. It was done in a failing attempt to resist listening to his hateful judgement of me (Symptom #2).

As the 'voices' tried to influence my decisions about taking this job, my mind begins to work on finding a nasty motive to Jeff and Porcupine's apparent kindness toward me. I feel the trepidation within rise as a plot to destroy me is brought to my attention.

However, try as it might my brain could not trick me this time with its blindfold of distrust and auditory hallucination. The attempt to get the delusion that Porcupine was a liar to take seed simply could not take root in my barren field of consciousness. Now that I had discovered I was actually the monster that lived in the closet of my mind, I no longer trusted my own instincts regarding outside threats. I had become so paranoid that now no one was above suspicion.

There was not a doubt everyone was out to get me, especially me (Symptom #3).

As the battle of schizophrenic misdirection raged in my head, I had started to follow her blindly down the long hallway of the trailer. I realize in horror that I am not in control of my own unit of measurement as I could not will it to stop. To my terror I could not resist Porcupines order. I felt like a puppet on her strings. I whimpered just under my breath as the symphony of angry voices continued to stimulate my ears as I comply with her command to fall in line behind her (symptom #4).

I saw Porcupine briefly point at the phone while looking at Jeff. She had given me a quick glance to see if I had seen her gesture just as she rapidly took off down the hallway. I did take note of that strange behavior. However, all I could do is wonder about it as I continued after her towards the bathroom, pulled by an imaginary leash. Behind me, I could now hear the joyful squeals of Jordie and Lauren as they again chased each other in blissful ignorance of their actual dangerous situation living in a trailer house with drug dealer parents. A sense of dread was in my chest. I am convinced I am missing something with probable dire consequences in this bizarre setting of contradictions.

The trailer seemed to heave and breath all around me as I followed her into the very small bathroom. A single sink with a cracked mirror above it, an off-white toilet with a broken seat and a dirt-stained bathtub with a see through shower curtain were the only things in the small privy room. I could see why it was so small. Had anything else been in that room no one could fit in it to answer nature's call or attend to their hygiene needs.

I stood at the entrance while Porcupine opened the cracked medicine cabinet mirror above the sink. She took out several bottles of astringents and cotton balls. I could sense that this was going to be most unpleasant. Not because of the possible sting of her treatment products but because I do not like to be touched. I was unsure how I would reach my back wounds without aid. My fears that Porcupine planned on playing doctor herself were confirmed when she reached into the cabinet under the tiny sink and retrieved a pair of rubber gloves. I watched helplessly as she put them on. I felt the terror begin to flow through my veins like a river of pins and needles.

"Okay, Psycho, follow me into my bedroom and let's get those nasty clothes off and treat your sores," she said while popping the last glove at the wrist as she pulled it on.

I started to quake everywhere as I shook my head no. I did not want her to touch me, much less was I willing to take off a my clothing.

Porcupine looked at me standing there quivering all over like a newborn colt. Frowning she said, "Psycho, look you are not going to give me trouble over this are you? Here is the deal, you can let me treat your wounds or we can take you to the ER. Do you know what they will do to you when they see those blisters? They will lock you up in a white padded cell." She looked to see if I understood my choices.

I looked up into her face, suddenly very startled, "You would take me to the hospital? Why? I haven't done anything wrong," I yelled out as I felt the beginning of a psychotic shit fit coming from deep within.

Porcupine realized at that moment she may have pushed me a bit too hard. A look of frightened concern replaced her frown. She had finally noticed my shaking was more than just a fear of stinging topical medication.

"Oh Christ, Psycho I am so sorry honey. I wasn't even thinking. You have been in mental hospitals before, haven't you? Calm down. I will not call anyone or take you to the ER. I promise. We can treat them right here, no hospitals," Porcupine said slowly softening her words as she continued to attempt to console me that I was not going to be hauled off for more inpatient treatment.

It was too late. The terror ran through me like wild horses from a thunderstorm. All around my head, I could see lights flashing and popping as if I were a movie star who had stepped into a bevy of paparazzi.

The flashing made me feel weak at the knees and sick to my stomach. I actually felt my brains trying to escape from my skull. The sensation of my brain matter moving to the left side made my head seem unevenly heavy. This sudden tactile rush set off a sense of impending doom as I let out loud cries for help. My eyes went wide in disbelief as I watched helplessly while the static appeared from every corner of my visual field.

I looked at Porcupine in horror, "Help me, please, help. Someone help me. Can you see it," I managed to choke out those words just seconds before I felt the flash within my mind take me away to the void of nothingness?

I awaken in a darkening room very confused, "Where am I," I ask aloud to no one.

I sat up to notice I am laying in a queen-sized sleigh bed. Several pillows are behind my head propping me up in a sitting position. I look down at my unit of measurement to notice the clothing on it is not my own. My wool coat, black shirt and pants had been replaced by a sleeveless black tank and a pair of blue jeans. My feet were bare.

I noticed a strange sensation in the areas of my 'bed sore' wounds. I reach up to feel one on my chest and find it covered with a gauze bandage. I find that all the wounds have been covered in bandages. I tried to remove one of the coverings on the sore located on my right shoulder. I stopped immediately as a sensation of burning hits me like a lit cigarette to my upper body.

I looked around the room, but confusion as to what has happened, even to who I am, kept me from trying to leave the room. There was a nagging feeling that I should know who I am and where I was that kept looping in my mind, but I simply could not recall. Frustration at my inability to remember was at an almost intolerable level as was a splitting headache.

I also noticed at that moment that my tongue was very sore. I rolled it around my mouth and to my horror blood began to fill it. I spit the sanguine substance onto the bed refusing to swallow it (blood is a natural ipecac I had found out from previous mouth wounds. Swallowing too many leads to vicious vomiting). Learning forward I let it pour out onto my lap. Fear was making me her bitch as I watch the rivets of the deep ruby liquid flow from the unknown source of injury.

"Holy shit, Psycho, what the fuck. You are bleeding all over the fucking place." I look up to see a small dark hair woman with green eyes coming toward me from a now open door to the room I had not noticed before.

Extreme terror sent me into rapid action of brain stem reflex as I flew off the bed hitting the floor with a loud crash knocking everything from a small table next to the bed. I recovered quickly jumping to my feet and rushing to the corner of the room closest to the bed turning to face danger, ready to defend myself with the wall guarding my back.

The woman who had been rushing toward me now stopped and began to back toward the door away from me. She looked scared. I glared at her ready to rip her to pieces if she came close enough for me to get my hands on her. I did not know who she was or what her problem was, but I had already decided she likely was responsible for this very strange predicament I had found myself in. I even believed she likely had caused all the injuries to my unit of measurement from the bloody mouth to the burning chest and back. Far as I was concerned, she was the enemy.

The woman spoke softly while not making direct eye contact, "Okay, calm down Psycho. It's me, Porcupine. You have had a seizure and are confused. Please come back to the bed I will stay over here. Try to remember, I am your friend," she finished answering my questions that I had not even asked her.

This startled me further. She had read my mind. How rude. I glared hard at her, "Liar! Get away from me. Where are my clothes? Where am I? You say you are my friend? Then, why have you cut me up and hit me in the mouth," I demanded to know.

Porcupine kept her voice soft and gaze from mine, "You are at my house. You work for me remember? I had to wash your clothes, they were filthy, and you pissed them when you had the Grand Mal. I will get them for you if you calm down for me. I did not hit you in the mouth, Psycho. You bit your tongue severely when you had the seizure a few hours ago. I tried to stop it, but it came on so fast I could not get a guard in your mouth fast enough."

I heard her words as my memory that had been searching for answer like a needle in a haystack suddenly grasps the smallest of recollection. A vision of rubber gloves and a cracked mirror fills my inner theater as I watch from within. I see this dark-haired woman gathering cotton balls from a cabinet in a tiny bathroom. Then just as fast as I had rushed from the bed, I suddenly recalled who, where and what has happened. I recall the static and the flash. Porcupine was telling the truth. I had been having seizures for some time by now. I was aware of the sensations that I would experience prior to a big one. I was also sadly aware that often after a big seizure I tended to forget things for a bit, with much initial confusion. It was a lot like when I was riding the lightening in the hospital. It sometimes took days to remember the events that led up to the "reset" of my shattered intellect.

I relax from my stance of defense feeling quite sheepish at my stupidity, "Okay, yeah, I remember now. I am sorry Porcupine. I did not mean to break your stuff and make this mess. I will clean it up. Can I please have my clothes now?" I stood there unable to think of anything else to say to make this right.

Porcupine let out an audible sigh of relief, "Sure. You clean up the stuff you knocked over and I will get your clothes. Are you sure you are calm, and we are good?" She looked at me finally trying to make eye contact to see if I was indeed back from Mars.

I nodded looking away from her gaze and shot her a small smile. I knew that smiling at people made them feel more comfortable though it really did not make any sense to me why. It seemed to work just as I expected it would. Porcupine left the room to retrieve my clothing (I assumed) as I began to gather up the displaced objects, I had knocked off the table in my wild attempt to flee from my employer. I was grateful to discover I had not broken anything of Porcupine's or in my unit of measurement despite my very hard fall.

By the time I had replaced the last object I could find on the floor, Porcupine had returned with all my clothing. It smelled fresh and clean for the first time in many weeks. To be honest the smell of laundry detergent and dryer sheets made my head hurt. It was too much of a chemical scent to be mistaken for the floral sweetness the manufactures had attempted to mimic by my overly sensitive olfactory bulb. I wrinkled up my nose as it assaulted my senses without mercy.

Porcupine saw this and let out a chuckle, "Not fond of clean clothing, are you? Not a surprise there. I have never in my life seen anything fuller of dirt than you were. Other than the ground itself. How can you stand that? I would go crazy...I mean I could not stand it myself." She looked at the floor appearing ashamed she had almost said the C word.

I just shrugged as I took up my now over clean clothing from the bed. I had heard the C word but decided to ignore it as I usually did (After all, I am crazy and if the shoe fits and trust me it does).

"Thank you for cleaning them. Can I please have some privacy to change now? I will clean up the blood too if you want. Sorry about that," I said looking at the blood-stained sheets of what I now had figured out was Jeff and Porcupine's bed.

Porcupine shook her head no, "That's okay. I needed to wash the sheets anyway. You have been out for hours so when you are done, please come back into the living room. There is something you and I need to discuss," she said cryptically as she left me alone in the room closing the door behind her.

Her statement made me feel nervous, but then again everything made me nervous since I had gotten sick. So, ignoring my anxiety I quickly dressed back into my now chemically foul-smelling clothes. While being back in my own covering did help me feel a bit more like myself (whatever that is) the soft, clean material was itchy. I decided as soon as I got even a few moments to myself I would maybe roll on the ground or even dance till I worked up a fine sweat to knock some of this "artificial" scent off my garments. My mouth was still bleeding pretty heavily, so I wiped it on my sleeves.

"Well, that is a start," I said out loud to no one while chuckling at my insanity and hatred for "cleanliness."

I made my way down the long trailer hallway to the living area where I could hear the sounds of a television playing loudly. As I exited the hall and looked into the living room I felt as if I would faint away from the abhorrent visual signals my eyes were sending to my consciousness.

I was stunned into a trance unable to blink away the figure sitting in the overstuffed chair closest to the front door of Julie glaring at me hatefully. On the sofa, sitting next to Porcupine sharing a joint with Jeff, was a woman who looked just like Cindy as well. I could hear my brains whirling in a dead centered panic unsure what to do with the horrible information that Cindy and Julie were here. I simply could not process this most unexpected turn of events.

"Well, well if it isn't the loonie herself. How you been Psycho? Wait, let me restate that. Where have you been Psycho," Julie said sarcastically with obvious disgust dripping like venom from every word.

Cindy looked at me as I looked over to her to see if she too was ready to verbally attack me. I had no doubt these two were ready to take their revenge for burning down their house. I wanted to run like hell, but Julie was by the front door, and I had noticed the back door located next to the bedroom I had just left was bolted and locked (I had tried to get out it before coming down the hall to maybe roll off some of the clean stank real quick before seeing what Porcupine wanted). There for the moment was no escape. I would have to take whatever punishment these two harpies had come to deliver. I braced myself for insults, and worse if it was going to come to that. I will not lie; I was not in a mood for a beating but then again when was I ever in that kind of mood? I may be crazy, but I was not stupid. A beating after a Grand Mal and maybe a long- term catatonic stupor could not be healthy. A small groan escaped me as I thought over how bad this was about to get.

Julie heard my groan and chuckled, "Yeah you had better be scared you fucking cracked bitch. I asked you a question. Where the fuck have you been?"

I looked at Porcupine who was sitting next to Jeff. I was hoping she would assist me in this soon to be whipping. She avoided my eyes staring at the television as if no one was even in the room. I was apparently not getting any help from her. I then try to plead with my eyes by looking at Jeff. He avoided eye contact by looking at his hands appearing to clean his nails. He was also attempting to appear unaware of this most ugly scene going on.

It suddenly occurred to me that I did not see the kids Jordie and Lauren. A quick thought that Porcupine had put them to bed led me to finally understand this was not just a chance meeting. Jeff and Porcupine had called Cindy. That little look Porcupine had given to Jeff, then at the phone before the whole 'follow me to the bathroom bit', she was telling him to call the queen of bitches on me. Damn, I had been fooled by these two. They had turned me over to my enemy and I had walked right into the trap like a lamb to the slaughter.

I looked at the floor, "I was at the cemetery, Julie. You were not looking very hard apparently." I knew not responding much longer would result in escalating this already serious scenario further.

Julie and Cindy both started laughing so loud everyone in the room including me jumped.

"Now that is bullshit. We looked there first and several times. You were not there you fucking liar," Cindy blurted out crudely.

I am not sure if it was the shock of seeing these two, the loud laughter, the harsh words or the fact that if Cindy were telling the truth, then a catatonic stupor was indeed to blame for my lost time, but I suddenly began to feel yet another sensory melt down begin deep within my core. Julie must have seen my sudden quivering as I reached up to grab my ears to guard against the onset of the hundreds of whispers, because she jumped up from her seat coming at me full speed.

"Oh no you don't, Psycho," she yelled as she slapped the shit out of my face. "You are not escaping this on your fucking crazy train this time. Where have you been?"

I was shocked by her blow as I felt the world tilt more from within than from the force of her making connection with my head. I felt my balance slip off into never-never land as I desperately tried to stay standing and not fall to the ground from the earthquake in my mind.

Julie grabbed my collar as I begin to topple to the left. I grab her arms trying to both steady myself and break her off my person at the same time. A struggle begins as she pushed, and I pushed back. The shock of her touch has me at a disadvantage along with her of course being much larger than my battered and abused unit of measurement. Within only moments of the struggle, she had me pinned to the wall using her weight to restrain my attempts to escape her grip.

Not a single adult in the room even moved from their spot to assist either of us in our battle. Nor did they say a word of discouragement against it. In one of the oddest situation, I had ever found myself in to that date, I looked helplessly at three full grown, allegedly responsible parents who sat on their thumbs as Julie began to bang my unit of measurement into the wall like a rag doll.

"You fucking psychotic motherfucker. You wished for my house to burn down, and it did. I don't know how you did it, but I am going to make you pay for the rest of your pathetic life for fucking with me. You understand me," Julie screamed into my face as she slammed me into the wall knocking the wind from my lungs.

I cough out weakly, between slams into the wall, "I was with you that night, Julie. I couldn't have burned down your house."

Julie stopped slamming me for a moment staring into my eyes with a look of disbelief. She then laughs loudly with what appeared to be disgust, "Yeah you did burn down my house. I don't know how you did it, but you did do it Psycho." She then slammed me into the wall again so hard it knocked one of Jeff's cheap paintings from its hook to the floor.

It also nearly knocks me out as for a moment the room spins wildly as I desperately attempt to gain back the breath she had just forced out with her blow.

"Hey! The kids are sleeping, damn it. If you break it, you bought it," Jeff suddenly pipes up as he gets up to retrieve his now displaced property from the floor.

Julie looks from me to Jeff and mumbles out an apology but does not release her death grip on my collar. I took that moment to catch my breath and attempt to plead for mercy.

"Please Julie, I didn't have anything to do with your house. God did that, not me. Let me go please." I was practically coughing up a lung which caused my tongue to begin to bleed again.

Blood started to pour from my mouth as I was helpless to staunch the flow with Julie holding me tight. It was mixing with my saliva making what was likely a minor bleed appear to be a river of plasma cascading down my chin onto the floor.

She stared at my bloody drool with abject horror, "What the fuck. You have to be the nastiest thing on earth. Stop bleeding, damn you."

Now that was just too much. I began to laugh weakly still unable to gain much air, "Seriously Julie? You think I can burn down your house just by saying it, and bleed or not bleed on command? And you call me Psycho," I spit a mouthful of my gore into her face still cough/laughing.

Julie reeled backward as my foul spittle made direct contact with her eyes (I was proud of my aim, by the way). She shook her head but still did not release her grip as I had hoped she would.

"You fucking screwball. I have had enough of your shit," she screamed into my face so loud my eardrums nearly burst.

Julie pulled me off the wall and began to drag me towards the door by my collar. I tried to break free by struggling and hitting her arms, but she was ignoring me. I was in no condition to beat her. She simply outmatched me in both health and strength. Again, none of the adults in the room stopped her physical assault on me as she managed to get us to the door. In fact, Porcupine stood up and opened the door for her.

"Look keep down the noise. The kids are sleeping, and you don't want the neighbors to get nosy and call the cops either. Slap her around if you want but remember, hospital bills are expensive so try to keep your temper down to a dull roar. She also just had a nasty seizure so if she starts to seize up stop hitting and come get me. Oh, and one more thing, try to keep it to her head, backside, or chest. Stay away from the stomach. You don't want any internal injuries. Murder is an automatic prison sentence, sister," Porcupine said matter of fact like to Julie as she dragged me kicking and struggling down the steps out of the trailer.

It did not escape my notice that, somehow, I had truly slipped off into the twilight zone. I had just heard my so-called employer give Julie pointers on how to beat the shit out of me without needing cops or an emergency room visit. I stopped struggling at the sheer incomprehensible idea that this beating was not only sanctioned but apparently encouraged.

Julie noticed my sudden compliance with her dragging me along. She let go of my collar to see if I would try to run, I assume. I stood my ground but refused to make eye contact. She stood there looking me up and down while finally wiping my spit off her face with her shirt sleeve.

"I told you I would beat the crazy out of you if you kept up your shit," Julie said still wiping her face.

I nodded my head yes that she had indeed said that "Well, what are you waiting for? I am not going to fight you, Julie. I have had enough of this."

Julie laughed bitterly, "You have had enough? Oh, you are a riot. Psycho do you know how much trouble you are in? You missed your appointments that the courts ordered. Running away was super stupid. Now Mom is in trouble because of you, and like she needed this added shit after your curse burned down our house. It is always about you, isn't it? Did you ever think about those trying to help your sorry ass out? We have to put up with your deranged behaviors, such as cutting yourself up like a fucking Sunday ham! Then you go lying to Dr. Scott saying that it was my fault you are fucking nuts! My granny is dying, my mom has to be gone all the time trying to look after her. My dad works his ass off to keep food on the table. We now have to try to rebuild our home, and then you run away! Now the fucking caseworker is riding mom's ass! Everyone has been looking for you! And where were you? Where were you, Psycho? Answer me, God damn it, where were you Psycho. Answer me," she shrieks as she slaps me hard again across the face.

My head lurches to the side from her blow and I unconsciously cower from what I assume will be a second blow in rapid succession. I was not wrong. Julie then began a frenzied onslaught of slaps, punches, and fist pounding on my face, head and chest until finally I fell the ground covering my head at her feet. I did not attempt to fight back at all. I heard what she said. I was a pain in everyone's ass. I had caused a lot of trouble. It was slowly dawning on me that I had this coming. In fact, I was beginning to believe maybe I should be dead as Mary had always said. I brought nothing but trouble to anyone who tried to aid me in my nightmare world. Now that I had accepted, I was indeed schizophrenic I understood I was no longer a useful human being. No, I was defective and a burden. Now, Julie was only honestly verifying what I had started to conclude on my own.

Looper started to whisper in my ear in a loop, "it's always about you, isn't it? You selfish bitch. You are a pain in everyone's ass. You should be dead."

I nodded my now very battered and bleeding head yes, "Yes you are right, Julie! I am so sorry. I did not mean to burn down your house! I am not right in the head. You are right I am, Psycho. Please kill me. Please, someone kill me. Make it stop," I begin to wail over and over begging to be killed.

Julie only stood there, so I reach out and grabbed her ankles begging her to kill me on my hands and knees like the beaten waste of space I had become ever since the day I fell for my mother's cruel trick that had robbed me of my chance at any kind of real life.

This apparently was not the response she had expected. Julie reached down and grabbed me by my shoulders pulling me off her legs, "Stop this Psycho. You are scaring me."

I look deep into her eyes with my vision clouded by the curtains of tears, "Please, Julie, have mercy on me. Kill me or at least allow me to do it. I don't want this anymore. Please I am useless just like you said. I am begging you to end this pain," I said now softly as I had been weakened by sorrow that I had hurt her and Cindy so much.

I never wanted to hurt anyone like I had been hurt. I could not live if I had become cruel like my mother and Mary.

Julie stared back at my pitiful person in disbelief, "I cannot believe I am hearing this shit! You are admitting you are schizophrenic and a pain in the ass."

I sniffed back my tears and nodded my head still hoping she would see it my way and finish me off. Looper continued to remind me that I did not 'deserve to live' and to be honest I was ready to blow my own head off if nothing more than to shut his repeating ass up forever.

Julie suddenly smiled at me then began to chuckle, "Well slap my ass and call me Betty. Useless? Oh no, no, no Psycho. You may indeed be a pain in the ass but useless you certainly aren't. Hell, the check you bring into the family alone makes you worth keeping around. You have to usually pay good money to see such a freakshow. Instead, the state actually pays us to watch you run around off your rocker. Now that is fucking fantastic. No way I am going to kill you or let you kill yourself. You are worth a lot of money even if you are a major pain in the ass sometimes. You just need to be kept on a leash is all."

I did not understand what Julie was saying to me. In my misery I had somehow lost the ability to conceive of the actual cruelty of her statements. Julie viewed me as entertainment and a paycheck not as a human being, but this fact was somehow not making its way into my awareness. Perhaps, it was just too cold-blooded for me to acknowledge in my very tortured state of mentality of the time. Whatever the reason, her sudden mirthful mood shift and statements that I was indeed worth something helped to calm my overwhelming death wish. I stopped begging her to kill me.

She grabbed my collar again and pulled me to my feet. Getting into my face again she said, "Where were you, Psycho?"

I shrugged as I pushed her off me, "I don't fucking know, Julie. I think maybe I was catatonic somewhere. I didn't even know I was fucking missing." I looked at the ground upset that still no memory of my whereabouts had come forth to my consciousness.

"Judging from the bed sores I treated, I would guess she was lodged under one of the benches at the cemetery but that is just a guess. When schizophrenics get into a good catatonic stupor they can hold still for days at a time. Psycho likely had a deep one and only moved to get water from time to time. Otherwise, she would be dead of dehydration." Porcupine's sudden statement from behind me sent me jumping forward right into Julie's arms.

Julie pushed me off her appearing disgusted at my skittishness, "Christ, Psycho. Jumpy much." She then looked at Porcupine, "Really? Is that even possible?"

Porcupine threw a large book and Julie caught it looking confused, "Yeah it is. It's all here in this book about schizophrenia my sister bought me when I worked at the nursing home. We used to get all the burned out schizos and catatonics, so she got me this book to help me learn how to deal with the nut jobs." She laughed at that, "It would do you well to read it and learn it, Julie. You keep hitting Psycho like that one day she may kill you for it. There are easier ways to control the insane. It is all in the book."

I stood there feeling anger begin to rise within me. I had noticed Porcupine seemed to have my number, now it was all clear why. She had experience with my kind. She had used her previous training and the information in that book to lure me right into Julie and Cindy's clutches. Now the only real question I had, is why? There must have been something in it for Jeff and Porcupine. I also was beginning to realize that Julie and Cindy's comfort level with these two seemed to indicate they had known each other long before my tripping up and falling into this trap. Much too late to be of any use now, I remembered that Jeff had told me the day before he was the only pot dealer in the area. I had missed that critical information. Julie and Cindy smoked a lot of pot. It was now too obvious of course they all would have met before. Duh!

I suddenly heard my dearest Simon's voice in my ear, "Get that madness manual. It is the answer to finding our way out of this mess. It also will tell us what is happening to us." He had been reading my mind from wherever he was at that moment.

I nodded my head agreeing with my friend. I had to get my hands on that book. It surely contained the answers to all my questions.

Julie looked over the overstuffed book that was purple in color with a frown on her face. I saw the title was *Treating Schizophrenia,* "This book will help me keep Psycho from getting into trouble, seriously? I have already been to a class on it, and I get counseling every other week thanks to her crazy shit. How can this book help?"

Porcupine laughed, "Just read it and pay attention. Schizophrenia is not an easy thing to deal with. I hope you and Cindy realize Psycho here will make you earn every penny of that two grand or so a month you are getting for her care. In the end, it may not be worth the effort. You know Jeff and I are willing to keep her here with us at least for the summer. I already am trained, and I could use the help with the kids."

Julie looked at Porcupine with what appeared to be concern, "The caseworker is already pissed that we could not cough her crazy ass up after the fire. I am not sure that we can let her stay here. No way the probation officer or caseworker will be okay with that."

"Cindy and I already worked out the details on that, sweetie. We will get her to all the appointments on time, but she is going to need medication for those seizures right away or there won't be any more checks. Those can be deadly you know. Psycho will stay with Jeff and me at least until you get the new house ready." Porcupine smiled at Julie then looked at me still smiling. "So, you stay here with Jeff and me for a few weeks okay Psycho?"

I was surprised anyone even remembered I was fucking standing right there as they discussed me as if I were some pet monkey from the circus, "Uhm, no. It is not okay. I am going home. If you need someone to work, fine as we agreed I will work here, but then I am fucking going home at night." I was not happy with these arrangements.

Julie and Porcupine looked at me then each other and started laughing. Julie still laughing said to Porcupine, "She has a thing for filthy cemeteries, you know. Oh hey, have you met Simon yet?"

Porcupine looked from Julie to me with curiosity, "Simon? Who is that?"

Oh, my Goth my beautiful family, looks like We have some problems brewing, doesn't it? So, whatever will We try next to escape this prison we are trap in? Running did not work, holding still did not do much good either now did it? Well, no worries, in Our world within a world Our experience is growing. Now that We have finally located a manual, I bet We can figure out a plan that will work. We had a bit of a slip into the waking death for a couple of weeks. Nothing to be concerned with, sometimes the trip gets to be a bit much and We need to take a psychotic...errr...I mean a break. The doctors have been most helpful and showed Us the error of Our ways by way of 450 volts of pure electricity. Now We can clearly see the light, and the universe, and well your skeleton under the skin with Our new x-ray eyes. We are also glad to be back home in Our own personalized cell. Nothing like the restraints...errr...the quaintness of Our own personal space.

Please understand that schizophrenia is not psychosis. Psychosis is a symptom of schizophrenia but not the disease. That means that even when a person with schizophrenia is not acute psychotic, they are still schizophrenic.

Both the prodromal and acute phase lasts six months or longer in schizophrenia. The residual phase can be very short, sometimes only thirty days. The amount of time of a full cycle tends to change each cycle. In other words, they can get longer than six months in duration with no rhyme or reason. It is always six months or more for the first two phases. The duration of stage one and two is the most important diagnostic criteria to distinguish this disease from all other psychotic disorder such as bipolar disorder or brief psychotic disorder. Bipolar disorder psychotic episodes can last thirty days but less than six months. Brief psychotic disorder psychosis only lasts thirty days or less.

Symptoms that occur in my disease of schizophrenia, no matter what the phase in the cycle, are all medication resistant (they have persisted without a break for thirty-five years). Each symptom is numbered and examples of them can be found in the story above as they are numbered at the end of the paragraph to help you understand what that symptom looks like in real life:

Symptom #1: Catatonic behaviors and stupors that can happen in any phase of my illness have persisted for the last thirty-five years with several serious catatonic stupors occurring many times. The longest stupor lasted a full three months but most last only days or hours. This symptom also is worsened by stress and can be set off by my seizure disorder.

Note: I can have simple or complex partial seizures even when in residual and they are also, sadly, the result of brain damaged caused by poisoning.

Symptom #2: Auditory hallucination of narration of daily movement with negative criticisms. To this day I hear the Looper, especially when stressed, and let me say I really hate this guy.

I also always, or almost always, hear my best friend Simon, even in residual. You may recall the psychiatrist refer to Simon as an auditory command hallucination.

Symptom #3: Extreme paranoia/distrust of anyone to delusional levels and suspicious of plots and/or conspiracies with a tendency to become delusional with very little suggestion, even if unintentional, to me from someone that there is a threat from: government, medical/psychiatric professionals, authority figures, and sometimes friends, even family.

Symptom #4: The unbreakable delusion that I am not in control of my own actions is mixed with the delusion that someone else's will has "hijacked" me, and I cannot resist their orders. Also called Avolition it is a negative "medication resistant" symptom of schizophrenia which means lack of will or desire. This is the most dangerous and oldest of all my symptoms. This is what schizophrenia really is or the core of the disease: the loss of self/will/desire.

All schizophrenics have this symptom but the level to which it impairs their day-to-day functioning is the determining factor to the quality of life they can achieve and level of independence possible for them. I have these symptoms severely and it is why I cannot live independently without a guardian's assistance. This is also the symptom that created Simon.

**Just so everyone knows I am in cute phase at this time (and also in this chapter) hoping for a residual to begin sometime soon. Fingers crossed.

CHAPTER 41: SWALLOWING BITTER PILLS AND HARD TRUTHS

Good day, beautiful family. Well, it does seem as though Our continued good health is dependent upon how well We preform Our side show acts now, doesn't it? We are so grateful to have you come along to cheer for Us and help Us put on an incredible show of illusions!

Oh, speaking of dependence on others, it has been called to Our attention that freedom is like everything else in the Real world, it is completely subjective. Oh, you did not know that. Well neither did We, but it is now becoming painfully clear that escape may not be such a smart thing to aspire to.

Why is that you ask? Well beauties, the discovery that Our biggest enemy is within Our mind has changed the rules so much, that the finish line is no longer the wisest of goals. Turns out We have been racing all this time toward Our own destruction.

Now, it is finally the time to stop, recalculate and chose a new path. To continue on this one is no longer a valid option. So now what? That is a great question, beauties. We were hoping you had a plan, but if not, that is okay too. We have always had interesting solutions to every problem We have encountered thus far. There is no reason to believe that We will not find which is the right way to proceed from here on out. At least We hope so.

So, thank you in advance for all your assistance in our choice of a new travel plan and for having faith in Us that this time We are indeed heading in the right direction, for a change. We shall see you all below, after we brush off the dirt from Our hardest fall yet. We keep tripping over Our own feet.

"There is no greater disability in society, than the inability to see people as more."
-Robert M. Hensel

Julie giggled as she grinned at me evilly, "Yeah, Psycho. Who is Simon? Porcupine asked you a question. Stop being rude."

I looked up from the ground glaring hatefully at her, "Simon is not here, Julie."

My chest was still smoldering with the left-over anger at realizing that Porcupine had used her past experience to lure me into this latest indignity. Julie's decision to bring my poor Simon into this fiasco by mentioning his name began to reignite my fury. This had nothing to do with Simon, and I was going to be damned if I would let her pull him into it.

Porcupine was still looking very confused, "Okay, I am not letting a sixteen-year-old girl stay in my house with a boyfriend, Julie. Cindy did not say anything about Simon. That is not going to happen in my house."

Porcupine's statement sent Julie into howls of laughter. "Oh my God. You think this loon has a boyfriend. Porcupine, now that that is fucking hilarious." She grabbed her stomach as she continued to laugh till tears came to her eyes.

I felt my cheeks heat up, but not with embarrassment. The fire of outrage in my middle was raging full force. The feeling of warmth was my face responding to the flames as they licked my head threatening to consume me. I was being blinded by it. I had become unable to see that my impulse to defend Simon would not be the most brilliant move given my now very serious situation. However, my agitation was now out of my control.

"Fuck you, Julie. Fuck you too, Porcupine. You leave Simon along, you whores. He is not my boyfriend. I would expect you to think that you fucking perverts. I'd better never hear his name come out of your twisted mouths again, you bitches," I spit out the vile words mostly glaring at Porcupine, but shooting a few looks Julie's way too.

Porcupine was surprised by my sudden vicious verbal assault. Her eyes widened as she took a step back from me trying to add a bit of distance. That was a smart move that Julie should have followed. Instead, the dumb girl only laughed harder at my angry tirade of insults.

That was all I needed to finally lose all my common sense (as if I ever had any). In a single smooth movement, I jumped onto Julie growling like a rabid dog. She did not have enough time to guard herself against my unit slamming into her body. She fell backward taking me with her to the ground. She was startled to confusion as I pulled back my right arm and punched her in the face with all the strength I had. She let out a scream as I took a second strong swing. Her mouth was wide open as I punched her directly in it. That not only stifled her cry immediately, but her upper front teeth caught on my hand. The fingers of my closed fist were cut to shreds just as a couple of her choppers gave way and shattered from my blow. I had finally gotten angry enough to literally knock some of Julie's teeth out (tee hee).

The blood from my fist and Julie's now broken front teeth splattered everywhere as I reared back, undeterred by her gurgling attempts to plead for the beating to stop. I had every intention to kill her once and for all. Nothing was in my mind but ripping her into tiny pieces. I did not even feel the injured fingers that now had shards of Julie's busted tooth material embedded in them.

However, before I could make another direct hit my arm was grabbed by someone behind me. I tried to use my strength to break the grip of this unseen person so that I could continue my attempt to murder Julie. The person was stronger than I was. My unit was suddenly pulled off of the flailing girl as strong arms locked my own, restraining me from further assault on her.

The inferno of anger within was not so easily held back. I began to try to get free of this yet unrecognizable person by wriggling, kicking, and reverse head butting. The unknown person held tight and did not let me go.

"Go and tell Dr. Scott I tried to kill you, Julie. Go ahead, because I am going to kill you, Julie," I yelled still under restraint as the now crying, bloody Julie tried to get up off the ground.

Porcupine had gone to assist Julie with her injuries as I continued to jeer and struggle against the very strong person holding me back from causing more damage. I still did not concern myself with the identity of this unknown interloper as the sight of the now front toothless Julie was all I could focus on.

I watched Cindy now come running out of the trailer house stoned to the gills but seeming suddenly concerned for her daughter. She had done nothing when Julie was beating the stuffing out of me. Jeff came out of the door trailing quickly behind Cindy.

None of them had been interested until the screams were not of the insane Psycho. Now that Julie was the object of a trouncing, it seemed to me the whole fucking neighborhood had turned out to aid her against her evil attacker. It was at this point it suddenly occurred to me that if Cindy, Porcupine and Jeff were aiding the blubbering Julie, then who the hell was holding on to my unit?

I turned my head around to find myself staring into the face of male I had never seen before. He had shoulder length brown hair and wore a tacky pair of glasses. He had a goatee and mustache and while appearing quite thin he was much stronger than his slight frame suggested. This man could not have been more than in his mid-twenties but was already showing signs of a receding hairline. He wore a black heavy metal shirt and pair of very worn blue jeans. It was pretty obvious this was likely one of Jeff and Porky's 'clients.' He had come by to make a pot purchase to find two teenagers fighting like it was a barroom on a Saturday night.

"Let me go, asshole. I do not like to be touched," I growled at the man while again trying to shake him off.

He held tight, "Yeah, bet you don't sweetheart. I will let you go when you calm your shit down. The girl is beat so let it go will you," he said, appearing amused at my demands to be unhanded.

"Fuck you," I gritted my teeth while stomping his sneaker clad foot hard as I could. That caused him to let go his grip.

"Crazy bitch," he muttered as he pushed me forward now limping on one leg. "Go ahead then. I am done."

I smiled at him, "Touch me again and I will kill you too." I turned and started back to finish Julie off.

However, Cindy, Jeff and Porcupine blocked me from her now standing body by standing shoulder to shoulder with Julie safely behind them. If I wanted to kill her, I would have to go through all of these adults first. I stopped to ponder if I could indeed kill all three of them.

"She will run away before you can beat down the first one," I heard Looper say in my ear.

I knew he was right for a change. My attempt to finally rid myself of Julie was thwarted for now. In fact, I had already forgotten what I was so angry with her about.

As I stood there trying to recall why I wanted her dead so bad, Cindy, who appeared very angry spoke up, "You are going to pay for this you fucking monster. We open our hearts and home, and you continue to abuse the privilege. Mary was right about you. If I would not go to jail for it, I would beat you to an inch of your sorry life," Cindy finished as she approached me with each word.

I stood my ground defiantly staring her right in her face. She did not scare me.

She finished by reaching out and slapping me hard in my face, "I can see why your mother wanted you dead so bad. Far as I am concerned the woman deserves a medal for trying to do the right thing." Cindy turned around leaving me there and aided her precious daughter to their car.

Cindy glared at me never taking her piggish eyes off my nit as she collected her stupid child. I boldly glared back at her in a stare down battle but all that was on my shattered mind was that Madness Manual. In the fray, Julie had dropped the book on the ground. Our struggling had pushed it into a cluster of bushes next to the trailer house. Even in the midst of the fight I had made mental note of its whereabouts. I was quietly hoping no one else had noticed the book had been left behind. Simon had told me to get that thing and now it seemed I might just be able to get my hands on it after all.

Julie was moaning as she held her bleeding mouth appearing to be in agony. I admit that made me feel pretty good. She had that coming as far as I was concerned. It was true I would likely go to jail or inpatient for that little pleasure of shutting her big mouth for her, but for that moment I believed it was worth whatever punishment I was going to get.

In my world of darkness, revenge was a luxury and like all luxuries, it surely would be extraordinarily expensive. So, savoring it was the right thing to do, no doubt. Cindy finally loaded Julie in their car. I shot an exaggerated smiled at Julie who was looking at me still holding her mouth from the passenger side window. Her eyes went wide as I begin to wave wildly at her.

See you guys later. Sure, will miss you Sister. Love you, get well soon," I yelled out loud enough for her to hear me above the car motor as they pulled away with me still smiling maniacally.

I have no idea why I did that. Lately, I did not know why I did most of the things I did. This was another of the odd behaviors that had been increasing as of late. Why I would tell someone I wanted dead I love them and wish them well soon was beyond me, but I could not stop myself.

The inner terror caused by the feeling of being hijacked by some unforeseen force overcame me. As a hostage to this nondescript bandit of my will, I was forced to stand there waving insanely at the Sloan's car as it faded into the distance. There were no true feelings other than fear behind the actions I was engaging in. I could no longer tell who was in charge of the unit of measurement at all.

There was no doubt in my mind at this point I had cracked a gasket. Looper informed me in his usual repeating fashion that, "there is no telling what horrible things you are capable of."

Once again, I had to agree with him. For some time now my 'accidents,' and fights seemed to be out of my control. If I am not the one in control, who is?

Suddenly, images of an unintended jump from a bridge, a bloody forehead cracked open by a headstone, a screwdriver digging into flesh, blisters all over the unit, flashing lights like a dozen cameras in my face, and a pancake covered in coffee grounds fished out from a dumpster flooded into my memory. An anxious feeling that these memories put together meant something important started to bite at my consciousness.

A sense of impending doom had been plaguing me since the car ride over, but I simply could not put the clues together to discover what was causing this perception of approaching calamity.

"Where were you for eleven days, Psycho," I hear Looper start to repeat loudly into my ears.

"Yes," I thought back to Looper, "Where was I? We have to find out." I turned around startled from my inner discussion with the Looper by the fact that I had not remembered that I was not alone.

Julie and Cindy had left me with Jeff and Porcupine who, until now I had forgotten about. I turned finally released from the hold of forced jubilant reactions to the Sloan's departure. Jeff and Porcupine were still in the yard watching the scene unfold along with the strange male who had pulled me off of Julie. All three were staring at me with looks of bewilderment.

"That was super brutal, Psycho. I mean wow, you are true cold blooded," Jeff said while shaking his head.

The strange male smiled at that statement, "Yeah, it was super funny though. Hey, sorry I busted out your teeth, but I do hope you get well soon. That was like classic," he began to chuckle as he appeared to replay the memory of my most insane behavior in his mind.

I looked at the ground feeling that sheepish feeling again. I wanted to explain that it was not me doing that mean stuff. I did not want to do that. I started to argue my innocence, but I knew no one would believe me. No one ever believes me. So, I stifled my urge to say anything about it at all.

"Psycho, you are probably in a lot of trouble. I am sure Cindy will call the cops on you for that. I hope it was worth it," Porcupine said while looking down the road nervously for the police cruiser that surely will be dispatched to pick me up in short order.

I shook my head no but did not look up from the ground, "No, Cindy will not call anyone, Porcupine. I am worth too much money. If I am sent to jail or inpatient, she will not get the checks. She would have called them from your phone if she intended to have me arrested. You can relax, I am not going anywhere. Not right this moment at least."

Porcupine did not argue my logic. She knew I was right. It made no sense Cindy would leave the scene of the 'crime' to call the cops. I was worth too much money to send away to a cell, for now. There was no doubt in our minds that Cindy would find a way to retaliate eventually, but until that time I was safe from legal intervention.

"Well, I warned Julie that Psycho was going to beat her ass if she kept it up. Guess she will learn her lesson about messing with schizophrenics," Porcupine said to Jeff who nodded his head yes.

"Why did you let her beat me up," I blurted out before I could stop myself. "You and Jeff just sat there. You even helped her, Porcupine"

Porcupine sighed loudly, "Look the Sloan's are hell bent you burned down their place, sweetie. I knew Cindy would not do a thing since you are a minor and all. But Julie, well she was going to beat you up one way or another. I thought it would be safer if she did it where Jeff or I could make sure she did not get out of control and really hurt you bad. That way Julie could get her anger out and you would not be too badly busted up. I was watching her from the window. Had she gotten out of hand I would have come stopped her."

Porcupine's excuse was so preposterous, I looked up at her in astonishment she would even bother to recite that utter bullshit to me, "Are you kidding? You let a fucking bully beat me up. A bully who believes I burned down her house using a curse. You allowed this shit to happen where you could watch so it did not get out of control? Well, thanks mom. Glad you had my best interests at heart, Judas," I finished yelling at her so loud the words nearly ripped open my scarred vocal cords.

Porcupine looked away from my glare, "Look she was going to get you no matter what. It was the only thing I could do. Would you had rather I let her ambush you out where no one could put a stop to her thumping your ass?"

"How about this, you fucking liar? Why did you fucking betray me to the Sloan's in the first place? Hummm? Go ahead, try to lie to me again! Asked around about me at Wanda's, my ass. You already knew Cindy and Julie. You knew the Sloans were looking for me. I know you called those bitches, and turned me in. You pretended to care, and to hire me so you could trick me into coming here. Why? What is your game," demanding a response to my questions?

Porcupine looked to Jeff for aid in quelling my angry demands for the truth of this compromised position they had put me into, "Yeah, we know Cindy and Julie well. You are right we knew who you are through their descriptions in the last month or so, but that is not how we knew to call them. We overheard the APB for you on the scanner. You've been missing for a couple weeks. The Sloans had called the law in on this. Their house just burned down, you were missing and now the cops were snooping around too. So, when Porky and I ran into you at Wanda's, we thought we could help everyone out of a nasty situation by giving you a job. However, we could not just hide you out forever. The Sloans are your guardian, so it was the best Porky and I could do, and this is the thanks we get for trying to keep you out of jail on the APB and out of the morgue from Julie's revenge," he answered my allegation with a bit of bitterness in his tone.

I set my hateful gaze on Jeff, "Bullshit. You could have just told me all this, asshole. You used lies and tricks. Why should I believe a damned thing you ever say?"

He chuckled at my response, "You want honesty? Okay here is the truth then. You are fucking off your rocker. When Porcupine and I offered you a job you did not even think we were real people. Even you know you are fucking insane. You thought you were hallucinating us. You are not even capable of knowing a real person from an imaginary one and you think we are going to try to have a logical discussion with you? Uhm, no way sister. So, yeah, we did call the Sloans like we had to, but we are not lying. We hired you to work for us. You were not tricked; you just were not told that we were calling your guardian. If we had told you, likely you would have run off and gotten yourself into more trouble."

I shook my head no at him, "I am not staying here. I am going home. I do not need a guardian or your job either."

Jeff crossed his arms and shot Porcupine a look of humor with his cat like smile, "Home? Do you mean that outhouse in the cemetery? Really? Psycho, face the fact that you are seriously messed up in the head. You can't take care of yourself. You do need a guardian. There is not going to be any more arguing about this. So, here are your choices; you can stay here with us and help around the house. I can call back the Sloans where I am sure Julie has a bone to pick with you. Maybe you would rather I call the police and let them decide what to do with your crazy ass? I will let you decide, but you are not going back to live in that cemetery outhouse. I have a family to protect and letting you go will bring trouble to this household. I will beat you down myself before I let that happen."

My anger was dashed as if a pressure hose of water had been turned on deep in the unit's core. As the flames of annoyance fade, it was quickly cooled by a feeling of icy alarm. Jeff had just put into words what had been unconsciously bothering me about the lost eleven days. It was what actually was causing my panicky feeling of imminent disaster. The reality was finally sinking into my shattered mind that I could no longer be trusted to not end up killing myself by accident, neglect, or act of insanity.

The confirmation of my failure at self-care was written on the unit of measurement in scars like a road map to hell. Whenever I was alone in my cemetery home, often the unit of measurement was being controlled by unseen forces that did not appear to have 'our' best interest at heart. The so called 'accidents' were escalating in both violence and in number over the last many months anytime I was not being continually 'watched' over by someone other than my Simon. The evidence that I had become disabled at attending to the most basic of needs such as feeding and cleaning the unit was observable in more than just the self-inflicted wounds. It was also evident in its covering of bed sores and emaciation of its frame.

The horrible truth was beyond appalling. I could no longer ignore that I was going to die if I tried to remain self-isolated. There was no doubt I had spent several months now doing or not doing all I could to end my life. I also had to face that I could no longer live without some medications. The addition of a deadly seizure disorder to my already impressive repertoire of brain damaging events assured that I could not ignore that ugly truth. I could often not recall if I had even eaten on any given day much less keep up with a rigid course of meds designed to keep my brain from a deadly reboot. Time and reality were not something I could easily understand anymore. That made me a slave to delusions, fantasy, and illusions. I could no longer wake up as I was forced to sleepwalk through a nightmarish world that threatened to destroy me at every turn.

My very survival was clearly dependent upon the charity of one who was in touch with reality. The person would have to be capable and willing to assist by protecting me from the perpetual danger caused by my abundant deficiencies. I would require help in both the real and unreal world, or my existence was well on its way to a gruesome finale.

The sun had just set as the dusk began to darken from shadows to full on blackness all around me as I looked in defeat at Jeff and Porcupine. The two of them stared back as I did my best to accept the latest misfortune my disease had brought down on my head. My choices were bad, worse, and downright ugly. No matter which group of so called 'guardians' I chose there was no hope of any kindness, or even basic human good will.

I sighed as it occurred to me, I really had only two choices here, impending death or impending cruelty. Somehow, I managed to pull up from deep within the ravaged recesses of my brain the final shreds of hope. Maybe if I could just tolerate the cruelty I would one day discover a way back to the life I had lost. If I allowed the unit to die, then I would forever be like this and perhaps what came after death would be as the Egyptians thought, the same only better.

A chill ran down my spine as I imagined eternal schizophrenia. Even on the disease's best day, a truer hell could not exist. That thought was on my mind as I made one of the hardest decisions of my young life. I had to give up my hope of independence and stay with a guardian. I promised myself I would try my best to stay on their good side. At least, until I could find a way out of this nonstop internal torture.

I looked down at the ground swallowing hard as I forced out my words of submission to Jeff, "Okay, you do not have to call the cops or beat me down. I will stay here. I will behave myself and do what you and Porcupine tell me to do without complaint." Although I was pretty sure that last part would not be truth for long.

"Well, see that was not so hard now, was it? I think this calls for a celebration. Come on Porky and Walter, let's go inside and fire up a bowl." Jeff said jovially as if he had won a decent sum from the lottery rather than just shattering the only remaining comfort I had left, my cemetery home.

I wondered if Simon and I would ever have the chance to dance outside the outhouse in the rain again as I watched Jeff and this Walter fellow go into the trailer. Porcupine stayed behind informing the two she would be in shortly and to 'save some for her.'

I did not look up from the ground as she approached me slowly as if cautious. She had no reason to worry. I did not want to fight anymore. I had just been beaten. It was not the fisticuffs with Julie, but one that was much more unfairly matched. I could not defend myself against the foe, not this time. The enemy I had just faced was me. My independence and freedom were now collateral damage from a catastrophic war within that had destroyed my mind and scattered it to the four winds.

"Psycho, we have to get something straight right now. Simon is not welcome to stay here with you. I cannot have you getting pregnant on my watch. No boys are allowed here understand," she said while keeping a safe distance I noticed.

I chuckled bitterly at that very silly rule shaking my head in frustration, "I told you Simon is not my boyfriend. I do not have a boyfriend, nor do I want one. I also will not sleep in your house. I do not like houses. I noticed you have an old shed in the back. I will sleep there for now. Otherwise, I will do what you say."

My response appeared to surprise Porcupine, "If Simon is not your boyfriend, then why did you beat up Julie over him?" She seemed very confused.

I shrugged, "Simon is my best friend and Julie hates him for it. You need not worry about Simon. In fact, you can't even see him."

"What? Why can't I see him? I didn't say you can't have friends over, just no boyfriends saying overnight." She was staring at me hard. I could tell without looking up as I felt her eyes prying through my unit trying to see into my mind.

I laughed out loud, "I will say it one more time, Simon is not my boyfriend. You can't see him because only I can see him not because he will not come here to visit. Now I will not talk any further with you about it. I may have to do what you say, but Simon is not your business, so I will politely tell you to leave him alone." I look up briefly glaring right into her face to make sure she understood I meant it. Simon was off limits to the likes of her and Julie.

Now it was Porcupine's turn to laugh but I could hear the nervousness in it as she said, "Oh, Oh. Okay got it. I am so sorry. I should have realized...well you know...oh never mind. Anyway, come inside in about thirty minutes and say to me that you just remembered my mom will be here by eight o'clock. I hate Walter and if I don't make some reason up for him to high tail it, he will smoke with Jeff all night. You got that?" I nodded that I understood.

She started heading for the trailer door and while looking back said, "I am okay with your sleeping in the shed for now, but remember if you run away next time, I won't be there to call off the probation officer and psychologist got it?"

I smiled at her and nodded. I really did not care for her threat, but she did give in to my not sleeping in their drug den. I would rather sleep with insect roaches than their blunt ones. I watched her go inside barely able to hold back my urge to run over and grab the forgotten book in the bushes.

Once the door shut and she was safely out of sight, I did run to the bushes and gathered up the forbidden manual, hiding it quickly in my jacket. It was far too dark to read it, but I knew I would need a good hiding spot, so I took a quick tour of the property.

I laughed as I walked around the front yard. One of the so called 'trained attack' pit bulls stood up and stretched lazily. Throughout both my beating and my knocking out Julie's front teeth neither dog had even barked. I had assumed they were just like me, objects of dark illusion. To my relief it was a correct assumption. I walked over to the now yawning canine and rubbed his head between his ears. He licked my wrist (likely because of all the blood on them) but did not offer any aggressive behavior. I just smiled at him and told him what a good dog he was as he happily wagged his tail. I certainly did appreciate the pit bulls.

Dogs and cats did not shock me when I touched them, in fact, I enjoyed their company very much. If nothing else, I would try to find consolation on being able to pet them whenever I could get the chance. It maybe would make my imprisonment here tolerable. I could hope at least.

I went around to the back yard and quickly approached the tiny shed. I had seen it earlier in the day light. It was not much larger than the small bathroom inside the trailer. Its wooden walls had been painted red but most of the color were faded to almost pink or peeling off. I opened the small windowless door to find it unlocked. I went inside and without even thinking began to search for a light switch. I had seen outside electrical wiring from the trailer to this outbuilding and rightly assumed that it may have at least the one convenience of artificial lighting. I found it to the right of the door and flipped it on. A single bulb in the center of the ceiling that was missing a covering immediately illuminated the small space weakly. Most of the corners were still shielded from view by deep shadows as the one light source was simply not large enough to scare away all the darkness of that place.

I looked about my new temporary home with some satisfaction. Jeff and Porcupine were not the hoarding type. This shed was practically devoid of any items other than broken shelves with a few musty blankets strewn about on them. I noticed a single grim encrusted window in the back of the building. It was so encumbered with filth from years of cleansing neglect that one could not even see outside through it. This did not matter to me as I quickly grabbed one of the discarded blankets from a shelf and hung it over the dirty window. I despised any opening from the outside into my inner sanctuaries. I never left them

221

without some kind of covering to keep the real world from prying into mine.

The center of the storage area was empty of everything but a crusty wooden floor. I would be able to curl up there and rest when I needed to without having to move a thing from its original placement. I took the madness manual and hid it under one of the old dusty blankets on a shelf farthest from the doorway. I knew my thirty minutes was soon to be up so discovering what mysteries it held would have to wait until later. For now, I turned off the light and closed the door making my way back to the trailer to follow the instructions Porcupine had given me.

I opened the trailer door as marijuana smoke barreled out seeking escape from the cooped up living room. The smell and thickness of it stung my eyes and flooded my orifices with its stench. Immediately I began to cough feeling the hazy foulness invading my lungs as it ticked and scratched deep within my chest. This was not something I was happy about.

"Porcupine, I almost forgot to remind you. Your mom is supposed to be coming over around eight o'clock." I feigned the behavior of someone who was apologetic that they had been remiss in alerting their employer of such an important detail.

I looked at Porcupine who was obviously very high indeed as she slowly turned her head to look back at me in what appeared to be a trance. Jeff was next to her with his head laid back on the couch in a sitting position staring at the ceiling. Walter however, appeared to be very intact as I noted his eyes looking up and down my unit of measurement with a smile that made me very uncomfortable forming on his face.

"Well, there you are Psycho. Now, I have finally smoked enough I can see you are truly a sexy little thing. I know some people think you are a bit weird, but I like it weird baby," he said still looking at the unit with a look I had seen many times before when I was still living with my mother.

I knew that look far too well and had never wanted to ever see it on anyone's face ever again. A cold bolt of electricity flashed down my unit's spine as I became very aware of the sudden threat Walter posed to me. This was not good. Until now, I had been able to frighten most would be sexually aggressive male away with my bizarre fashion sense. Walter, however, seemed to actually like it. He was much bigger than me and I already knew from the fight earlier much stronger too. I unconsciously backed away from him into the kitchen making sure not to make eye contact with this creep.

"Hey Walter. Didn't you hear what Psycho just said? My momma is coming man. You have to split. I need to clean up this mess, clear out the pot smoke and look presentable or she will threaten to take my kids away again. If she sees you here, she will flip her shit. So, go home man. Now." Porcupine had stood up and began trying to pull Walter up off the couch to his feet.

He shrugged off her attempts to grab him easily, "Whoa their little momma. I am going to get going. Stop wigging out baby. Let a man have a minute to enjoy the view, will you?" He never took his sleazy gaze from my position in the kitchen.

Porcupine appeared distraught. I did recall she told me she hated Walter. Something about this entire scene did not seem right. A suspicion that Porcupine had good reason to want this man to leave that had nothing to do with me was voiced by the Looper.

"She is acting overly defensive and afraid of Walter. She is hiding something from you idiot," the Looper began to repeat in my ear.

I looked up at Porcupine to read her mind. I agreed with the Looper, she definitely was hiding something here. As Porcupine and Walter mildly argued about his departure, I could hear Porcupine's inner thoughts in my own mind loud and clear.

She told me she had once been Walter's lover. Walter had betrayed her and now she allowed him into her life for...I could not quite catch the reason, but it was very important to Porcupine. She feared Walter, more than hated him. He was a predator, and she did not want him in her house except to get from him whatever it was she needed.

I broke my communication with Porcupine's mind off as I saw Walter finally stand up and start to head for the door. He looked back at the now sleeping Jeff, "Your bitches are running me off man. Catch you later on, bro."

Walter than briefly stood at the kitchen entrance blocking my escape to the front door. I backed up keeping as much distance between he and I as possible given the very small size of the room.

"I will be seeing you real soon cutie pie. Next time you want to be held by Walter here, you need not knock any teeth out. Just give me a call anytime. Porky here has my number." He blew a kiss at me as he turned and exited the trailer closing the door behind him.

Porcupine shot me a look of terror as she rushed to the living area window to watch and make sure Walter was leaving, "Psycho, listen to me. Walter is not a nice guy, okay. You stay as far from him as you can. Now that he has his eyes on you, he will try to lure you in. Do not ever let him get you alone, or in his car. Do you understand me?" she looked back at me as I slowly emerged from my kitchen hideout. Porcupine had a stern look of concern in her drug glazed eyes.

I nodded my head but already knew better than to ever get compromised by a male of the species in such a fashion. Walter was a real threat to our unit and there was no way I would ever allow him to get within range to hurt us.

Porcupine then sat down on the couch and sighed loudly. She dropped her head into her hand as I hear her begin to sniffle. She was crying.

I watched her quietly weeping and felt no sympathy at all. She was a horrible mother. I could not stand mothers who would put their children so low on her place of importance that she would allow men like Walter into her house for some greedy purpose. Lauren was a beautiful little girl and though she was very young, men like Walter who would hit on an obviously mentally ill sixteen-year-old minor may just as easily not be above molesting a child of a much lesser age. Porcupine allowed strangers into her home to buy dope, smoked it to abhorrent levels, and allowed predators in as friends, with her two most precious and helpless gifts only a room away.

It seemed to me she was an even worse mother than my own. At least my mom did not pretend to care about me. Porcupine played with the kids, acted upset when Jordie nearly got ran over and ever bathed and dressed them in fine clothing. However, that was the shallowness of her true love for them. In reality, a mother is supposed to protect her children and even sacrifice her own happiness if need to be assure their safety. Porcupine failed in even the most basic task of motherhood. A sudden intense sense of hatred for her came to my attention. There was no longer any question. I had incorrectly chosen my place of guardianship.

The Sloans, my only other choice, were certainly beginning to look like the only selection I ever really had. Cindy was at least a decent mother. She completely loved Julie and that was quite evident. It really was too bad Cindy hated me as much as she loved her daughter.

The Sloan's home promised me a life of humiliation as Julie's entertainment and toy, cruel verbal interactions, and beatings. However, bad that seemed, it was still better than what I now could clearly see was being promised by my residing with Jeff and Porcupine. A life of unwanted sexual advances, being surrounded by criminal activity, and the likelihood that in time I would become a victim of a violent crime, again. I was simply not going to return to that life. My mother had made me an unwilling expert in the area of the dark twisted underworld before I was even ten years old.

Everyone from Simon to the Dude was forbidden to discuss our past life before the sickness but at that moment I realized I was standing on the edge of a very familiar abyss. If I did not leave immediately, I would surely fall in. I had already paid with everything I had to gain the pathetic life I had now to escape my mother's drug fueled world. My body, my soul, even my mind, had been taken away in payment for my freedom from her. I did not have anything left to dare attempt another evasion of such a horrific existence.

I also realized my impulsive attack on Julie was going to have consequences I had not considered at the time of that lunatic frenzy. I was going to be forced to try to get Cindy to take me back into her home no matter what punishment she may demand of me. I winced slightly as I thought it likely Julie would be knocking my front teeth out in repayment for my evil deeds of earlier that day.

For a brief moment I considered the last alternative of ending the life of the unit once and for all. Actually, the Looper brought that to my attention as he repeated "death may be better" over and over again in my ear. However, I waved that out of my sight. I had already given up so much to make it this far. I just was not ready to give up, yet. I would be eighteen soon enough and then I would finally be free of them all. Then I would get a job, a home, and my own family. I was aware I had a lot of obstacles in my path, but somehow, I was going to find my way through this maze of confusion I was just sure of it. Now that I had my hands on the Madness Manual, maybe I could get there even faster than I had ever hoped to. Until that most glorious day of my rise into adulthood, I would have to submit to whatever horrors the Sloans decided to dish out. The Looper could try all he liked to change my mind, but it was useless. The decision was not going to be argued any further.

Suddenly Porcupine who had been quietly crying, spoke up breaking me from my deep discussion with the others from within. I had forgotten she was even there.

"My life is horrible, Psycho. You cannot even imagine what I have been through," she said hoarse from her smoking and weeping.

I looked at the floor immediately bracing myself for what was sure to be an unleashing of her burdens onto my, already, over weighted shoulders. I tried to choke back the irritation that began to well up inside me as the very high Porcupine began to spew out her evil history to me as if I were her Father Confessor. I could not escape the irony that for the first time ever I was invited to a party. Unfortunately, it was Porcupine's pity party and I had not even been granted the right to deny her RSVP.

"Do you know why they call me Porcupine, Psycho," she moaned out still wiping the salty fluid from her eyes.

I shrugged. I have to say I did not care why. That did not stop her from telling me anyway even though I did not say a word, hoping my lack of engagement would prevent her from persisting in the sharing of information I really did not care to hear.

"Walter is my old boyfriend. When I was just about your age, I met him and thought he was so cool. We hung out and he introduced me to pot. It was so much fun, you know? Then one day he introduced me to crank. I was hooked on it before I even knew what hit me. I just wanted so bad to be grown up. My mom, she tried to stop me, but you know I just knew everything and thought she was stupid. Well, turns out Walter was a pimp. So, soon I was using crank so bad I could not afford it on my after-school job money. I quit school and Walter started getting me customers to help me pay for my habit. I was so tweeked out, I did not mind it so much. I actually was doing so much crank I carried needles so I could shoot up before a trick you know. Make it more fun and all. So, this one time a John is reaching for my ass, and I had a back pocket full of syringes. He impaled his hand so bad Walter had to give him his money back for the trick. After that Walter started calling me Porcupine and everyone else did too. I thought it was funny at the time, but now I am a mother. I have two kids and I am still addicted to crank. I tried to quit a couple of times, but I just need the rush, you know? So, Walter still comes out and takes care of me and all. I really hate that I need it and him so much. Psycho, listen to me. Don't be like me. Now that Walter has his eyes on you, he will try to make you one of his whores. You have no idea what it is like to be trapped in a nightmare, where everyone calls you by a name that actually means you are a loser," Porcupine finished as she looked at me with tears in her eyes.

I looked up from the floor making direct eye contact with Porcupine. Anger flashed as the demon from within took my unit as its hostage, "Really? I do not believe you just said that to me you self-absorbed bitch." I wanted to run away horrified as I heard from within the ugly words spill out of the unit's mouth.

Porcupine realized too late what exactly she had said, and to whom she had said them. Ignoring my verbal insult, she quickly said, "Oh my God, Psycho. I am so sorry. I did not mean to; well I just was not thinking is all. Please don't pay any attention to me. I am just high." She back peddled appearing genuinely apologetic.

That meant nothing to my demon. It was far from sated. I could do nothing but listen helplessly as the next insults flew out of the unit at Porcupine, "Of course you are sorry. The sorriest mother I have ever seen in fact. As for not thinking? Yeah, I believe that too. You seem to have a habit of not thinking, then blaming everyone else for your bad choices. As for not knowing what it is like to be trapped in a nightmare. You are not trapped. You can get out, but you chose to stay because to get out would require work. You wear a name that means loser, well so do I darling, but unlike you I did not ask for it, I was cursed with it. So. you have nothing to worry about from me, I have no intention of ever paying any attention to the likes of you." I began to laugh maniacally as I stare at the now very hurt Porcupine.

Porcupine looked at me in shock, "Psycho, why are you attacking me? I thought we were friends. Look I did not mean anything disrespectful I was just talking. Maybe Cindy was right about you all along. You are an ungrateful bitch."

I bared my teeth as the demon spit back at Porcupine, "Yeah, Cindy is right I am ungrateful to those who do not deserve my piss if they were on fire. Friends? You thought we were friends, huh? Well, I should have guessed if you don't know what it means to be a mother you certainly do not have a clue what it means to be a friend. I would never allow a friend to be beaten up without getting my ass whipped too. I also would never tattle on a friend either or lure them into a trap with lies. You can kiss my ass, Porky, and tell you what since we are such good friends, I will let you kiss it for free. Now that is a real friend darling. I know you would expect me to charge for it like you do." The unit began a laughing fit as it finished cutting Porcupine right to the heart.

Her eyes glistened with torrents of tears as I stood there laughing at her. Inside I was ready to cry with her. On the outside I laughed at her pain. That creature that was demonstrating such cruel levity at her expense was not me at all. It was something that more resembled the evil girls Julie, Joni, or one of the scores of other persons who had ruthlessly tormented me throughout my very short life span. No matter how hard I tried I could not stop this monster from lashing out at Porcupine. I was not in control at all.

Somehow. I gained enough control to turn the unit towards the door and with all the strength I had I forced it outside slamming the door behind it as I quickly retreated to the shed in the backyard. I was sure all was lost now. I needed time to talk the Sloans into letting me stay with them. I needed to get to those appointments tomorrow. I seriously doubted Porcupine was going to help me out anymore after the asshole I had just made of myself!

How could I do something so horrid? Porcupine had just opened herself up with honesty and trust. I had stomped her down with cruel judgement for her effort. It seemed to me that all she was doing was trying to show me a piece of humanity that I often was denied. As I walked briskly back to the shed, I cursed myself for being so unstable. This new symptom of blurting horrid things at people, even if they were true, had to stop. It was getting me into a lot of trouble. I needed to learn a way to treat this problem and I had no time to spare. I turned on the light and retrieved the book "Treating Schizophrenia" hoping that somewhere in its pages the answers to what was happening to me would be there. More than anything else, I hoped it would tell me how to gain back control of my unit of measurement.

Okay that is enough for now beauties. It seems like We have gotten Ourselves very lost now and can no longer tell right from wrong as We had suspected for some time now. Turns out that in the real-world people do not like to hear the truth any more than We do in the world behind the cracked looking glass. Truth is often quite ugly, with many edges all designed to cut you right to the bone. We suppose that is why so many chose to cover up the truth with a bright sugar coating to help one swallow it more easily. Sometimes, it appears the coating becomes so thick it is really all coating with only a memory of the actual truth deep within. It is always the lie that goes down smoothly but will ultimately make you sick from all the sugar. Swallow enough and you can even become diseased. Now that We see that very clearly, We can help you better understand the reasons for delusions, the way a schizophrenic thinks, and why sometime you need not be psychotic to actually be behaving (at least in a mild way) like one. Perception is subjective, at least it is if you are schizophrenic.

CHAPTER 42: BE STILL MY BEATEN HEART

Good day most beautiful family. Well, what can We say? We are in total shock. All this time behind the shattered looking glass We had believed the world of the real was the delusional. Turns out we were wrong. It would appear that We are indeed the ones who were the problem all along. Now that We realize that all of Our troubles, as of late, are because of the brain disease We "shall not call by name" We are at a loss for what should be done. Let's correct that, what can be done is the real question. Acceptance of Our fate is now in the review mirror, Our path is now recalculated with the new coordinates (the right ones this time, we hope) toward an unsure future. Is everyone ready to start the engines and begin the race again? Great! Now see that is what We love about all of you, you do not hold past errors against Us. Despite all We have been through together you are still willing to trust Us and get back into this trip to, well, wherever the hell We are going. Too bad most people do not have that attitude. In fact, most people We have had the displeasure to know, are never going to let Us forget our mistakes, ever. The trouble with never looking forward but always having to watch behind Us, is that We cannot see where We are going only where We have been. With that in mind We would appreciate it if you would keep an eye out for obstacles in our path ahead while We continue to watch Our backs. Awesome, thank you all so much for the help. We are all going to have to work together if We hope to make any progress in any direction at all. Start the engine and whatever you do, do not worry about what is behind you. That is Our job. See everyone below.

> *"Imperfection is beauty, madness is genius and it's better to be absolutely ridiculous than absolutely boring."*
> **— Marilyn Monroe**

Sitting cross legged in the middle of the shed I began to read through the Madness Manual. I actually still had a bit of hope that it would turn out that the behaviors and problems I had been demonstrating would not be close to the disease discussed within the pages. However, before reaching the end of the first chapter my heart had sunk. There was no longer any doubt, the symptoms listed were ones I recognized very well because they had been plaguing me for months now.

I had to stop and put down the book and pace the shed for a bit as I felt the stress within rising to dangerous levels. The hope that everyone had been wrong about me, and that this was all really a plot to drive me crazy, had been dashed. I could no longer believe the delusion that I was not really sick. It was simply impossible to ignore that the author of this text had never met me, had never spoken to me about my perceptions of the world, and had no reason to write an entire book about it. Worse still this author was citing other authors, works, and research into the matter. In order for my plot theory to work, now the entire psychiatric world would have to be in on it. I did not assume that an impoverished, cemetery kid in a Podunk town would be that important to have so many going through so much trouble to destroy her life.

All of these highly educated people from the manual stated clearly that when a person starts to see, hear, taste, and smell the things that I had been for the last many months, the person has a thought disorder." That thought disorder was a disease with a name when it was not improving after six months. I was now almost into my seventh month of odd perceptions, and strange behaviors. Dr. Scott, Dr. Huff, everyone around me, and now the Madness Manual, agreed that I was indeed schizophrenic. I had to admit now that; I was not faking it, it was not a plot, everyone else was not sick instead of me, and I had not been misdiagnosed. I tried to stay calm as these facts now sank into my understanding as I sat back down and picked back up the manual.

I returned to reading on through every chapter, more horrified with each discussion of my disease, and theory of what to do with a person who had it. I did not stop until I had read the entire thing. The sun had not even risen as I finished the final page. As I closed the book and pushed it away from the unit, I sat there stunned into silence. Not even the Looper dared to say a word. I stood up and began to pace the small area wringing my hands, trying to wrap my mind around what I had just learned of this monster disease that had destroyed my sanity.

There was a crushed, heavy feeling in my chest as I paced the floor realizing I was so screwed. I not only had schizophrenia, but there was also no treatment for it available. There is no cure. It is progressive and life-long disabling.

According to the book, I could look forward to a lifetime of humiliating symptoms, numerous hospitalizations, painful treatments, and medications with side effects so horrid it would make my disease symptoms almost more desirable. I had been told all this prior to reading the manual. I had already been a victim of most of the 'so called' treatment plans in my very short duration of the illness.

However, seeing it stated like that in clinical, professional, cold terms from a total stranger drove it into my chest like a stake into a sleeping vampire. Just like the undead night creature of lore, I had been hunted down and pinned to the earth. I had indeed accepted prior to reading the book I had the disease, but now I was finally accepting that I would never be unimpaired for the rest of my life.

The tiny flame of hope that I would someday find my way out of the confusion, was completely extinguished. I finally fully understood several terrible facts:

1. I was never going to escape the nightmare.

2. No one could even offer any kind of real comfort while I suffered through it.

3. I would have to learn how to survive without any chance of truly enjoying anything ever again.

4. I would forever be insane because this disease was the mother of madness itself. Hiding it from the world of the real would be close to impossible.

5. I am dependent on others for survival and therefore possessed lifetime vulnerability to those who would exploit my serious impairment (broken from reality, disordered mind).

I was going over these disturbing facts in my mind when the door opened, and my best friend Simon came in.

He found me babbling and pacing the floor repeating over and over again, "I cannot do this, I will never make it."

I could see him standing there watching me as he began to roll his smoke. The look of concern was very evident in his eyes, but I was too agitated to even say hello. I knew he would understand. After all, he was just a symptom of my disease according to the Madness Manual.

Some time passed before Simon could take no more of my obvious short circuiting, "Okay, enough of this shit. What is your problem? It is not the end of the world you know. We can manage this if we work together girly," he said as he sat down on the floor motioning me to do the same.

I did not want to sit down but I knew Simon was right. Pacing and wringing my hands was not going to solve my problem. I needed to calm down and think this out. I needed a plan and Simon was here to help me create one. Simon always has my back and as my best friend he and I are a team in all things. So, when Simon says sit down and we can manage this together, I listen to him. I sat down immediately ready to hear what he had in mind.

Simon sighed loudly, "Let's think this out. I know what the book says about no cure, no treatment, and that we need help to survive. I know that you and I have not properly managed the unit, so we do obviously need help. But what are our choices for this help? Neither option is good. We need a third option, Psycho," he looked at me quickly, he knew I did not like to be called that.

"Simon, really? You think it wise to pick a fight right now? You know I fucking hate it when people call me that. What is wrong with you," I said in sheer disbelief that my best friend would dare to be so nasty when he knew I was on the edge of a meltdown.

Simon smiled at me and chuckled, "I will answer that question when you answer one for me. You read the manual. You know you have schizophrenia. You going to deny that" he looked back at me hard.

I shook my head no, now very confused what his question had to do with his calling me Psycho. "No, I do not deny it Simon. I have the disease okay. Are you happy now? Now answer me, why are you picking a fight with me," I was quickly getting pissed off at my friend.

Simon reached out suddenly and took my hand in his. I was startled out of my anger for a moment as he leaned closer to me staring deep into my eyes, "Listen to me, no do more than that, hear me. We are Psycho. People are not going to let us forget that because they are not. If you get angry at them for it, you allow them to damage the unit."

"What the fuck are you talking about Simon, Psycho is not my fucking name," I said pulling my hand from his.

Simon grabbed my hand back again aggressively which actually frightened me a bit, "I said hear me, damn it. Anger allows the unit to be damaged and you are giving them more and more control of us," he had a fire in his glare I had never seen before.

This time I did hear him, "I don't understand, Simon. How am I giving them control," I asked now frighten enough by his weird behavior to squelch my initial irritation.

Simon let go of my hand and leaned back smiling again, "You know I am right. When you let them make us angry, you hurt the unit, or they do. They are making you angry so they can control us by getting others to see us as crazy and dangerous. You have to stop getting pissed over shit that does not matter. Let them call you Psycho. Who cares? We are Psycho, even the book says so. We have to embrace it. Can you not see the bright side to this? Their rules no longer apply to us. They have made that clear. We do not matter anymore to anyone other than they get money or work from the unit. No one believes us either. Since they have minimized us, then their rules do not apply to us anymore. If you look hard you can see the real freedom we have. The unit is their slave but not you or me. We are not even real. They don't see us. We can do whatever we want because we are Psycho," he began to chuckle at that.

I realized that what he was saying was the truth. I had been a fool. No matter what I did from here on out no one would forget I am schizophrenic. I had become the freak show that everyone wants to watch but no one wants to pay to see or take home to hang out with after the show is over. They treated me like an incompetent, overlook my feeling, and assume I was unable to do anything worthy of merit.

I was not expected to succeed, I was expected to be insane. The definition of insanity is: in a state of mind which prevents normal perception, behavior, or social interaction. No one believed I could be normal. So why was I trying to be?

I was having no difficulty being schizophrenic but learning to act like I was not one was making my nightmare even more unbearable. I was so busy focusing on the terror of submission of my independence, that I had forgotten the special freedom that comes with the loss of such a precious gift.

Insane people can do things normal persons are forbidden because if the normal did them no one would accept them back into society. I was now among the outcasts and branded insane. Simon was right, social rules no longer applied to me. I could do whatever I wanted (within the laws of government, of course) because of my label. I would of course have to give up my dream of normalcy and embrace my insanity.

It was not really a fair trade, but I now realized I had no other viable options. The choice was made for me when I had trustingly eaten my mother's cooking. I was only just now realizing I had been wasting my time trying to fight a war that I had lost a long time ago. I was the loser and now I would have to learn to find a life in the battle ravaged landscape as a prisoner to my disease for the rest of my existence.

As I thought it all over, I decided to listen to Simon's advice. I was ready to learn to love being

Psycho. He was right, if you are going to do the time, may as well do the crime. If they wanted a freak show, then a freak show they would get. One small comfort was that at least this way I was likely to gain a small bit of peace by no longer restraining behaviors that were the most useful at calming my inner terror. I usually refrained from pacing, dancing, repetitive movements, and talking to the Looper in an effort to not upset the normals around me. Now I would not bother to be so polite. Those things helped me feel better but upset those around me. Since I'm Psycho, then I no longer had to worry if they got upset, because my name said it all.

I looked at Simon as he sat there focusing on rolling another of his cigarettes. He was giving me time to consider his suggestion. My dear Simon could be polite when he wanted to be. I thought that a life of dark places, friends no one else could see, pulsating lights, reading minds, static, pacing, trances, and the Looper in my ears was not what I had aspired to when I was just a child dreaming of a future. The tragedy of it made me start laughing for some reason. It was not funny, but then again it was. Something about my whole situation was just well so insane who couldn't find it darkly fascinating at least. I had been looking at everything wrong now, I could see everything so clearly. My laughter got harder the more I thought of all the crazy shit I had been through all my life.

Simon looked up and read my mind. He too began to laugh wildly. Yeah, he got it. This was just simply too funny. No one could be so fucking unlucky and lucky at the same time. I was a creature of contradictions; I was both beautiful and ugly, realistic and fantastical, smart and stupid, cruel and kind, logical and illogical, witty and robotic, and wise but a fool. The only thing that was not contradicted was my sanity. In that area I was wacko!

The first light of the dawn spilled onto the floor as the door of the shed was opened. Porcupine stepped inside to find me sitting on the wooden floor laughing like a hyena with Simon at our most heinous circumstances. The madness manual laid discarded at my side now forgotten as the information contained within it was now safely locked away inside my head.

I had found out in the last few weeks before I was 'taken out' of school that I had a photographic memory for things I saw or read. Unfortunately, that did not hold for things I was told so I had to write things down to recall them. I now assumed it was just another oddity that likely had been caused by the damaging effects of my brain disease. Prior to the onset of my illness, I did not have that ability.

"Jesus, Psycho. What is so fucking funny. Do you realize it is seven in the morning? Nothing is funny this early in the morning." She looked at me with puffy, red eyes that indicated she had not slept much, or had smoked a lot of pot recently. I was unsure which it was.

I stopped laughing immediately. My little outburst the night before led me to believe that Porcupine would be looking to boot my ass to the streets. I had not expected it to come so early in the morning though. I looked at Simon who was also looking at me with a look of surprise. He had not expected this early morning bum's rush either apparently.

"Well? What is so damned funny," Porcupine repeated, this time a bit of irritation in her tone.

"Uhm, Simon just farted, I thought it funny," I lied while looking at Simon whose jaw dropped at my accusing him of such a rude behavior. I flashed him an apologetic smile and shrugged.

"Sorry my friend to throw you under the bus, but I had to say something," I thought to Simon who was now giving me a go to hell look.

If Simon's look was of dubious surprise, Porcupine's was triple that, "What the fuck. Are you getting into our stash, Psycho? There is no one in here but you. Oh my God, you are beyond crazy," she said shaking her head in disbelief of my lack of grounding.

"Are you here to throw me out," I asked, still smiling at Porcupine.

My affect was not congruent with my inner feeling of fear. I was really very scared at what she may do to the unit, but I was unable to express that on my face for some reason. I had read about it. The madness manual had called this inappropriate affect. It is the inability to express the proper emotion to match up with any given situation, like laughing at a loved one's funeral or crying at a funny joke. This strange smile to such a serious question along with my insane laughter was definitely upsetting Porcupine. I could see it in her eyes.

She cleared her throat and looked at the floor, "Psycho, what you said last night, it was all truth. I am a shitty mom. Jordie and Lauren deserve better. I need to quit the crank for them if not for me. You were right that I made bad choices. I thought a lot about what you said all night. I could not sleep. I realize that I needed to hear that, maybe I even said what I did to get you to tell me what I needed to hear. I will try again to kick the habit and talk with Jeff about getting legitimate jobs. I want to thank you for being a real friend by being honest with me. Most people lie and go along with anything, so they do not have to deal with the drama. Not you. You told me like it is. So, no I am not throwing you out."

I could not believe what I was hearing. Porcupine was thanking me for saying she was a waste of space and bad mother. She also said she is going to stop being a drug user and dealer. This could not be correct. I wondered if maybe I was hallucinating that everything was going to be great. I did tend to do that shit. I sat there looking at her blankly, waiting for the hammer to smack me in the head that she was surely hiding behind her back.

Even Simon was shocked. He began to cough wildly as apparently, he had gasped so hard, he sucked down saliva into his windpipe. He could not catch his breath as he stared at me bug eyed unable to speak to tell me what to do now.

I rubbed my eyes, but Porcupine still stood there staring at the floor, "If you are not here to toss me, then why here so early? Surely this could have waited," I said cautiously still waiting for the punchline.

"I came to help you get ready to see the doctor and probation officer today. Did you forget we have appointments this morning? Your bed sores need treating, and your hand is all busted up. You did not even clean off the blood. Psycho, you have to start to take better care of yourself," she pointed at my blood, dirt encrusted hands.

I looked down at my hands. They had taken a beating during the fight with Julie, both of them. I had not even noticed they were cut up. Some of the cuts were pretty deep and had been bleeding off and on all night. They had been unable to clot without pressure (which I never bothered to apply) and some type of bandage. I never attended to the unit with any regularity unless Simon or someone reminded me. I don't know why but I just always seemed to forget the unit's needs. I had even gotten blood and gore all over the madness manual while reading it. I had completely ignored it as unimportant.

I nodded at Porcupine but did not look up at her. I was in no mood for her touching me and I already knew she intended to treat my wounds herself, "I don't like to be touched," I said simply.

Porcupine shifted her weight to one side, "Yeah, I got that. I figured out a way to treat you without touching you. I have a wooden salad spoon that I can hold the cotton balls with. I will not come in contact with you that way. You can treat the wounds you can reach at my direction. I will use the spoon for the ones you can't. Will this work for you?"

I looked to Simon who now had finally caught his breath and stopped coughing. He looked back at me and shrugged, "Sounds reasonable."

I nodded at him. Porcupine thought I was nodding at her.

"Great! Now let's get going, okay? Jeff is asleep. He could sleep through an earthquake. My mom came by already to take the kids to the zoo today. They are staying with her tonight so we can deal with these appointments without that added responsibility," Porcupine said appearing more alert than she had when first entering the shed.

I stood up and gave Simon a quick 'see you later' mind message as I followed Porcupine out of the shed. He shot me a quick wave as he began to roll yet another of his smokes. We both knew our mission roles. I would protect the unit by being Psycho, and he would help me watch for danger from the real world. We were finally working as a well-oiled team. I felt pretty satisfied this plan of ours may just work to keep us safe for a change.

The weak morning light made me narrow my sensitive eyes a bit as I step out of the dimly lit shed. I briefly felt a pang of regret that my stone clad residents were not there to greet me as they had in the past. I had slept in cemeteries for so long now, seeing the well mowed lawns was a bit disorienting to my senses. The world below my feet tilted just slightly and I swayed trying to maintain my balance against it. Porcupine turned around to say something only to see me standing there, arms outstretched leaning to one side as if balancing on a tight rope at the circus.

She raised an eyebrow, "Okay not even going to ask what the fuck you are doing now. God damn Psycho, you are too fucking weird. Laughing at an imaginary friend farting, and now walking like a retarded chicken trying to take off in flight? Are they giving you any medication for this shit?" She put her hands on her hips waiting for my response.

I stumble just a tad as I take a step again trying to maintain my balance against yet another sudden shift of the ground, "I don't have any. They burned up in Julie's house I guess."

Porcupine rolled her eyes at that, "Well fuck. Okay, today you make sure that psychiatrist of yours gives you some samples. I should have known you were off the meds. No wonder you are flipping out. You have to take medication Psycho, or this will get out of control fast. Come on quit playing around, we don't have a lot of time to get you cleaned up." She took off toward the trailer.

I steadied myself against the tilt and walked somewhat clumsily following behind her. I heard what she said about the medication. I had read about that too in the manual. I was not happy to hear that meds were necessary, but I did understand without them it would not be long before I was running headfirst into objects again or jumping off of bridges. The medication would not stop all of the insanity, but it would at least take some of the worst symptoms down a notch. I agreed with Porcupine that I would need to get some from Dr. Scott and there was no time left to waste. It would take weeks to work. I had already lost at least two weeks which had allowed my symptoms to grow very strong. There was no doubt I was rapidly losing ground in the battle with my psychosis.

I petted the lazy pit bulls who greeted me with happy faces and wagging tails as Porcupine went into the trailer first. I did really like these two fellows. I thought to myself that when I got my very own place, I would have lots of dogs and maybe even cats too. It seemed to me that if people were more like dogs, life would be more worth the effort. I was deep in thought and belly rubs having forgotten my task when

Porcupine opened the door and yelled at me to get inside to clean up.

I quickly went in to find Porcupine had set up a makeshift treatment area on the kitchen table. She directed me to use the kitchen sink to wash my hands (berating me when I tried to not use soap) and face. Once finished she directed me to sit down at the kitchen table after I had removed my jacket and shirts down to my bra.

I shot her a nasty look at that direction. I was not going to just strip down on her fucking command. My mind whirled as the Looper repeated over and over, "she's a pervert you know."

Porcupine let out an irritated sigh, "Again with this? Look I have seen plenty of tits in my day. I am a woman too. You have to take off the shirts to get to those bed sores, which is the bottom line. Jeff is out cold it is just us gals, plus I already seen all your business honey. I did have to undress you yesterday when you seized on me. Now let's go. We don't have all day. It will take you thirty damned minutes as it is to remove that ten pounds of rags you are wearing. How can you stand all that in this heat?"

I looked at Porcupine hard, "Easy, I am Psycho, remember?" I then began to remove my jacket and shirts as she directed. I was not happy about it, but I did know she was right.

My response took her by surprise. She began to chuckle, "Yeah, that you are sweetheart. And I am Porcupine."

I just sneered at her statement as I continued to disrobe. I did not like her games, but for now I was stuck playing them.

She watched me then apparently thinking on my statement said, "I just realized you don't know my real name. I would be happy to tell you what it is so you can call me by it instead of Porcupine." Porcupine smiled at me appearing to want me to seem pleased she would share such information.

I was down to my last shirt so before removing it too I stopped then looking at her with an evil smile, "Do you know my name?"

She was still smiling, "Oh yes, I do know your name, Cindy told me."

That is exactly what I expected to hear, "I do not care what your fucking real name is. I will not give you the respect of using your real name since you never showed me enough respect to call me by mine." I then pulled off my last shirt and sat in the chair as she had instructed.

Porcupine gasped at my statement and grabbed her chest as if I had hit her in it. "Psycho, which is not fair. I did not know you would be offended by a stupid nickname. Hell, had I known I would have never called you by it."

I had to laugh at her stupidity on that one, "Porcupine, if you thought calling someone who is mentally ill Psycho was not offensive, then I have to wonder if you need to wear a life preserver when you take a bath, so you don't drown. You knew my name all this time and never bothered to use it. So, you can fuck yourself. I don't give two shits what your real name is."

I finished by grabbing some of the astringent she had laid out on the table and began to cover the cuts on my hands with it. I had already tired of this conversation.

Porcupine stood there unable to think what to say in defense of what she now had realized to be the truth. She watched me for a bit in silence as I treated my hands with the topical antibiotics. I had begun to wrap my busted knuckles in gaze when she finally found her tongue again.

"Yeah, you are right. It was shitty of me not to think of how hurtful calling you Psycho might be. I am sorry for it. Do you want me to call you by your real name then?" She would simply not let this touchy subject go.

I stopped wrapping and shot her a hateful glare, "Drop it. I am Psycho and you, darling, are Porcupine. Now are you going to help me with this shit or at least tell me what to do with the bed sores or what?"

In truth, I did not allow her to call me by my real name when given the chance because I had already decided I did not want to get any more personal with this woman. I did not like her and keeping as much distance from her as possible was my new goal. Nicknames can be used in families as pet names, terms of endearment, and even private jokes, but in this case our nicknames were equal to the way we were viewed by society. Far as I was concerned, I was going to play the role I was forced into. She should stick to the one she had chosen for herself. We were not family, and never would be friends. There was no need to ever know the person behind the nickname.

Porcupine realized I was not going to give in to her attempts at familiarity, so she helped me remove the old wrapping on the bed sores. I was able to treat most of them without her aid but a few on the back I could not reach. She had to treat them clumsily with her salad spoon method. It was not a pleasant experience but necessary.

After the treatment and all the wounds were bandaged, I quickly dressed and began to comb out my very tangled wig. Porcupine watched me silently as I applied my usual corpse make up and did my best to clean off the worst of filth acquired from my battles the day before. I then added my derby as the final touch to my now signature look.

"Why do you dress like that," Porcupine pipped up, breaking her silence and nearly startling me into a heart attack with her sudden noise.

I smiled at her trying to calm my internal terror that she had just stirred up by both speaking without warning and by the nature of the question, "Because I am Psycho. Shouldn't we be going?"

Porcupine blew out her air in frustration, "You are not going to tell me anything about yourself, are you? I am trying to understand you better. I am trying to help, can't you see that?"

I shrugged my shoulders, "You cannot help me. You are not qualified. So shouldn't we be on our way?"

I had suspected her questions were dripping with motive that would likely work in her favor. I now believed I had heard the evidence that I was correct. Porcupine had said she read that madness manual. If she was telling the truth than she would have no need to ask me such probing questions because she already knew she could not help me. Porcupine was trying to develop a relationship but exactly why I still had not discovered. There was no doubt in my mind there was something very sinister afoot. I had no choice but to wait it out while thwarting her attempts to gain my trust. I knew it would all come out in the wash, and I was very patient.

She nodded it was time to go. We left the trailer and loaded up in her black Chevy headed the thirty miles to the west to settle up my bill with the probation officer and Dr. Scott.

All the way there, Porcupine prattled on about her childhood, family, and other personal information such as hopes and dreams for the future. I just sat there staring out the window watching the world of the real race past my visual field doing my very best to tune her out. I did not care a fig for her life, memories, or dreams. Despite my very obvious lack of interaction, she was just like Stephanie. I could not for the life of me understand why these people felt the need to rape my ears with their foul histories. I had enough bad dreams for several lifetimes and certainly did not appreciate all these attempts to add extra to my overload.

The Looper was repeating every fucking word she said to top off my misery. I now understood he was the reason I could hear an echo whenever I heard human speech. It had been his voice echoing that day so long ago in Stephanie's house when she was making hamburger helper. I did not understand then what was happening to me, now I was painfully aware. His hollow, monotone voice was never quiet. I had gotten used to it but in long conversations such as this one, I admit I wanted to jump from the speeding car and end it all. If my head ripped off in the fall, then I would no longer hear Porcupine or that blasted Looper repeating her.

The thought of my head being wrenched from my unit's shoulders made me giggle. I really found that a bit disturbing that such a violent image would make me laugh but then again, I tended to laugh at the strangest things anyway. I laughed a bit harder as I imagined even with my head laying yards from the unit Porcupine and Looper would likely approach and keep on talking to it anyway.

"Psycho! Hey, wake up Stop that laughing now. We are almost there and I don't think you want to get thrown into the rubber room do you? Laughing like a loon will get you put away. Try to get that under control," Porcupine said appearing alarmed.

I looked at her, "I was laughing at your ability to talk non-stop for your information. I was not laughing like a loon." That really pissed me off when people insinuated, I was the one acting crazy when they themselves were acting much more psychotic.

Porcupine's eyes went wide in fear, "What? What did you say?"

Now she was really getting on my last nerve, "What? What did you say," I repeated her words even using her inflection and tone, "You talked my ears off, but I say one damned thing and you can't fucking hear me?"

Porcupine turned and looked at me like I had morphed into a giant rat, "Psycho, I haven't been talking. No one has said anything since we left the house. Jesus Christ, you need to get some medication."

I rolled my eyes at her, "What? What did you say," I again repeated just as I had before in a mocking manner then started to laugh at her stupid attempt to fuck with me?

I knew she was lying. Why people felt the need to fuck with my head was beyond me, but I was not falling for it this time. However, something went wrong as I began to laugh.

I felt a pop in my head and suddenly I began to repeat "What? What did you say?" over and over again.

I tried to stop but was stuck in the Loop. I also could not move suddenly other than rocking my head back and forth as all my unit's limbs went stiff. To my absolute horror drool began to pour out of my mouth because even my ability to swallow had gone stiff and useless.

I could hear Porcupine pleading with me to stop my behavior, but I was helplessly at the mercy of the Loop. I could see the static starting at the corners of the visual field as electricity from the grid rolled like a Jacob's ladder making the scenery ebb and flow in waves. I felt my head come to a halt suddenly. My gaze fixated and froze in a look of horror as I began to slip away from consciousness. I could hear Porcupine yelling at me from farther and farther away. I was not falling into the darkness of sleep. I was collapsing inward toward the white light of the waking death. The catatonic stupor overtook me within minutes.

I began to slowly recognize light and sounds as my head began to rock. The sights and sounds were so confusing as I began to fight hard to try to understand what was going on. Confusion and terror stung me like a million hornets as I came out of the stupor very rapidly. I suddenly began screaming bloody murder and flailing wildly.

The nurses expected this, so I was quickly held down as I battled to regain control of the unit of measurement. Only moments pass and I am able to move again with some consciousness that I am not in the Chevy with Porcupine. I see white walls and two large female nurses holding me down on a gurney. The word hospital comes to my whirling high centered brain.

"Where am I," I yell out very upset and frightened, "Where am I, where am I. Help! Someone please help me."

"Calm down sweetie, you are in the ER. You are going to be okay. We gave you a shot of Lorazepam. You were catatonic, give it a few minutes and you will feel better. Hang in there, sweetie we got you," the larger dark hair nurse said softly.

She does not calm me. I continue to yell begging for help and asking where I am located for several more minutes. The kindly nurse continues to repeat her answer softly and calmly. Finally, I am free enough of the static to understand she is answering my question. I then recall what an ER is and that I should stop fighting the nurses. I calm down and stop yelling. She said I was catatonic, and I am in an emergency room somewhere.

The nurses continue to restrain me a few more moments after I stop fighting them. They ask me if I know who I am and I tell them. They ask me if I know the day of the week, month, and year. I answer correctly. Satisfied that I am back from whatever planet I had flown to, they release me and help me to sit up in the gurney. They even help me with a drink of water as the medication had caused a nasty cotton mouth like it always does. My head feels like it is about to blow off my unit's shoulders with a headache from hell. I am rubbing it and looking at my boots when I hear an all too familiar voice.

"We have to stop meeting like this, kiddo," Dr. Scott says as she enters the treatment room.

I look up startled, "Huh? How," I sputter out unsure if I am not hallucinating her.

Dr. Scott walks over to me as the nurses ask her if she needs them to stick around. She tells them I am likely fine now and she will yell if she need help. I watch them leave as Dr. Scott looks me over a bit too close to my unit than I would like her to be.

"You were brought here in a catatonic stupor by a Mrs. Evans. Apparently, you were on your way to see your probation officer and me but looks like the stress got to you. Why are you not on your medication? This is what happens when you don't take it, we have discussed this before. You are very lucky that Mrs. Evans got you here fast enough that the shot of Lorazepam was able to pull you out. Had you stayed down much longer we would have had to give you ECT to bring you back," Dr. Scott lectured me as she used a pen light to look into my eyes (I never understood what the fuck she was looking by doing that, my brain maybe?).

I was frightened that she mentioned the horrible lightening of ECT. Please don't do that. I didn't mean not to take my medication. I don't have it. It burned up. I swear it did. I would take it, but I didn't have any." I felt myself begin to shake with terror despite all the sedative in my bloodstream.

Dr. Scott could see I was becoming upset. She backed away from me and softly said, "No it is okay, no ECT today. You are responding to the Benzo so it won't be necessary. Okay, so I was told about the house fire. Mrs. Evans said you had a seizure yesterday too. We are going to give you a shot of Prolixin and some Phenobarbital. I will get you new prescriptions for the medications, but you have to start right away do you understand me?"

I looked at the floor avoiding her gaze but nodded my head yes. I hated the shots, but I hated ECT and hospitals far more. So, this time I would not argue with her about it.

Appearing satisfied that I was going to comply with her orders she began to question me about the last month and a half. She had been told I had run away, but I quickly cleared that up by telling her the night of the fire was stressful. Somehow, I had wandered off in a catatonic stupor. She had already spoken to Porcupine, so she did believe me regarding my explanation of the missing days.

Dr. Scott pulled up a chair sat down and began to write down what I told her I remembered. She asked a lot of questions about what I could recall of the events of the last many weeks since she and I had last spoke. I left out all details of the brutal treatment from the Sloans, the Stephanie delusion, the Julie fights, and of course my latest developing situation with Jeff and Porcupine Evans. I stuck to my medication compliance, side effects, and promises to continue to take the medication as she instructed.

It all was going very well until she asked me to show her my arms. I was confused by the question. I looked up at her, "Why? I don't understand."

Dr. Scott glared at me hard, "the nurses told me that you have fresh self-inflicted wounds on your arms and wrists. Want to tell me about that?"

I looked at the floor again and shook my head no but did not respond verbally.

"You have been looking for the radar again, haven't you," she said hollowly. "Let me see your arms. Do I need to get the nurses back in here to restrain you or are you going to show me them on your own?"

I rocked back and forth a bit with anxiety. She was right, I had been looking for it again but not in the last couple of days since I had discovered that Stephanie was not with me those three days. I had finally realized the radar was probably not real either, but I doubted Dr. Scott would believe me. I was unsure what to do.

"I am not going to ask you again," Dr. Scott was getting testy.

I rolled up my sleeves and put out my arms as she had told me to do. I heard her gasp in horror at the sight of my latest attempts at radar retrieval. She began to write again in my file. I felt the need to try to persuade her to understand I was done looking for good this time, while I still maybe had a chance to change her mind from doing to me whatever it was she was writing down.

"Yes, I did go looking again, but it was a mistake. I did not realize at that time that there could not be a radar there," I said now pleading as I dropped my arms and rolled back down my sleeves quickly.

Dr. Scott looked up at me appearing quite cross, "What do you mean you realized there could not be one there? What changed your mind? I have heard this before; I am warning you now. Whatever excuse you are about to give me had better be damned good because right now I think maybe you need to be in the hospital for a while to get you stabilized and stop this self-injurious behavior."

I felt that cut through my force shield like a knife to my unit. I knew it was time to finally say everything this woman had ever wanted to hear and maybe even throw in a few exaggerations for good measure. I knew if I could not convince her of my sincerity, I was going away for a long time again. The Evan's and Sloan's were bad news for sure, but the hospital was hell on earth. I was looking for a third option, but this was not the one I wanted.

"I realized that there is no radar because I realized I have schizophrenia. The disease made me believe Julie's lies," I said trying hard to sound genuine.

Dr. Scott's eyes went wide in disbelief, "Did you just say you realized you have schizophrenia?"

I nodded my head yes. "I understand that I have a thought disorder and sometimes what I think is real is not real. I read a book on it called *Treating Schizophrenia.* I now understand there was never a radar. I know I need medications. I know I hallucinate and believe delusions if I don't take the medications. I just didn't have the medicine." It seemed to me she was maybe buying this story.

Dr. Scott sat back in her chair looking dumbfounded, "I don't believe it. You finally admit you are sick after all this time just from reading a book?" I nodded my head yes.

She looked at me hard again, "And Simon, who is he?"

I felt my chest ache a bit as I heard my friend's name cross her lips, but I steadied myself, "He is a command hallucination made up of my scrambled emotions just like you said. He is not real. He is just in my head."

I almost blew a gasket as I told that lie to her. For a few moments, I believed I may explode in a frenzy of anger that Dr. Scott had made me say it to save my ass from a rubber room. However, my friend, true to his promise to do his part as a team came through just in time.

"Tell the bitch whatever she wants to hear, girly. If she says the sky is fucking green, agree that it is the finest shade of baby shit green ever. If they put you away, they will fry our brains again. Lie if you have to, but don't get angry," Simon said to me with his mind.

My temper went back to its slumber and fear quickly regained control of the unit's helm. I continued to look at the floor quietly pleading with any God who may be listening that Dr. Scott would believe me this time.

She let out a long breath, "Alright, I may be a fool on this but if you are admitting you are sick and need help then, I can admit that maybe you are finally insightful enough to do what you are told to calm your symptoms without the supervision of the mental hospital."

I felt relief poor over me like a bucket of soft leaves floating from my head down the unit. We had been saved one more time from a near miss and rides on the lightening. I held back the urge to let out the breath of extreme tension.

"I will get your shots ordered, prescriptions filled, and I have already talked to the probation officer. You are forgiven seeing him for a month long as you see me every week till the medications are working again. Understand? Miss one appointment and I will finish these commitment papers. I mean it," Dr. Scott said sternly.

I nodded that I completely understood and trust me, I did indeed. She was not kidding, and I was not going to test her.

Dr. Scott stood up and called for the nurse ordering the horrid long lasting Prolixin and anti-seizure shots to be prepped for my ass (literally). I was sure the danger had passed and that shortly I would be headed back to the Evans' shed again. Thoughts of how to get the Sloans to take me back began to trickle in my mind as I sat there listening to Dr. Scott give the instructions to the nurse.

"Oh, one more thing kiddo. I almost forgot. The Sloan's guardianship request has been stalled in the courts because of their lack of a suitable home at this moment. Luckily, Mary has agreed to continue her guardianship until this matter can be resolved. Otherwise, we would have had to place you in a group home for a bit," Dr. Scott said as if she were ordering a burger and not just ripping my heart from the unit's chest.

I blinked my eyes hard and tried to understand what Dr. Scott had just said, but before I could ask her to repeat it, Mary appeared at the entrance of the small examination room. She was just standing there evilly smiling at me.

I secretly hoped that damned nurse would hurry up with that medication, because I needed it bad. As I looked at Mary looking at me, there was now no doubt in my mind this could not be real, and I was having one hell of a hallucination.

Uh oh, looks like some nightmares do come true, huh? Well, We were looking for that third option were We not? Looks like We should be much more careful about what We wish for! So, everyone enjoying the very first leg of Our new path? We do hope you all are because beauties, the roads are just icy, and now We must drive very carefully, or We will skid off into the ditch or worse hit someone else head on. So, everyone remember to buckle up. Seat belt's help to save lives and they are also very useful restraints to keep all of you from bailing out on Us.

CHAPTER 43: THE PSYCHO PATH

Good day most beautiful family in the multiverse. We were wondering if maybe you are all ready for another leap of faith? You are? Now that is a big relief to Us. Especially since most of the damage done from the last few failed leaps have yet to heal. We were unsure if you would be game. You know sometimes We think far too long to make wise decisions. Impulsive choices can sometime be dangerous, so We have learned a nasty habit of never engaging in it, on purpose anyway. However, in these last few weeks taking too long to make a move has put Us all in a very bad situation. Now We are at a crossroads in our journey and unsure which is the correct path to take. Problem is that all roads behind the shattered looking glass lead back to the middle of nowhere. Really it is only the difficulty of the path that matters since the destination no longer is a goal. So, which way do We go? Oops, We just remembered a very important detail about Our existence. Often what choices We think We have are not real. You see in order to survive in Our world you must give up your innate belief that We have any control, because we do not. Look deeper and you will realize We have been fooled into believing there are several options, when really there is only one. Heeheehee, it is okay, We used to be fooled too, but We finally are looking at this delusional world with schizophrenic eyes. Now all you have to do is think like a Psycho. Okay everyone, let's start this tale and see if you have truly been reading the road map right side up when you should have been reading it upside down.

"True strength is doing what you know is right even though you don't want to."
-extramadness

Mary just stood at the door of the emergency examination room grinning her old 'gotcha' smile at me as Dr. Scott came back to stress yet again what she expected of me.

"Remember miss one appointment you are headed to State. I will not accept any excuse do you hear me? This is very serious. Catatonic stupors and self-injurious behaviors in a schizophrenic are a sign of a cataclysmic psychotic break well on its way. I will not have your permanent profound break from reality nor death on my conscious or my books you hear me," she said staring at me hard with a coldness in her voice I had never heard out of her before.

"Cataclysmic psychotic break?" I asked now very frightened, "what is that?"

She shook her head, "You need to be aware that sometime when a person develops this disease so severely at such a young age and shows serious symptoms like you have been, there is a chance they will become so broken from reality all they can do is scream and pee their pants. Those profound cases do not live long and are locked away forever in a cell, restrained for their own good. Basically, brain steams with only terror left. It is not common, but it can and does happen. If you don't follow my instructions, it could happen to you. If you do not kill yourself nipping an artery looking for fake radars first!" She looked deep into my eyes to be sure I understood this most upsetting news.

Terror gripped the unit as goose pimples raised on every inch of it. I suddenly had a vivid memory of the mental hospital just after my third ride on the lightening. I recalled one day the usual quiet of the ward became filled with the tortured screams of a woman. One night they had brought her in secretly and locked her away in the very back of the psychotic ward behind a closed door.

When I had asked another inmate about it, he had said, "Oh that is the Hebephrenic they have lashed to the floor back there. If they let her go, she will tear out her own eyes. She is gone, psychotic forever and one day soon she will die of heart attack from the stress of it or manage to chew out her own wrists, if she is lucky.

I shuttered at the memory of her never-ending screams. I was the only other schizophrenic there. While the other patients had often complained of the noise she made, I felt empathy for her. I wanted to scream with her. I just did not think it would get me out of this hell or I probably would have.

In her screams I could hear the language of the schizophrenic. Even though a very new psychotic, I had already become fluent in the language of the insane. I understood what she was really saying all too well. I also knew, no one could understand her but another of her kind. Sometimes, late at night I would do my best to send her my thoughts to offer any kind of comfort I could. I used to like to imagine it did help her, the poor girl. When I did call out to her mind it seemed she did scream more softly, but likely it was only my delusion and wishful thinking. Probably not real at all. I understood on some level even then that nothing and no one can help us, not even one of our own.

I looked to the floor and nodded my head yes letting Dr. Scott know I understood. I decided I had heard enough. I did not ask another question.

Dr. Scott left me sitting on the gurney. I glanced up to see her take Mary by the arm and pull her away from the door.

"Come with me I need to discuss this very serious situation with you," I heard Dr. Scott's voice trail off as she hauled Mary away to a more private place to discuss my case with her.

The big, dark-haired nurse that had been very helpful in my return from the Catatonic stupor stepped into the room and closed the door. I saw she carried the horrid shots in her gloved hands. I stood up and sighed. I dropped my pants down to expose my upper buttocks as I assumed the position for the shots that would be a reoccurring event for the rest of my life.

She was quick and gentle as she administered the mostly useless so called 'treatment' for my madness. I noticed as she injected the unit her breathing was somewhat labored as if she were stressed or nervous. This was a curious thing as in my mind she was not the one having to submit to nasty medications with heavy side effects and with little to no benefit.

I was busy pulling back up my pants when I realized she was still hanging around. The woman was rather rotund with large beefy arms. She was about average height with dark hair cut short around her attractive round face. She looked to be in her late forties but had flecks of white in her hair. This nurse had kind, large brown eyes and a very charming voice. I looked at her to see her looking at me with a sad look on her pretty face.

I stared at her thinking I maybe should read her mind to see what her problem was but suddenly a feeling of grief overcame me. I actually staggered back slightly as I tried to button my pants still keeping my eyes on this strange nurse.

"I am sorry. I did not mean to stare," she said suddenly appearing to have seen my slight wobble, "are you okay? Do you want me to get you anything? Are you thirsty?"

I shook my head no, "How much longer do you think they will keep me here." I asked feeling the grief spreading throughout my unit.

I was so confused about this feeling. I could not understand where it was coming from. I sat back down on the gurney.

"I am not sure sweetie. Your doctor has ordered you get a full look over and treatment for any cuts or scraps you may have. I would be happy to do that for you or I can get another nurse if you would rather? I know you likely do not like to be touched so I will be careful to do as little of it as possible if you would allow me to examine you," she said looking toward the floor appearing to avoid eye contact on purpose.

I was not happy to hear of this latest indignity. An examination was not something I was prepared to submit to. I began to burn away the grief that was flooding me with the rising temps of anger. I was now ready for a fight as I realized this nurse was saying I was to be checked over from head to toe.

"I will not be examined thank you very much," I growled at the kind nurse, "not by you or anyone else."

The nurse winced at my words. I found that very odd indeed but did not care to ask her why. I was about to lose my temper and go "Psycho" on the first asshole who even attempted to put a paw on my unit.

"I am really sorry, sweetie. Please understand I do not want to invade your privacy, but the Doctor said if you do not comply to have you restrained and notify her immediately." The nurse looked up quickly to see if I was looking at her. I was.

"Sweetheart, if you do not do this willingly, she will have you committed. I overheard her telling Dr. Ingles that if you argued she wanted him to sign the papers and contact the State Hospital. I am not supposed to tell you that, but I know what you are going through, and that hospital is a snake pit," she said softly with almost a pleading tone.

That statement stifled my anger briefly. I heard the voice of Simon ringing in my ears like thunder, "Psycho, stop it. Let this nurse do her job. Do not get angry. Do you want to ride the lightening? This is a test. Dr. Scott is trying to trap us. She expects us to fight. Do not fight."

I grab my ears trying to shield them from Simon's screams into them. He did scream often, but not so damned clear before. I shook my head yes as I told him with my mind I would do as he said and submit to this nurse's examination of the unit of measurement. Simon then quieted as quickly as he began to scream.

The nurse saw me grab my ears becoming very disoriented and agitated. She had back up to the wall but left me an escape route to the door appearing willing to allow me to run if I felt I needed to do so. This along with her keeping a distance and soft truth telling statements allowed me to restrain my anger demon enough to regain control of the unit.

I dropped my hands from my ears and looking at the floor doing my very best to appear calm despite the now rising terror within. I said to her, "Okay. I will let you examine the unit of measurement but only you please ma'am. I will not fight you. Do what you must but please do this quickly and help me get out of here."

The nurse looked up at me with what appeared to be gratefulness (weird), "Okay, tell you what. I can make this as painless as possible. I will leave and get the paperwork and stuff for your treatment, and you put on the gown I will get for you. I will also get you a blanket to feel more covered. I need you to remove everything even your wig and makeup, okay? I am sorry but doctor's orders, not mine." She looked down again as she said that. I nodded that I understood the instructions.

I watched as she put a rag with soap and water to remove my make up next to the small sink in the room. She then grabbed a blue hospital gown laid it on the gurney, with a blanket and left the room closing the door behind her.

I could feel my unit shaking with fear as I began to disrobe from the many layers of clothing I had on. Once all was removed, I clumsily got the hospital gown on and wrapped the blanket around me. I needed the added protection from the air as it began to assault the unit without mercy. It was sending the sensation of sandpaper scrubbing the skin from every direction. I approached the sink and did my best to remove all traces of my make up. Last of all, almost down to the unit of measurement without any of my armor I engaged in the purest of humiliation by removing my wig. I placed it gently atop my pile of discarded clothing I had stacked on the chair that only a bit before, Dr. Scott had grilled me from. I had barely finished what I had been instructed to do when I heard the knock at the door signaling the kind nurse was ready for the torture session to begin.

I called out that she could come in. The nurse came in holding a medical chart and a tray of various items such as astringents and gauzes of different sizes. She sat the tray down on the sink counter and walked over to my bundled-up unit with a pen and the chart.

"I have a picture of a body here front and back. I am going to first examine you and show on this picture every mark, bruise and scar, okay? If you get nervous about it let me know and I will show you what I am writing. I will not hide anything I say about you. All you have to do is ask me to see it. Do you understand?" She kept her eyes downcast as she showed me the paperwork with a drawing of a woman with no face or hair.

I did not say anything as she tried to show me the items. I was not interested. I just wanted to get this crazy shit over with. The nurse finally realized I was not going to thank her or even look at the chart, so she stopped trying to get me to agree to it.

Since my face and head were easily visible, she started her exam there by staring at my head and neck front then around the back, marking on the chart wherever she saw injury fresh or old. I again noted that she appeared to be uneasy, and her breathing was shallow and labored. I assumed maybe it was her girth giving her some difficulty.

She then asked me to lower the blanket and I did so. She saw the bandages from Porcupine and mine attendance of the bed sores. She asked me to remove them and gasped as she noted the wounds once I had uncovered them.

"How did this happen," she asked still stunned.

I shrugged, "catatonic stupor."

She nodded and looked very sad as she continued marking on the images in my chart every single scar, wound, cut, bruise, and noted the condition of the overall health of the unit of measurement.

She finished the exam and put down the chart and for a moment held her eyes with one hand appearing to be trying to kill a budding headache. When she removed her hand, she looked up at the ceiling and I noticed she seemed to have the beginning of tears in the corners as if she may be about to cry. The nurse cleared her throat and went back to her forms by asking questions about my unit from eating to bathroom habits and everything in between. I did my best to answer without giggling at the stupidity of this game.

She asked questions about my period and that did make me laugh despite my best effort to stifle it. I had not had one of those in many months. I was too thin, and they had stopped coming. I had considered it a blessing since I often did not have enough food, much less feminine products, to deal with natures little monthly joke on the mature female of the species.

That information along with other answers I had provided appeared to work on her last nerve especially as she heard me chuckling at the lack of a menstrual cycle. She stopped writing and looked down at the floor.

"This is unprofessional what I am about to say but I think it should be said so please forgive me. The people who did this, and have allowed this to happen, to you should burn in the deepest pit of hell. I hope everyone involved either through their neglect, active involvement, or just standing around letting it happen, one day wakes up and finds themselves being treated like this. No, I take that back, I hope they get it one hundred times worse," she said now tearing up openly as she spit the words out.

I was stunned into silence from my laughing fit. I too looked at the floor not knowing what to say to that. I was not even sure she wanted me to say something. In fact, I was very confused.

She took a deep breath, sniffling as she began her story: "I guess since I probably will lose my job for what I just said, I may as well tell you why I said it. I was only sixteen when I gave birth to the light of my life, my son Kevin. He was my pride and joy. I had been adopted myself and was a troubled teen, but Kevin came, and he saved my life from what was sure to be a world of drugs, abusive men, and other self-hating habits. Once he came, I straighten myself out, went to school, became a nurse. Kevin and I we lived happy as anyone can ever be.

Then when Kevin was nineteen, he made my already outrageous pride in him go to outer space as he was accepted into a fine college on a full ride scholarship. It meant he had to move to another state, but I wanted the best for him, so I let him go with my blessings to pursue his dreams of being a physician. His grades were amazing as he quickly excelled in every area.

The first two years of Pre-Med he was so busy, but he still made time for his momma never missing a phone call or a visit home for the holidays. Then when he turned twenty-one, he stopped calling. I got word he was failing classes and was not coming out of his dorm. I could not get him to answer his phone. I took time off work and flew out to see him unable to understand what was going on.

When I arrived, I found he was missing. His friends and I went looking and finally found him on the streets wandering, dirty, rail thin, paranoid and injured all over like you are now. My beautiful intelligent son had rotted into a babbling shell, completely destroyed by the onset of paranoid schizophrenia. I had no choice but to have him hospitalized to help him try to find his way back from his deep psychotic break.

After a full year of treatment with the finest clinics I could afford, he finally came home to me. But he was not my Kevin anymore. He was suspicious, broken, and without emotion. I was beyond heartbroken. I still loved him, but his struggle and pain tore me up inside the way only a mother could understand when she is forced to watch her child suffer such torment.

I tried everything, from therapy to vocational rehabilitation but my Kevin was no more. I took extra work to support us and his escalating psychiatric bills. Then one day when I was working extra over time to make a few more dollars to help support us I got the call.

Kevin had decided he could not live like that. He had taken a sawed-off shotgun and ended his life. The neighbor had heard the shot in the woods behind our house. Kevin was dead the second he pulled the trigger. I was devastated beyond human understanding.

Then I found his final words to me in a note he left on my bed. It said: "Mom, I am sorry, but I am already dead. I am lost. That is more than I can bare, but to watch you die with me, that is not something I can do anymore. Thank you for loving me when no one else can or should. Love forever, Your Kevin." The nurse finished her story and dropped her head weeping softly into her hands.

I sat there looking at her unsure what to do. I looked wildly around the room wondering if I was going to get into trouble that she had told me this stuff. Her story caused me to feel very nervous and respectful of this mother who had truly loved her child. I had never encountered a person who had lost a child, and I had never encountered a parent who loved a child of schizophrenia (that is what people with this disease are called by the way including myself). I also realized why this nurse had been so capable of managing me and my many demons. She was experienced on how to placate the prisoners of this hellish disease on a very personal level.

As she continued to cry, I thought of Kevin and how he had chosen a path that I myself had often considered. One that was sure to end this suffering. I did uniquely understand why he had done it. However, then I realized that Kevin had given up with so much more than I had ever known to live for.

His mother weeping in her hands exuding grief beyond heartbreaking sitting before me made me think to myself, "She is something that would be worth anything someone had to endure to just see her brown eyes smile." I decided Kevin was an idiot for hurting someone who loved him so much.

I stood up and ignoring the shock I wrapped my arms around this lost mother and said, "I am sorry for your loss ma'am. Kevin was a lucky young man. I want you to know it was not your fault. You could not help him. He did not do it to hurt you. Kevin just could not handle the undeath this disease brings. He is out of pain now. Please understand that. He has the peace this life denied him, I am sure he would want you to have peace knowing that he suffers no more," I finished trying hard to let her know I did care even thought I really had no reason to do so.

She cried a bit harder when I first held her and began to speak but as I finished, she started to relax in my grip. I gritted back the pain of this embrace as I continued to grant her what I believe she needed, one last hug from Kevin. I understood to her I was his ghost. My disease is different for everyone who get it, but for this woman I resembled his expression of the illness and she had bonded to me mistaking me for

284

her lost son. I knew she needed to hear what I knew Kevin would say to her if he still could speak. I also felt that despite the fact that Kevin had given up too easily in my eyes, I could not blame him either. If I could assist her to heal the deep sorrow of his loss, then I should try. I could not escape my own sorrow, but maybe helping another out of theirs would make my own suffering worth more than cruel entertainment for a group of soulless teenage girls or the carnal pleasures of some hedonistic foul unloving male.

The nurse finally stopped weeping as I dropped my hold on her glad to be free of the shock sensations. I sat back down on the gurney as she wiped her eyes and looked at me both grateful and a tad ashamed, "Thank you so much. I will never forget your kindness. I suppose I will have to find a new job now," she chuckled at that.

"No, you won't. You just attend to all my wounds. I thank you so much for doing such a fine job. If they ask me that is all I will ever say. Just that you are the finest nurse I have ever been treated by ma'am," I smiled and winked at the nurse to let her know her secret was safe with me.

She appeared surprised as it finally dawned on her that I was not going to tattle on her. What would I say anyway? I would never do such a thing to anyone for making the mistake of being a decent human being. I smiled at her realizing as she looked at me that I had gotten what Kevin had lost, I saw those brown eyes smiling. I had been right, seeing that would definitely be worth anything one had to endure just to see that once in a while.

The nurse got up and finished the evaluation by re-wrapping my bed sores and my arms from my most recent "radar retrieval" surgeries. She often would sniffle appearing upset as she dealt with each wound of neglect, violence or self-abuse. When she was finally finished, she told me that someone would come get me for check out as soon as I was dressed and ready to go.

She went to the door to leave and give me some privacy but stopped looking back at me once more, "My name is Shirley. I wrote my phone number on a note, and it is on the tray I brought in. Please keep it and if you ever are in need of anything, don't hesitate to call me. I don't know how much I can help you, but if there is a way I can, I want you to know I always will. Kevin and I would like to thank you for listening and for understanding. Please take care of yourself." With that she walked out shutting the door behind her.

I rushed to my clothing and put them on in record time. I then got my wig back on and wondered where my purse may be. Likely it was still in Porcupine's Chevy, so for now I was without my make up. I assumed I would live but I did hate being without my mask to hide my scarred and bruised up face. I almost forgot about Shirley's phone number, but Simon reminded me by telling me having such a lifeline could not hurt us. I took the handwritten scrawled phone number and put it into my pocket feeling a bit dizzy as the first signs of the Prolixin side effects began to overtake the unit.

I shrugged it off and began to pace the room and wring my hands trying to quell the anxiety at having seen Mary waiting to pounce on me earlier. I knew a big problem had just fallen on my head like a boulder dropped from the cosmos. Now that the Sloans would not be getting a check on me, the escape route through them was blocked. I also realized that Jeff and Porcupine were a dead issue now that the Sloans could not provide monetary compensation for my care in their household.

I was crazy but not stupid. I was very aware that none of these people gave two shits about what happened to me at all. They all wanted the money the state paid for my pathetic existence. They were happy to provide minimum care, such as meager food, shelter and water but none of them wanted the problems that I could cause.

The Sloans were greedy and wanted the money and extra free labor with entertainment but did not want to have me even speak, much less act up.

The Evans were greedier still. They wanted labor, entertainment, and quite probably had some plan to literally use my ass to collect extra cash on top of whatever the Sloans were giving them.

However, none of that mattered now that Mary had the leash on me. She would no doubt take me to the appointments and pick up my medications. She would even likely provide meager supplies, but she would not provide shelter for us. Worst of all she would not give us what we needed more than anything else, supervision. Simon was right, we were failing at caring for the unit of measurement. If I returned to the cemetery as I truly wanted to, the unit and all of us were doomed to Kevin's fate no doubt.

As I paced that room, I even briefly toyed with the idea of calling Dr. Scott back to the room and begging her to go ahead and commit me to the mental hospital. The whirl and smell of the shock shop stopped that idea in my shattered mind almost before it got a foothold as a plausible alternative to our very dangerous situation.

"What are we going to do, Simon," I finally said out loud in pure desperation, unable to figure out what to do now that I had this new most disturbing news.

He responded quickly, "Calm down for starters. Okay, Mary we know. Just the usual with her. Get the meds so we do not end up Hebephrenic. Make her buy us supplies and take us to the appointments. With the medication and Prolixin maybe w can take care of the unit this time without help?"

I had not considered that. I would be on medication this time. Maybe with the right supplies and Simon's guidance we could reclaim our independence from these slave masters! I. smiled as I thanked my friend for his most sage advice. Simon always seemed to know the right thing to say.

Again, I never was any good with reality. The truths that had been overlooked by both Simon and I were the most dangerous to the unit. I would indeed be able to get the medications but remembering to take them would be another matter. I also had already forgotten my numerous nasty open wounds and the need to receive constant care for them. Not to mention a catatonic stupor was possible or a Grand Mal at any time with no warning. The very things that had caused me to realize we needed aid were cast aside to the garbage heap called 'lack of insight' almost as fast as they had come to our attention in the first place. That was the real reason schizophrenia is so disabling. The inability to recognize the serious of our sickness and its limitations make us unstable as well as unable to care for ourselves with any regularity.

I finally heard a knock at the door. I gave permission to enter, and Mary's deplorable form opened the door, "Psycho come with me. They have released you into my care." She was smiling that irksome grin again.

I rolled my eyes as I sighed following her out. We did not speak as we traveled to her awaiting station wagon parked outside the hospital. I did look around for Porcupine's black Chevy nervously as we went through the somewhat crowded parking lot. The light of the day was still strong enough to cause a bit of a glare on my now very dry eyes. Mary saw my visual search of the cars around us.

"If you are looking for that druggy whore, you can stop now. She left hours ago," Mary spewed out dryly.

I stopped a bit stunned, but to be honest I expected she had abandoned me to my fate now that there was no check to gain. "What about my purse," I asked miffed she took my things with her.

Mary snorted, "You mean your demonic make up bag? I have it in the car. That horrid woman gave it to me before she left to go fornicate some more."

I did not respond to Mary's baiting me to defend Porcupine. That was not going to happen. Porcupine was a loser, and worse still a liar too. I was not in the habit of fighting for assholes.

Mary and I got into the station wagon as she took off headed for supply gathering without my requesting it. She knew the drill. Nothing was going to ever change between us.

At first, the ride was quiet as I gratefully collected my bag and reapplied my make up with the use of the cosmetic mirror in the passenger side sun visor. She shot me hateful side way glances as I worked on my mask.

"Since we last saw each other it seems you have really spread out your leathery wings, demon. Drug dealers, prostitutes, and arson. I am sure the devil is impressed with you," Mary sourly stated.

I smiled at that, "Gosh, Granny I sure have missed you. Yes, the kids are doing great. Jack just graduated from Yale and Kim is studying hard for the SATs. I just got the promotion at the firm myself. The husband and I are planning a trip to the Caribbean as soon as he can get a break from his big contract deal. Thanks so much for asking. How the hell have you been? Is the arthritis acting up or did the new medication work like you hoped it would," I sing-songed out happily in response to her statement?

Mary blew out her breath in irritation, "You are as insane as ever. What in Sam Hill are you spouting? You know I should turn this car around and have that nice Dr. Scott lock you away in the loony bin if nothing more than to protect decent people from your evil."

I laughed out loud, "Go ahead Mary. I already know you won't even if I stripped naked right here in the car and mooned all your neighbors. Do you know how I know that? Let me give you about two thousand reasons you hypocritical bitch."

Mary started to get angry I saw her grip the steering wheel till the veins on her hands popped out heavily, "Sinner. Demon. Who told you about the money? Well, they lied. You cost more than your worth."

"Hahaha, really? Then what the fuck are you doing here? I know it sure as shit is not because you missed these little loving chats of ours. Look just get me the medication, the supplies, and take me to the appointments. Drop me off at the cemetery and cut the shit, will you? I do not want to fight with you anymore. I have had a rather trying day and I am in no mood for this bullshit," I said already getting another of my famous psychotic driven headaches.

Mary looked at me surprised, "Well, finally something we can agree on. That must be a first. I am going to warn you now, I will not tolerate any trouble out of you this time. I am ready to hand you off to the Sloans if you so much as look at me crosswise."

I rolled my head on my neck trying to release some of the tension building in the back of my head from the Prolixin side effects, "If you don't want trouble then stay far away from me. I already know the

Sloans guardianship is only held up. Once they get the house replaced, I will be back in their care so quit your lies. I am not that stupid kid you took advantage of several months ago darling. I am on to your games."

That statement cut Mary to the bone. She knew I was right, and she knew I had her number. Her nasty demeanor suddenly went to a syrupy sweet overly dramatic charm, "Okay, you are right. Let's just forget the past. I don't want to fight either. We are family after all. In fact, you remember that awhile back I promised to give you a gift. Well, I bought it. It is in the back seat. Go ahead take a look. It is all yours," she motioned to the back seat with her head.

"Huh," I said wondering if this was another of her tricks. "What gift did you promise? Eternal damnation is all I ever recall you promising that I would get," I chuckled at that.

"Look will you," she said again appearing sincere as she ever could be.

Curiosity got the best of me as I looked into the back seat expecting she would reach up and clobber my noggin as I had to lean closer to her to see behind us. I saw a manila envelope, not too unlike the old psychiatric records she had once thrown at me in a fit of anger. At first, I thought that was what I was looking at, those damned records. I had thought they burned up in Julie's house but for a second, I was not so sure.

"Get it Psycho. It is from me to you. A special gift," Mary insisted.

I raised an eyebrow but decided to bite. I reached back and grabbed the envelop. I opened it up and gasped in horror. I was staring at a paid in full receipt for a burial plot complete with headstone in my cemetery. That was bothersome enough but the reason I gasped was the headstone had an order for my name with an also known as Psycho just under it compete with my year and day of birth. Mary had not only bought my death plot she had also made sure that I would not escape my reputation long after the unit had passed away.

I stared at the certificate in disbelief. Now I had already known incredible cruelty, especially at the hands of my family, but this was fucking cold blooded even for Mary.

"Why," I squeaked out almost despondent with the gravity of such a perverse gift from my own damned grandmother.

Mary started to laugh satisfied that she had finally done something so heinous it had reached my jaded heart, "well to be honest I got it as a birthday present for me. You know birthday presents should be something you really want and normally would not get for yourself."

I heard that loud and clear, "very clever you snake. You know what Mary? I believe I will take this gift and thank you for it. I promise you right here in front of your God that it is now my only goal in life to live long enough to bury you in this grave you have dug for me. I swear I will put you in it, and every day for the rest of my shitty life I will come and visit you. Do you know why? So, I can piss on your bones." I felt the rage start to unfurl inside stretching out like a cat waking from a nap while sunning on a window ledge.

Simon's voice again raged in my ears like a thunderbolt, "Stop it, Psycho. She is not worth it. Remember what happened the last time you hit this useless piece of shit. Let it go, now."

Once again, my anger was restrained as I grabbed my ears feeling the eardrums were going to burst from Simon's demands that I let Mary get away with this insult. It hurt so bad, I actually let out a moan of agony.

Mary just chuckled as she watched me grapple with Simon's commands and my anger demon, "Yeah, sure you will outlive me. Psycho I would be willing to bet the farm that you won't make it to Christmas with that daft brain of yours. You will kill yourself and I will be the one to come piss on your grave."

I did hear Mary, but the ringing of Simon's voice now joined by the Looper's chants of "she will piss on your grave" in a repeat like a scratched record in my mind kept me from responding.

I held my ears and rocked in the seat moaning actually thinking that Mary could be right. If this was my future, then fuck it let her piss on my bones. Let the town come to see the Psycho grave. I would at least not have to hear another damned one of them. In those moments as I began to think that Christmas was far too long to wait to start my eternal winter nap. The noise of this nightmare world of mine was truly threatening to drive me well past the edge of insanity.

Mary and I arrived at the shops to buy my supplies and pick up my medications. I had been reduced to a rocking and agitated psychotic by her most nasty prank. She had likely enjoyed watching my torment as I wrestled with my symptoms trying to regain control of my unit and my stability.

As she pulled into the pharmacy parking lot, she looked at me, "You going to be stupid all day or get off your lazy butt and go get your medications? I will not get them because I will not be seen with a filthy schizophrenic in there. I have friends unlike you, and I intend to keep them."

I no longer was too interested in getting the medications, but I got out of the car and went inside to pick them up anyway. I was greeted by a sea of offended faces. The other customers in the pharmacy there to pick up their own elixirs, liniments, and balms, were not happy to see the corpse like disturbed teenager in their vicinity. As I stood in line waiting for my turn to pick up the useless medications prescribed by Dr. Scott, I heard several verbal insults both under the breath and out loud from the staff and patrons. The words "freak, weirdo, nut, druggie, and wacko" flowed more liberally than the beer from a good old fashioned hillbilly cookout.

I did not pay any attention to the insults. Inside my head the chaos and horror were far worse than anything these rubes could even have the intelligence to imagine much less use in a clever enough taunt to hurt my almost non-existent feelings.

I managed to pick up my medications to find the only real break I had gotten all day. Dr. Scott had ordered a 90-day supply of all my prescriptions to be given to me at one time. I would not be running out of anti-psychotics, benzodiazepines, or anti-conversant meds for some time to come.

I returned to the car with my stash of weapons against the onslaught of psychosis only to be told by Mary that I was completely on my own with regard to shopping for supplies. She would give me the money to buy them but would not 'be seen' with me anywhere in public. That was fine by me. I did all my shopping with only the jeers, belittling, and verbal abuse of total strangers to deal with without the added hatefulness of Mary's mouth.

I managed to get through almost all of my shopping for clothing, blankets, and camping items without too much serious incidents from the rudest small-town people I had ever encountered to this point. However, when making my final stop to acquire food for the unit I did have a run in with a nasty pack of so called 'ladies' at the grocery store.

I was trying to load my staple baby food and very simple carbohydrates that the unit of measurement could still digest onto the checkout belt. Three older women approached and stood around behind me like a flock of old hens. They rattled on loudly about how my "parents should be smacked" for allowing me out of the house in such a "bizarre almost demonic" outfit not to mention "that obscene make up job." They loudly questioned everything from my morals to my religious preference to my sanity (well they were correct on that one anyway).

One of the old, wicked bitches actually gasped as I loaded on the baby food jars stating, "Oh my God look at that. I pray those are for its little sister and that this thing is not a mother herself."

I heard the other two witches agree with her, as I was then discussed in terms of 'it' not even dubbed a human any longer in their insulting argument of who it (referring to me) was with regard to a the 'baby' I was buying 'tons' of baby food for.

As I finally paid for my goods and prepared to leave, I could no longer take that shit without saying something back to them as I looked at the three now obviously frighten woman.

They had realized to late they should have kept their traps shut as I approached them smiling and said, "I need a lot of food to fatten the little fucker up you know. I hate eating the skinny babies, too stringy. Have a nice day ladies."

They all about fainted as I said that most foul thing to them. I would like to say I was wrong to do it but since I never have eaten a baby yet. I believe if they were allowed to make up lies and spout it where I can hear it, then I am well within my rights to respond to them with more lies.

After all the shopping was done, Mary and I traveled back to the cemetery I had called home for some time now. I was not quite as happy to see it as I had thought I would be. Now that I was aware of catatonic stupors, delusional friendships, and other nasty events that had taken place there while I was trying to live independently, I actually was a little afraid to be alone there.

I was afraid I would hurt myself beyond repair this time to be exact. Despite the fear of myself as my roommate, I got out of the station wagon and unloaded my supplies quickly. One thing was for sure, I wanted to see the back lights of that damned vehicle as soon as possible!

Mary watched me pull my items through the iron gate but did not offer to assist. She did not even get out of the car. That too was fine by me. When she was sure I had everything, she motioned me to her window. I did not want to go see what she wanted but I did know it likely had to do with a future appointment. No doubt she would try to threaten me again if I dared to not be there when she showed up.

I walked to her window, and she rolled it down looked at me and smiled, "You forgot one thing."

I shrugged then looked at my stash just inside the gate trying to recall what I had missed. I felt something hit me in the back of the head just as Mary started the car putting the pedal to the metal as the car speed backward rapidly.

Mary had a huge grin on her face as I stared at her bewildered by this strange behavior, "Welcome home, Psycho," she yelled as she drove off leaving me standing there in the dust stirred up by the station wagon's spinning tires.

I looked down to see she had thrown the manila folder at me as she had done so many months ago only this time instead of it containing the records of my destroyed future, it held the contents of a promise that I did not even have a future. I picked the bill of sale for my burial plot she had purchased for me. As I walked into my cemetery gate, I could not help but feel very lost and terribly alone.

The problem was that I was far from alone. The one person on Earth that posed the greatest threat to me knew exactly where I was. I was now her prisoner. I had just discovered there was no one on Earth who could help me escape her attack. But worst of all no one could even hear me scream.

Doesn't look like We are faring well does it, Beauties? Who ever said 'sticks and stones can break my bones but words can never hurt me' must have been hearing impaired? In the world behind the cracked looking glass words can actually cut deeper than any blade, or shall we say words can cause a deep cut from a blade. Many disasters, accidents, and misfortunes have thus far plagued our journey to nowhere, but few have been so full of potential catastrophe as the path We have just been forced onto. You see you thought We had the power to choose, didn't you? Well, no Beauties We are never going to truly be in control so long as We cannot look out for Ourselves. That is the secret to all choice, no one is ever really free to choose what they want. They can maybe choose from what they are offered. Sometimes, the offers are not even real in the world of the delusional. Whatever shall become of Us now? Well, no worries the story shall continue just keep taking that leap of faith with Us.

CHAPTER 44: CROW IS A DISH BEST SERVED WARM

We are preparing ourselves for our switch from the stability of the earth to the changeability of the ocean. Now you surely knew that in our path to nowhere eventually we would come to a body of water, didn't you? You ready to test your sea legs? That is wonderful, then just climb on deck and join us as we set our sails for destinations unknown. We know that the wind does not seem to be in our favor and those clouds headed our way appear pregnant with rain, but we are not going to let that stop us from putting everyone at risk...errrr...launching on time. The troubled waters of our journey will be brackish, so we hope that everyone is able to get their sea legs. Nothing worse than a case of motion sickness. Especially with the onslaught of rolling waves tossing us about without mercy now is there? Oh wait, yes there is something worse, a boat that is sinking.

Yes, beauties we really should have checked to make sure this hull was watertight before we pushed off, but it is really too late now, isn't it? You start a lookout, so we do not crash upon the rocks. We will do our best to keep us afloat by bailing the seeping swill with this teaspoon. Why not a bucket you ask? Well, that is the damnation of it all, we never seem to have the proper tools to deal with these potentially deadly situations. It does look seem we will need to abandon our craft soon as all is lost no doubt. We did bring one lifeboat and we insist you get in it and start paddling for shore. We will see all of you below because as the captain of this vessel it is our fate to go down with the ship.

"We all make choices in life. The hardest thing is to live with them."
-unknown source

I had only been away from home for a couple days, so everything was still just as I had left it. One of the things I had learned about my disordered senses is that time is often distorted in my mind. While only a day or two had actually passed, it seemed like months had.

I sighed and began to haul the many boxes of new supplies I had purchased with money Mary had given me. From clothing to cooking utensils this time I had made sure to select items very carefully for someone living 'off grid.' I had learned many lessons about survival without proper shelter over the last several months. My gear this time would help to make my meager existence as tolerable as possible.

I grumbled under my breath as I thought of all the money over these many months Mary and others had withheld for themselves that was actually meant to pay for my care. While unloading the many jars of baby food, packages of batteries, lighters, and new blankets I thought hard on how shitty a person had to be to rob from someone who had so little left the state sent money to substitute for an income they would never be capable of providing for themselves. Now that was just as low as it would be to beat up a baby mouse. I was indeed helpless as an infant rodent. I really hated that my brains had not leaked out enough for me not to realize that fact.

I unpacked the last of my items while rubbing my upper hip that smarted from that vicious shot of liquid mental restraint called Prolixin. That too was pissing me off. It seemed to me very unfair that I was being sedated heavily to stop my fit throwing but everyone else got away with behaving like assholes. When I threw a fit it was honest. I was in a lot of mental torment, pain, and terror. However, in most cases, I would have never thrown the damned fit in the first place if the people around me would stop picking at me. It made absolutely no sense at all. They surely knew I was already doing my very best. Every second of everyday it took all I had not to rip off the skin suit from my unit of measurement and run screaming like a white girl from a summer camp slasher. Yet still they insisted in pushing me ever further into unbearable torment.

I wondered about Shirley's statement that someone should be helping me out. She had cursed even those who saw but did nothing not just those who had. I wanted to tell her this was not the first time, hell not even the tenth time, no one would come to my aid. I had told of my mother and her many friends torturing and raping the unit of measurement many times before she poisoned us. No one ever came to help then either. Not until after she managed to dash out our brains with the living death called schizophrenia, did they even believe us. We were well aware had the denim brigade not nearly killed us that night in the cemetery we would have not been in this situation we now had found ourselves in. Their cruel trick saved our unit's life, but not our soul. It was already too late for that. Shirley had indeed suffered a nasty blow from reality with the loss of her son Kevin. Somehow, she still managed to believe that when nightmares come there is always a hero coming to save the damsel in distress.

Well, for being dubbed insane we were more grounded than Shirley, which was for sure. We gave up that bullshit fairy tale the day our prince came and pushed us off the bridge. Our prince had been named death and our princess died when he kissed her in her fine castle with a moat. He even killed the dragon with his sword dipped in poison. As we recalled it, with great sorrow, the murder of our princess occurred when I took a swan dive right into the lake below. We had gone into the water alive and whole but crawled to the bank undead and shattered. Now, just like all corpses, we are trapped in a cemetery where the diseased are stored and forgotten. We knew that no one could bring back the dead. So, of course, we were not being helped out. There is no cure for death and no hope or help either.

I sat down on my privy bench after my task was done with those thoughts cascading through my malfunctioning brain pathways. I was very careful to avoiding putting pressure on my sore bottom. I reached over and grabbed the manila envelope laying on the bench next to me that contained Mary's cruel gift. I opened it up and stared at the bill of sale and descriptions of 'services/property purchased.'

All at once, I started to giggle as I realized I was holding the title to my very first home in my hands complete with a large fenced in and gated yard and outbuilding. It was dark irony that I finally could claim I had a real home, and the real estate was simply to die for.

I got up and went out into the yard with the map of the cemetery from the purchase file. The summer was now in full force, so the late setting sun offered enough light for me to quickly find my plot on the grounds that on the map was marked with an X. It was actually a very nice spot with a lovely view of the mountain that I called the sleeping giant. My outhouse was clearly visible, and a lovely tall tree granted a canopy shade above. I smiled as I thought this was the nicest home I had ever lived in...uhhh...died in...uhhhh...had. Mary was a shit for doing something so sadistic but at least she had chosen a lovely spot to torture me in.

"What the fuck are you doing." Simon's voice suddenly called out from behind.

He scared me so bad sneaking up like that that I let out a yell and took off running blindly. I was rapidly tripped by a broken headstone. I went face first into the ground with a thud knocking the envelope, its contents, and my wind all over the area around the unit.

Simon began laughing hard at my one-yard dash into the ground, "Jittery, are we?"

I gasped for air as I lifted up onto all fours. "Go...fuck...yourself," I said taking big breaths between each word, "You know better than to sneak up on me, you toothless drunk bastard."

He really started laughing at my colorful description of his person, "Yeah, when was your last bath, you skanky schizophrenic Psycho?"

I winced a bit at the last word, but I was slowly getting used to being called that without getting angry. I stood up while glaring angrily at my best friend as he was doing what he always does, rolling a smoke. I walked about picking up the map, bill of sale and work order for my headstone.

"I cannot recall. Probably before I left Julie's place last month sometime," I attempted to brush some of the dirt that had just been ground into my pants from my nosedive.

"Psycho, it is called soap and water, you should check it out sometime. It is the best way to win friends and influence people you know. Right now, you are the Lady of the Flies, with the smelliest reputation in the land," he chuckled, thinking himself very clever.

"Ha ha ha," I clapped at that. "Bravo! I may be Lady of the Flies, but you are the God of Gas, my friend." I totally ignored his calling me that name this time.

Now Simon's eyes flashed with irritation. "I did not fart, you lied. I could not believe you said that. How fucking foul can you be," he said somewhat childishly.

I shook my head laughing. "Get over it. She bought it and I couldn't think of anything else. Look sometimes you just have to take one for the team. Isn't that what you are always telling me? Hey, what the hell was with the screaming at me today That was not cool man. You almost set us over the edge, Simon," I said suddenly becoming angry recalling his screams at the hospital and in Mary's car.

He stopped rolling his smoke and looked up at me. "Psycho, I told you to mind that temper. Twice today you almost got us locked up. Do you want to end up lashed to a floor in some padded storage cell forever? Keep it up then. Look, we are not always going to get our way. They own us, Psycho, and that is the bottom line. Until the unit turns eighteen, we have to behave, or they will make sure we are prisoners."

"We are prisoners, stupid. Look around you, Simon. We are trapped. Mary has us right where she wants us. They gave the unit another fucking shot of that zombie juice. Dr. Scott says the unit has to get a shot every three weeks or else. That makes us prisoners," I yelled at Simon, while headed back to the outhouse.

I did not wait for his pathetic response. This time I was not interested in his opinion. He knew I was right. We never had any choices. If we dared to stand up for ourselves, they threatened to haul us off to the State Mental Hospital or shoot us up with some mental straight jacket. In the end we always got forced to do what we were told. If that was not a prisoner, I did not know what one was.

In the outhouse I threw the envelop into the old storage bin with the bible, broken mirror and my broken first mad box. I thought of how Stephanie had stolen my psychiatric records from me and started this whole mess. I privately cursed her for it.

"Did you get everything we are going to need to live here this time," Simon said as he entered the outhouse behind me.

I nodded my head yes as I rifled through one of the new boxes to show him the books I had purchased. I had bought several hoping to help alleviate my boredom in the long empty hours that I would spend alone in this wilderness. I had found several on subjects of interest for my survival such as mental illness, biology, a dictionary, history, and understanding human behavior.

Simon watched me pull them all out of the box. "Seriously? These are all stuffy books. Didn't you even get one fun book, Lord of the Rings, or Stephen King? Damn, Psycho, you are boring as hell."

I flashed an angry look at Simon, "I do not have time to play. I did not buy fiction because we have all the fucking fiction, we could ever want just by getting up every morning," I raised my voice as irritation with his criticism stirred my anger demon.

He started laughing hard, "Shit, you got me there. I suppose your time would be better used learning to understand these shitty people around here."

I looked at him as I did my best to calm my rage. "Yes Simon, that is the plan but I also plan to go to get educated so I can get a good job. I do not want one with drug dealers. I want to buy a house and have a family someday. I am not going to let Mary, Porcupine, Julie, or even fucking schizophrenia stop me from having a real life. These books are the start. I have to learn their lies so they will give me the paper that says I am credible. Since I cannot get them to stop putting that label in my records, then I have to find a way to get a stronger one. That is the plan. First college, then a professional job. I am going to get out of this world of death one day. Just wait, you'll see. When I do, I am never coming back."

Simon smiled wide, "Now we are talking. Finally, you are thinking. Maybe that medication isn't so bad after all. It seems to have helped that single brain cell of yours to work a bit better."

"Watch it, Simon," I cautioned him. "Okay now some problems we have that I have thought about. I need your help to figure out how to fix them."

He nodded, "Okay yeah, the medication and eating on time right." I nodded back.

"Get out your pen from the supplies and list all the medication and the food. I have been thinking if we drew a grid on the privy bench marking it off in days, then cross grid it for hours too using the dosage on the bottles as a master key. Then put the pills required for that day at the hour in the grid drawing so if you haven't taken it you will know. As for the food put it with the grid. You will see it and remember. Simple," he said as I listened intently.

"Yes, this could work," I said smiling at him.

I quickly got out the pen, medications, and food. It took me an hour to work out the drawn grid, but I did as Simon suggested and left empty "squares" in which to place the pills that corresponded to the right time and day of the week. It was quite a memory tester with the anti-psychotic needing to be taken every four hours. I was glad Simon had a plan. I would never remember the meds without some way to keep up with them.

Finally, I had finished the grid and the pill placement project. The privy bench now looked like it had a miniature checker game with colorful pills instead of red and black discs. I noted that it was time to take them, so I did without too much bitching from Simon. I was just too tired to fight with him about it.

Though he seemed pleased about the pills and food he still seemed bother by something, so despite my fatigue I asked him what the issue was.

"Bathing, which is the next big problem, Psycho. I know I tease you, but you are beyond filthy. The unit is already wide open to infection. You have to at least clean wounds and the entire unit from time to time. I noticed you did not bother as usual to buy a single fucking thing for hygiene, you skank. I think I have a plan for that too since you keep failing at cleaning the unit," he finished while still admiring our pill grid.

I rolled my eyes, "I can jump from the bridge weekly if you like," I laughed, "Queen Elizabeth the first used to say she was the cleanest monarch in the land because she took a bath once a year whether she needed it or not. So, if it is good enough for a Queen of England why do I need to do more than that?"

Simon's jaw dropped, "Are you serious, Psycho? You surely know you smell. Look tomorrow go to the

312

school and sneak into the bathroom and take some of the soap. You can clean wounds and use some of the old clothes as rags to give the unit a sponge bath at least twice a week. At least then you can maybe keep down infection, and the flies."

Now my jaw dropped, "You want me to break into the school to steal soap? Are you fucking insane? No way."

Simon laughed at me, "The doors are open when the summer staff is there to do some repairs. I saw them. Just slip in around noon when they are at the picnic tables eating lunch and grab some soap. They won't see you. It is not breaking in if the door is open, fool."

I just shook my head at that, "Okay, whatever Simon. I will do it if you say so, but I am going to look real fucking stupid when they ask me about it in prison. I can hear it now; what are you in for Thema. Oh, for murdering my hubby. How about you Marcy? I held up a bank and shot two tellers. What are you in for Psycho? I stole soap from a high school. Shit."

Simon started laughing at my response so hard he snorted. I looked at him as he held his stomach nearly on his knees at my statement, "Jesus, Psycho. Now that is fucking hilarious. You are killing me here."

I started giggling at his laughing till both of us looked like the fucking loons, we are rolling on the floor of the outhouse at dusk in a cemetery at the idea of needing to steal soap.

I had two kerosene lamps, so as the darkness began to overcome the outhouse, I lit them. By lamplight I ate my dinner while Simon entertained me with stories of all the places he had lived when he was still a brakeman with the railroad. I knew he had never been to any of those places, and I knew he had never been a brakeman either. However, I did not care. In our world, fantasy was often readily accepted as fact. We both were feeling pretty confident that this new arrangement could work despite our initial misgivings. We went to sleep peacefully hoping that the next day would bring nothing but boredom. Simon and I were very tired of the drama our lives (or whatever we have) had become as of late.

The next day at noon we went to the school and just as Simon said the doors were unlocked. I went inside cautiously but found the coast clear. I managed to squirt a whole baby food jar full of hand soap and get out without being caught. I took off with Simon back down the road to home. Even though I seemed to get away with it I still couldn't help thinking about Marcy and Thema thinking me a lightweight if I got caught and sent to prison for stealing soap. I was overly nervous the rest of the afternoon over it.

Simon of course had me dance with him to work off my nervousness and keep the melt down from happening. As usual it did work. That night I read to him from our books and ate my meal. Things were going smoothly. I had not missed a single dose of the medication, had eaten three times a day and now even had a way to bath or clean wounds. Things were starting to look up for us.

The rest of the week was like the first. No problems, no melt downs, no missed medications or meals. I managed to do a fair job getting a "whore's bath" in which I could clean my face, underarms, and well the unmentionables (in that order by the way – never do that in the reverse order). I did not think to buy soap or toothpaste, but I did by astringent and bandages with a rag designated for that only. I cleaned my wounds daily with soap and water and treated all of them I could reach. I could only pray the ones on my back were doing okay. I left them wrapped in the original bandages from Shirley.

The week flew by as Simon, and I appeared to be improving. Looper still plagued me non-stop, but I was hallucinating less, and able to focus a bit better. I even seemed to remember things better without Simon's constant reminding me. Finally, the day of my appointment with Dr. Scott arrived. I awoke that morning to find I could no longer see Simon. I could hear him, but the medication had ended my vision of him by closing off the pathway that caused the hallucination of his physical form. I was not happy about that, but Simon reminded me the benefit of memory, focus, and less florid hallucinations was worth the sacrifice.

I knew he was right but not seeing my friend made me feel lonelier than ever before. I could talk to him and that was a comfort, but not seeing another person again for a long time (other than that monster Mary and hideous Dr. Scott) would be hard. I dealt with the disappointment the way I deal with everything, stoically. I did not choose to be sick, but I was. I could cry all I wanted; it would not change that this was my fate. I would have to learn to get over my wish to be around others. They did not want to be around me and when they did usually it was for rotten reasons. I decided I was much better off alone.

Now that no one was around I had somewhat improved. I was still mad as a hatter, but at least I was not trying to rip off my skin or cut up my arms anymore. I also was screaming in terror a lot less. I could even sit still for a few minutes at a time without moving about like a Parkinson's sufferer. I also had stop needing to pace and dance so often. I still had not had a single melt down. It seemed to me that there was a defiant correlation between social interaction and my most violent symptoms. I decided to give it another week before I was sure, but at that time I had to assume I may need to stay in isolation for life. If only to protect the unit from further damage at my own hands.

Mary arrived right on time to find me leaning on the gate killing time by watching a couple of squirrels chase each other in a tree across the old dirt road. She pulled in almost running over my feet. Now that was a first. I had been bullied many times by some of the best, but being bullied with a car, that was really special.

I just scowled at her as I went and got in. She took off down the road before I was completely inside almost throwing me from the station wagon.

I scrambled managing to get into the seat and close the door as she sped down the road at quite a clip. "Gosh Granny, so kind of you to want to take me out for lunch, but really I have already eaten," I said obnoxiously.

"Foul sinner," she spat back at me, "Why aren't you dead yet?"

I chuckled. "Because I keep waking up alive darling. I am feeling great Thanks so much for asking," I finished loudly in an overly happy tone.

She snorted and frowned at that, "You smell like you died, Psycho," she said overemphasizing the last word, "how can you stand it?"

I shrugged. "I am used to putting up with disgusting things, Mary. Like you for starters, but I have a list somewhere, give me a second to find it," I said while pretending to look through my coat for the imaginary note.

Mary's eyes bugged out, "How can you wear a coat? It is 99 degrees outside, you wacko. Well, makes sense because you are a demon. I will say it will be even hotter where you are going."

I stopped looking for the list and glared hatefully at Mary, "If I were you, I would be nice to me, Mary. I could tell Dr. Scott you are keeping my checks and making me live in a cemetery outhouse. Then they will make you take me into your home and do right by me. Hey, do you think Bob has been missing me? I bet he does. Bet he will want to give me big old hugs and kisses all over. Gosh, you know what, I would be thrilled to see old Bob. Of course, he will want me to thrill him back, but that can be arranged no worries, darling."

Mary slammed on the brakes nearly sending the unit right through the windshield. Her face was red with anger as I recovered from my near headfirst trip through the dashboard. "You shut up, Psycho. You are never getting your nasty hands-on Bob. I think I will do the world a favor and kill you. No one would ever suspect me anyway. Everyone knows that you are a schizophrenic, and they all expect you to kill yourself."

I laughed at her attempt to frighten me, Really? You think I am stupid don't you. You are not going to kill me. First you are a pussy, and I would like to see you try it. Second, I don't draw you a check dead. Nice try bitch. Not going to work, I am not scared of you."

Mary got a look so evil that I had to look away for fear she would turn me to stone just like medusa, "I can kill you easily. As for a check, you are worth more to me dead than you ever were alive. I have a life insurance policy on you, sinner. I really should do it for free, but your dead body will afford Bob a nice retirement. In fact, it pays double for accidental death. You know what I am going to do? I am going to call up your mother to ask her to send some of her drug dealer pals down here to finish the job she started. Didn't anyone tell you she was let out a couple weeks ago because of overcrowding. Oh yes, she is out. I can get you the proof if you want it. She is on parole right now, but her friends are not. I am sure she will be happy to do it as a payback for your getting her arrested. It makes me smile just thinking of what those beasts will do to you before they finally end your demonic existence. I sure they will have a good time, but I doubt you will enjoy it much. If I were you, I would kill myself before those drug dealer friends of your mom's make sure you get what you deserve."

I felt the blood rush from the units face as I stared blankly out at the dashboard trying to get her words to stick in my mind. I felt the terror from my core begin to course through the unit's veins freezing every tissue cell it touched. Mary could see that she had pushed the one button even Simon could not stop me from reacting to. She had pulled the mother" "card on me. I was well aware that Mary was still in contact with her. I knew this likely was not a bluff. My own mother had no problem doing, and allowing others to do, unspeakable things to me even as a small child. Then she had done her best to murder me. Mary was the mother of this atrocious woman. So, calling my mother and asking her to send rapist or killers to murder me so she could collect on a life insurance policy was certainly not unlikely. No this was a real threat and I realized I was in big trouble.

Mary was smiling at me as I looked at her observably shaken, "I will run," I said.

She laughed hard coldly, "No money, on foot, with a daft brain? You won't get far. Those fellows that your mom knows are professionals. Run if you like, they will hunt you down."

She was right there. I knew these people and I was aware of how without money, a car, or anywhere to go I would be easily tracked down.

"I will tell Dr. Scott," I said now desperately searching for any answer to stop this woman from making that call. I was bracing the unit to prepare for killing Mary before she could make sure I was destroyed.

Mary kept laughing. "She won't believe you. I already told her you have a crazy delusion that drug dealers sent by your mom are after you. I know you may not believe that, but she will verify that for me today when you see her. You have no choice. Kill yourself and make this easy for everyone. Oh, and if you are thinking of attacking me right now, I wouldn't do that. I think you'd better remember one more scratch on me and you are locked up in the Criminally Insane Unit for a long time. You know the drug dealers will be kinder than those inmates will be. So, you think on it. Kill yourself anyway you like. If you need something to help you do it right, I will be happy to make sure you have it," she finished by pulling back onto the road with a smug smile still chuckling under her breath.

I sat there the rest of the ride in stunned silence. Mary chuckled under her breath really enjoying my distress. Even Simon was hushed in awed muteness. Neither of us had any idea what to do now. This was grimmer than any outcome we had experienced since we had tried to commit suicide. My mother was the one person on the planet who wanted me dead bad enough to do whatever it may take to make sure that happened. If she really was out of prison our disease was the least of our problems. Worse still the state had never terminated her parental rights. That meant she could easily get permission to come here to visit her mother. The only thing the Looper could say repeat is "Fuck! Fuck! Fuck!" This time I had to agree with him.

Mary pulled into the parking lot. I started to get out as she happily said, "Don't forget to ask Dr. Scott what she thinks about your mom sending drug dealers to kill you. Oh, and you can ask her if Debbie is out of prison. I bet you will be tickled pink to hear your loving mother is out and feeling fine."

I staggered a bit as if Mary's words punched me in the head. In truth they did. I felt them smack into my force shield as I walked into the clinic feeling almost like I was floating from sheer disbelief at how my day had become such a shit show so rapidly.

I signed in and waited without being able to do anything but listen to the recurrent cursing of the Looper in my ears. My heart in my chest was banging like a metal head at an Iron Maiden concert. I was sure I was going to faint, but I never was a lucky bitch. Somehow, I managed to stay alert as my name was finally called back.

I walked into Dr. Scott's office to find her, as usual, going through my records. I sat down still stunned from Mary's proposal.

"Hey kiddo," Dr. Scott said not even looking up at me. "How is the week been going? I was happy to see no more visits to the ER. Are you taking your medications?"

I nodded in a zombie fashion but said nothing. I did not know if I should ask her about Mary's telling her of a false delusion or of my mother's alleged release from incarceration or not.

Dr. Scott finally finished whatever she was writing down in my file then looked up, "Well you look better. Mary has told me that you are doing better this week except that you fear your mother will retaliate now that she has been released. Is that true?"

My eyes went wide. So, it was true all of it. The Looper yelled out "Oh shit! We are so dead," so loud in my ears I winced at it.

I looked at Dr. Scott hoping she would help me. I was that desperate, "Please send me to State! Like right now." I jumped up and started pacing the room.

Dr. Scott sat back in her chair calmly watching me, "No. I am not going to put you in State. You are delusional. Mary assures me that your mother is not only in counseling for what she did to you but is remorseful. Have you spoken to her yet? I think that may help; you know."

I stopped cold and turned and looked at this incredibly stupid fucking waste of motherfucking space (okay so I am still pretty angry about this so forgive the string of obscenities...no wait fuck it, I mean that), "Are you fucking joking. I am done with this conversation; do you understand me. Put me in the fucking hospital or I will kill myself or someone else will kill me, do you hear that," I yelled at her almost insane with fury.

Dr. Scott sat there just staring calmly at me despite my threat, "Yeah, I expected you to say that. Listen to me, you are delusional about this, and I am not locking you up and feeding this delusion. What I can do is get a shot of Valium in here and make sure you calm your shit down if you threaten again. I can also send home enough of the stuff to keep you from moving off the couch to take a piss."

I could not believe this was happening. My jaw was practically hanging low enough to trip over as I looked at Dr. Scott, "Are you serious? You are not going to lock me up? Mary got to you that much. Well, fuck me. I am so finished."

Dr. Scott was unmoved as I sat back down and covered my face with my arms. I could not afford to have her call in the shot. A dance with my Prince Valium right now would likely cost the unit precious time we now needed to figure out a way out of this horror.

Dr. Scott waited a few moments then said, "So, let's talk about this delusion shall we? I have gone over your files, and I can understand why you may have some trouble forgiving your mother. She did some pretty nasty stuff to you."

I dropped my arms and for the second time in ten minutes stared in disbelief at this ignorant, knuckle-dragging, piece of shit. "Oh my God. Are all of you just alike? Some pretty nasty stuff? Really," I looked up and rocked a bit in the chair. "Tell you what, I am going to tell you that Mary has bought me a burial plot in a cemetery that I live in. She is married to a child molester who beat the terror out of me when I was placed in the home. So, all this time she has left me to rot out there because my choice was to be raped repeatedly again or be homeless. I chose being homeless. As I was saying, Mary bought this plot because she wants me to kill myself so she can collect the life insurance money. She told me that if I don't, she will have my mother send down the very same people who fucked me for life to finish the job and get the money that way. Do you believe me? Please Dr. Scott, I am telling the truth, please believe me."

Dr. Scott had listened to my blurting of the situation I should have reported in the first place with a look of boredom. She now began to write something in my file as I sat there sweating and shaking worse than a crack addict that was in bad need of a fix.

"Okay kiddo, the meds are apparently not working fast enough so I am upping them by 25 mgs every four hours. I will let Mary know the new dose," she said pushing the new prescription to the corner of her desk.

I felt like I should cry but no tears could break through my absolute terror at this inconceivable turn of events, "You don't believe me?"

Dr. Scott looked at me calmly, "No, I don't kiddo. I have the report from the DCFS case worker right here says you are doing well and thriving in Mary and Bob's home. It is dated two days ago; would you like to see it?" She pushed the paper in her hand toward me. "But more than that, I know you. You are often given to delusions of persecution and your high IQ makes them very believable too. I will not be taken in by this. I think if you think it out carefully you will realize, like that discounted radar, this is all in your head and not real."

I sat back in my chair as a calmness overtook me. I understood. I was not going to be able to run away, get locked up, or get anyone to believe me. I could push my luck with Dr. Scott and get shot up making it easier for Mary to push me off a bridge somewhere without a fight. I could attack someone and get locked away in jail or worse the Criminal Insane Unit. I could also take Mary's advice and end it before my mother's goons did it in a more humiliating manner.

My shattered mind began to realize that I was trapped like a fly under glass. However, the Prolixin held, and I did not melt down amazingly. Instead, I just sat there staring at Dr. Scott nodding, shaking my head, or shrugging my shoulders as she asked me stupid questions about my medications over the last week.

Suddenly, a thought came through loud and clear, "Did the Sloans get a new house yet? How is that guardian thing coming along?"

Dr. Scott was shocked out of her bullshit checking off items on her list so she could pretend she was actually treating me. "What? Oh yes, yes, they did and the Guardianship court is scheduled for the end of the month. There will be no need for you to be there. This is pretty much a done deal. They have complied with counseling and passed the home study. It is really just a signature at this point. Why?" She looked at me curiously.

"Just wondering is all. Simon told me to ask you about it. He hates Julie you know," I babbled to her making sure to sound just a tad immature.

Dr. Scott raised an eyebrow, "You are not going to give us trouble on this transfer, are you?"

I smiled but covered my mouth and looked to the floor faking a psychotic move. "Oh no. Just Simon being nosy is all. He thought maybe now that Julie does not like me, she will make sure the Sloans don't do the guardian thing," I giggled just for good measure trying hard to give Dr. Scott what she wanted, Psycho.

This worked as I saw Dr. Scott lean back and relax assuming she was dealing with a mentally ill child with poor insight again, "Oh, now we have discussed Simon and you are never to do or believe what he says. Do you remember? I just saw Julie yesterday and she said she is excited to have you home again. See that is why you never take his advice. Simon is never right and gets you into trouble."

I sighed and looked down hard while shrugging, "Yeah, I remember. Simon is trying to get me into trouble."

She smiled and went back to her list to check off her fucking boxes. I sat there smiling inside. I was not deft today as the medications were working. I also had been reading up on human behavior. I had learned how, when someone has an image of who you are fixated in their mind, nothing you do can change that. Dr. Scott viewed me as incompetent and unable to think for myself in anyway. In order to get information that I really needed without allowing Dr. Scott to alarm Mary to the question I needed to convince her that I was still off my rocker. Just as the book said it would, my acting job worked. It was so accepted that I was too gone to know anything of worth she had even forgotten I asked about the Sloans and focused on my friend Simon. I had to cover up my grin of this victory with a forced giggle fit. Dr. Scott briefly spoke about inappropriate affect then finally cut me loose back to Mary's would be murderous claws.

I had just come up with a new plan to escape my mother and Mary, but I needed to be sure that the Sloans were still willing to take me in. It would be very hard to explain a suicide or murder if I was always at someone's side. I needed someone everyone found credible to watch my back. Like it or not, I was now Julie's new bitch. It was a far better projected outcome, as far as I was concerned, then being the victim of a vicious murder/rape, a long-term inpatient prisoner, or a suicide statistic. I knew it was going to be a rough ride. I knew Julie would make me regret choosing to live rather than die, but I also knew this was my own hope for now. There was always hope that if I could buy more time, in the future some better alternative would come along. For now, this was the best I could do.

As I left the clinic to get back into Mary's station wagon, I got prepared to keep this horrid creature chasing after my carrot on a stick until I could get to the Sloans and see Julie. I took a deep breath and got inside the car.

Mary smiled her "gotcha" grin at me. "Well, how did it go, Psycho? Did you learn anything new?"

I looked down appearing forlorn, "Yeah. You were right Mary. I have to kill myself. There is no need to call in Debbie. I will need a good knife though. I do not have one. I will make it look like I went radar hunting again. No one will suspect, but I want something in return." I knew better than to give in to her demands without something being in it for me.

In order for my plan to work she had to believe I was sincere. Just giving in to a woman I had now been fighting for almost a year would suggest I was up to no good.

Mary looked both happy and suspicious, "What do you want besides the knife?"

I continued to look at the floor, "I would like a motorcycle. I know you may think I will try to run on it so you can get me one with almost no gas in it if you like. Even with a full tank I know I cannot outrun Debbie's people, but I always wanted one all my life. Since my life is over, it is my last wish. In fact, if you will get me one today, I could even use it to end my life by running it off the road or a bridge. That would be the accident you need even more than the knife, but I understand if you do not want to take the chance. I am sure just an accidental suicide may be enough," I finished my devil's deal offer to Mary.

*Note: Devil's Deal Offer: this is when I offer to give someone what they said they want from me, but the deal is always swayed in my favor. Like any Devil's deal once you sign over your soul you cannot quibble about the details you never bothered to read in the fine print.

Mary's face brightened to a most heinous shade of old lady grey as she realized I had found a way to get her an assured double payout on my demise. She knew I could not ride a fucking motorcycle. Hell, I did not even know how to start one much less run away on one. Besides, I am Psycho, right?

"Okay, do you care about the color," she asked, and I knew right away she had taken the deal. I also knew by her question she knew where to buy one cheap and fast.

"I like black, but all the colors are so pretty," I said immaturely while smiling.

Mary smiled even more evilly at my childlike statement buying the act, "Well black it is then."

We rushed back to the tiny town of our residence and to my extreme relief I was correct. Mary knew right where a black Honda 1100 shadow was for sale. Not too far down the road from Stephanie's old house was the beautiful bike. It was a brand new 1987 model. She assumed that for what I was going to pay out in my blood it was a reasonable sacrifice of cash since the last thing she wanted was my "accident" being held up more than a few weeks waiting on parts for a broke down cycle.

She had me wait in the station wagon while she went inside the residence and made the purchase, ashamed to the very end to be seen with me. I sat there smiling at my clever plan. Mary never would see it coming. I wished Simon was around to see me finally find a way to manipulate a manipulator.

However, the thought of the second part of my plan quickly turned my smile downward because now that I had the bait, I would have to lure in the wolf. I was well aware that in the end, even if I got a best-case scenario, I am going to end up the dog in all this. So even if I win, I will actually lose, but then again, I will at least live to fight another day. My disease had robbed me of the ability to enjoy life but not the need to survive. The continuation of the unit was the only thing on my mind as I watched Mary cross the yard and get back into the car.

She was smiling her "gotcha" smile as she handed me the keys to a motorcycle I now owned outright. "Here are the keys and your bill of sale. I will give you till next Sunday. That way Bob and I will be at church when it happens. Mr. Taggert says you are welcome to pick it up on Sunday and he will be around to help you start it. Do not make a mistake and survive the crash, you hear me? If your plan is just to get into the hospital let me remind you that soon as you get out your mother's friends can make sure you wish you had broken your neck as you had agreed to do," she finished her most cruel statements while handing me the rest of the items for my first vehicle, and my last if she had it her way.

I nodded my head grateful to have a few days to try to find out where Julie had moved. I assumed I would have to go to the Evan's home by foot and find her through them. I was okay with walking the thirteen miles to their trailer, but I would need time to get there and hunt her down. Sunday was four days away. I was satisfied this could indeed be done with time to spare. I had no idea how right I actually was.

Mary took me to the gate and for the first time ever she left without throwing dust all over me. It should have bothered me that in order to get someone to show some polite behavior to me I had to offer to die in a horrible fiery crash, so they could make money off my death. However, it didn't. I knew no one loved me, well except Simon and he was me. So long as I loved myself, I decided there was a reason to try to keep on battling for breath no matter how dark my world had become.

I watched the vile woman drive away with nothing but contempt for her in my unit's heart. I really could not wish anything bad enough on her, so I gave up trying and went inside the cemetery to talk with Simon about our plan.

I was only halfway to the outhouse when I heard, "Hey Psycho," I turned to be knocked clean out of my senses by a blow to my temple from a fist.

I staggered backward confused as my knees buckled and I fell back onto my ass still wobbling from the sucker punch. I was trying to clear the stars from my vision to see who had called my nickname, and also who had punched me, when I heard the very voice I had been planning to seek out.

"Well, well if it is my old friend, the Psycho. Where is Simon, Psycho? In your shithouse? Maybe I should burn down your house with him in it? Hummmm," Julie said while peering down at my sitting unit.

I blinked hard as Julie went from blurry to the regular pulsating but clear vision now standing above me, "Hey Julie. I was going to go looking for you.

Wow, you look great. Did you get a haircut?
Something is well, just different, did you lose
weight," I said sarcastically.

Julie raged as she realized I was referring to her
now replaced front teeth. She grabbed me by my
collar and pulled me up ready to punch me again,
"You fucking Loon I had to get a fucking partial.
Now I am going to knock your fucking teeth down
your throat see how you like it, Psycho."

I readied myself for her blow trying to pry off the
arm holding my collar and rapidly shot off, "Okay, go
ahead, but I am sorry Julie. I am just a fucking
psycho, you are right! I got you something to make up
for what I did to you."

"Fuck you," Julie reared back farther to make sure
she knocked me hard.

I closed my eyes tight, "I got you a motorcycle
Julie. Please don't hit me and I will give it to you.
Black just like you said you always wanted. I swear
it."

There was silence. Julie still held me, but she had
not hit me yet. I opened an eye to see her standing
there in shock.

"What did you say? Are you serious," she said
almost in a whisper?

I opened both eyes and looked into hers. "Yes. I
got you a 1987 Honda Shadow. Brand new."

Julie let go my collar and I was not expecting it, so I fell to my knees off balance, "You bought Taggert's bike for me?" She was almost squealing with glee.

I stayed on my knees thinking it safer there until I was sure that she would not punch me again, "Yeah, I have the keys and pink slip here. I will give them to you as an apology but look you cannot knock my teeth out or burn down Simon in the outhouse if I give it to you. Swear it." I did not think her word meant much but I was really in no position to argue her honor code at that moment.

Julie asked to see the keys and pink slip. I took the out of my jacket pocket and showed them to her. She smiled big showing off her new front partials like a mule about to 'hee haw' (hahaha, it still kills me to this day, sorry not funny, yes, it is)!

She reached down and offered me her hand to shake. I shook it despite the shock and handed her the items. Julie did a weird dance and twirled yelling she finally had a bad ass bike (it only cost her a couple front teeth). I watched her victory dance still on my knees trying to figure out how to approach my real reason for buttering her up. Finally, she calmed down from self-absorbed party and recalled I was there.

She stopped smiling as she looked at me still on the ground. "Okay, that makes us even about the teeth, but there is a lot of other shit I am super pissed at you about. You know at the end of the month you are leaving this place and living with us. I came here to knock out your teeth and to beat you into submission so I guess I will leave your front teeth and just beat the rest of you till you know who the fucking hand is that feeds you."

My initial gut reaction was to yell that it was my fucking money that they were using to 'feed me' and several other insults. However, the Looper reminded me that if I fucked this up, I was "dead meat.:

I looked down at the ground swallowed my anger as I said, "You do not have to beat it into me. I will do whatever you say, no fight not anymore. Just please take me with you right now. I will never give a reason to hit me again. I am begging, you Julie take me away from here, right now."

Julie almost choked as I said those words (hell I almost choked myself), "What? Wait, you are wanting to go? What about Simon, and this damned stinking graveyard you love so fucking much?"

I kept my eyes down trying to not feel the terror rising, "I don't want to live like this anymore. Please Julie I will do whatever you want, just get me the fuck out of here."

Julie gaff haws aloud, "Did you hear that, Joni? Psycho says she will do whatever I want and all I have to do is get her out of here."

I hear Joni approaching from behind me. Likely she was hiding somewhere waiting to see if Julie needed help beating me half to death. She must have decided to come closer to be noisy as to why I was not bleeding from every orifice yet.

"Yeah, but that is bullshit, and you know it. Psycho is a clever little nutjob. I wouldn't trust her as far as I could throw Simon," Joni said as they both began to laugh at that joke at my friend's expense.

I gritted my teeth fighting the urge to rip them both new assholes as they taunted me about Simon, my lack of personal hygiene, and of course my mental instability. I took it all, never responding no matter how cruel or personal they got with their jeers. As I knelt there on my knees, I finally understood what it must feel like to be an ant trapped under the magnifying glass of a towheaded young boy as he fries the hapless creature to a crisp. I already was thinking maybe suicide was a preferable outcome.

Whew! What a fucking close call huh beauties! I am so glad you made it to shore before all was lost, oh wait, shit, this is a deserted island and looks like we are stranded. Alright, let's not panic, okay, maybe if you start a big signal fire and we start the hunt for water we may just pull through this. Have a little faith in us. We can survive several days without food and surely some ship will come by and rescue us, right. Now we know, you beauties are readers or you would not be here still (this thing has gone on forever, eh).

Okay so we are off to the coffin at last to restrain our shattered brain and get prepared to entertain you will the next book, entitled "The Key and the Collar", in this trip to the center of nowhere.

Alexandria May Ausman was born into a dangerously neglectful home environment. She was the helpless victim of numerous incidents of psychological, physical, and sexual assaults by her parents and peers. She dressed in an unusual manner to 'fightened' off bullies and to appear less attractive to sexual predators. Despite her cries for help her pleas for aid were ignored until she was finally placed in foster care at age fifteen. In her sixteenth year, her mental health began to deteriorate. Alexandria was quickly abandoned by her foster parents when she was diagnosed with Schizophrenia. While still only a teen, she was forced to battle this devastating illness alone.

Alexandria has struggled with lack of a support system, numerous psychotic episodes, exploitation, homelessness, and an uncaring mental health system.

Alexandria raised two healthy children. After obtaining her bachelor's degree in psychology she worked as a child abuse investigator and became a diagnostic psychologist while acquiring her Master's in psychology. Alexandria never forgot the experience of 'slipping through the cracks.' Her life's goal is to help people suffering abuse and/or mental illness have access to necessary services. In 2018, Alexandria's fashion expression gained notice. By accident, she became a model of 'gothic attire'. That summer she won the World Gothic Models contest. Henceforth, dubbed the Goth Queen, Alexandria didn't miss an opportunity to offer a helping hand to those in need.

She began writing a fictionalized account of her life experiences after a catastrophic return of psychotic symptoms. Today, Alexandria is retired, and homebound due to crippling symptoms of Schizophrenia. She currently lives in Tallahassee, Florida, with her loving husband and a loyal support dog.

Made in the USA
Columbia, SC
17 August 2022

65554102R00189